Smit

Smitten

J'Sat Necolle

SMITTEN

Smitten

J'Sat Necolle

Also by J'Sat Necolle

Still Got Joy

A Change Gonna Come (Winter 2019)

SMITTEN

A NOVEL

J'SAT
NECOLLE

Smitten

AnaBooks

A Division of Ana Productions
Atlanta, GA 30313

AnaBooks and colophon are trademarks of Ana Productions, Inc.

For more information about special discounts for bulk purchases, please contact Ana Productions Special Sales at 404-655-0458 or sales at j'satnecolle.com

The Ana Productions Speakers Bureau can bring authors to your live event. For more information or to book an event, contact the Ana Productions Speakers Bureau at 404-655-0458 or visit our website at www. jsatnecolle.com

Manufactured in the United States of America

Library of Congress Cataloging-in Publication Data

ISBN 978-0-9961234-2-6
ISBN 978-0-9961234-3-3 (ebook)

Smitten

"It's Tooda and Grammy, and Grammy and Tooda…"

J'Sat Necolle

Smitten

This book is dedicated...

To the second little girl that stole my heart, Carson Shontia Baker. Thanks for coming into my life and filling it with joy. You have made these past four years of my life more exciting than it has ever been before. From the time you entered this world, you have brightened my life in ways you can never imagine. The way your eyes light up when I enter a room is the most extraordinary feeling I have ever experienced, and I sincerely thank you for always making me feel special.

While, your entry into my life stalled my budding writing career, putting it on the back burner for years; it is also because of you that I am encouraged to try it again. My hope is that my trials, tribulations, defeats and triumphs, will always encourage you and your mother...To never give up. To always chase your dreams. To love and live without fear. To always remember how much, I love you both.

"Go Tooda...Go Grammy. Go Grammy...Go Tooda..."

Smitten

.

J'Sat Necolle

Smit-ten

/smitn/

Past participle of smite

2. be strongly attracted to someone or something.

"she was so smitten with the new boy"

Smitten

J'Sat Necolle

Not sure if you're...

Smitten

This is what it sounds like...

http://cueyoutube.com/wsly/ WslyLanding/?r=WslyAppInde x&code=hcB

*I **DO NOT** own the rights to this music!*

Chapter 1

"*M*an, damn Hallmark with all this happily-ever-after crap," Zahiri whined as she grabbed the remote from the empty pillow lying beside her on her double pillow-top mattress. Looking at the DVR recordings she had lined up on the menu bar, she amusingly realized that this Hallmark movie marathon may not have been her best idea, especially considering the fact that she had been on a 3-year hiatus from men. *And why the hell don't Hallmark ever have any black romance movies?* I suddenly thought to myself. "Racist bastards!" *Shoot, black people need love too!*

Picking up the silent cellphone, I glared at the empty call log, trying desperately not to go on yet another rant about the blatant racism black folks succumb to everyday at the hands of white America. Releasing a heavy sigh, I grumbled, "Fuck love," to no one in particular. "At this point I just need me some dick!" I exclaimed.

Sure I'd decided that I would stay celibate until I found someone that was worthy of my goodies but after downing a half a pint of Absolute with my best friend, Yana, and watching two movies about love and romance on the Hallmark channel, the only and quickest cure for my ailment is some good sex, because I absolutely know that the prospect of love or romance is nowhere in my near future.

Staring at the etched gray lines in my cracked I-phone screen, I couldn't believe I was actually lying here contemplating potential prospects that could come thru, fuck me good, then haul ass back to the rock from which they'd crawled from under. That was until my phone's cursor inadvertently scrolled through my contacts and highlighted the name Smitten on my screen.

Kenyan Warner. The name alone quickly sent me spiraling down memory lane, which is why I still had his old number listed as Smitten in my phone. It doesn't matter how much time has passed, one thought of him instantly made me wet. *Hmph... The Kenyan Warner*, I thought to myself. That wasn't just any old dick. Kenyan had that grade-A, write home and tell your mama, certified premium and dipped in gold dick!

Oh, hell nawl! I definitely can't do that! Quickly trying to create a distraction from my throbbing pussy before I did something, I knew I would regret, I quickly began jumping up and down on the bed, playfully kicking Yana in her side, "Wake up, Bitch!" "You have been MIA since the first movie. Who in the world has one drink and passes out?"

Smitten

Groggily, Yana slightly lifted her head from the bottom of the bed where she had been lying sound asleep for the past four hours. "My bad, my bad," she said mournfully, "I was just so tired," she said, letting out a long yawn.

"Tired of what?" "Girl you haven't worked in over two years and your man is out of town, so what the hell have you been doing to get so freaking tired?"

As soon as the words left me mouth, I regretted it. I instantly felt awful and the scowl that abruptly appeared on my best friend's face did not make me feel any better. Immediately rushing to the far end of the bed, I gently stroked the side of her face, "Yana, I'm so sorry. I'm such an ass!" Wiping the single tear that now fell aimlessly down her chubby cheeks, Yana nodded her head in acceptance of my apology and plastered her rendition of a smile across her face.

But I knew better. That smile was as fake as that no-good, two-timing husband of hers, who was probably down in Miami riding another man's dick even as we speak. And no, I don't know for a fact that he's gay or bi or whatever the politically correct term is nowadays, I just know that he can get secondary pussy anywhere, especially here in Atlanta. So why in the hell does he have to live an entirely separate life? Away from any and everybody that knows his ass. And... at the bottom of the damn map, might I add. Sounds to me like he has a lot more than some pussy to hide. I'm just saying.

J'Sat Necolle

Smitten

But what the hell do I know, I haven't had a man in three moons and a Sunday, as my Grammy used to say.

Supposedly Gavin had temporarily relocated to South Beach to oversee a new project and would only be gone for six months to a year. The hotel chain he worked for, Charloz, was opening another luxury resort off the coast of Miami and he was spear heading the building project. Well hell, that was three years and two miscarriages ago. Not to mention, the resort has been open for business for over two years now.

When he first left, he flew home every two weeks like clockwork, just like he had promised Yana he would when he first accepted the promotion. However, about a year or so into his reassignment, the visitations became less and less frequent. He would always come up with some clever excuse why he could not make it home. This deadline had to be met or someone dropped the ball, blaze' this... blaze' that. And when he did manage to grace Yana with his presence, he seemed distant and unresponsive. Hell, I still can't figure out just how she had managed to get knocked up, not once but twice during that time.

Not just that though, in addition to the bastard's blatant lack of respect for his wife, his entire personality has changed, too; along with his wardrobe. Where he used to be fun and down to earth; always the life of the party, he was now

Smitten

self-righteous, stuck-up and pretentious. He
never hung out with his homeboys when he
came home, but then again 24-hours, because
that's what his visitation time had dwindled
down to, doesn't leave him a lot of time to just
kick it. Not to mention, this negro, slash once
country bumpkin, went from wearing three-
piece K&D suits for $139.99 when he first started
with the company, to now wearing two and three
thousand-dollar Hermes suits. Don't get me
wrong, I'm not hating on a brotha for stepping
his game up because I realize better than anyone,
that to be successful, you've got to look the part.
But hell, I also know that when you are not on
the plantation, you can put down the cotton;
won't nobody tell Maser'!

The melancholy mood that had sucked the air
right out of my bedroom and killed my tequila
high had almost made me forget the reason I'd
woke Yana up in the first place...I need some
dick!

J'Sat Necolle

Chapter 2

Yana Yearwood-Smalls looked down and shook her head in disgust at the frilly pink robe she had worn several days too many. The remnants of her many tv dinners and take-out orders had soiled what was once considered a sexy ensemble. Her husband of eight years, Gavin, had brought it five years ago as a gift for their second honeymoon in Punta Cana; and while it has definitely seen better days, she refuses to get rid of it. Much like her husband.

"What happened to me?" Yana asked as she peered at herself in the large vanity mirror in the spacious master bathroom. Glaring closer at her once smooth, blemish-free, caramel-latte complexion under the bright florescent light, she could see the years of pain and loneliness deeply etched in the lines around her eyes and mouth. Lightly touching a dry spot on her face, she began to cry, which is all she seems to do lately.

Abruptly turning from the disturbing image peering back at her from the mirror, she practically sprinted to her bedside table and snatched the marble drawer handle open. Pulling out a folder marked confidential, she mulled through the architectural drawings on top and stopped when she reached her designated area.

Quickly pulling out the stack of take-out menus she had so cleverly hidden after Gavin horribly joked during one of his visits after her second miscarriage that she had probably accidently ate the baby with her fat ass.

Her mind instantly remembered how that belittling insult had hit her like a ton of bricks, momentarily sucking the breath right out of her chest. But instead of hurling the plate of food she was holding at his head like something was telling her to, she instead turned and retreated slowly up the winding, iron staircase, and walked into the guest bathroom at the far end of the hall, away from the master bedroom.

Turning on the multi-faceted showerhead, she hurled the pile of Chinese take-out at the broken reflection of the woman she used to be, starring back at her from the mirror and began crying like a baby. After emerging from the bathroom an hour later, she'd found a note on her side of the bed that read, *"Something came up, had to take the red-eye back tonight. Gav."*

Instead of being angry or hurt that he had left without walking 15-feet to tell her goodbye, a small part of her felt relieved he was gone. That was eight months ago and incidentally the last time she had actually seen her husband in person.

Picking up her cellphone, she called her favorite Japanese restaurant, Nakota, and placed her order. Catching her voice, the little Asian waitress on the other end of the phone said, "Thank you, Miss. Yana, we will put it on your tab."

"Thanks," I mumbled. *How pathetic*, I thought. *In a city the size of Atlanta, I call the freaking restaurant and they know my freaking voice.* "I've got to do better," I said to no one in particular, shaking my head in disgust.

Instead of wallowing in my self-pity, I decided to do something I rarely do, while I waited on my lunch to arrive. I climbed in my bed, grabbed my laptop and logged onto my Facebook page and turned my privacy notification off. Since my last miscarriage, I hardly ever post anything on Facebook; however, I honestly think I spend a good 35 hours a week on here just lurking around in people's business. I always have my page set to show that I'm inactive because I don't want anyone to know that I'm logged on… and in their business.

I must admit though, being nosey on here keeps me thoroughly entertained. You'd be surprised at the kind of post people put on here about two or three in the morning when they know the person or persons, they are talking about are at home fast asleep, minding their own damn business.

Some mornings I am so tempted to just screen shot that shit and send it to the person being talked about as their anonymous wake-up call. That would teach those Facebook popping bullies a lesson, because half of the time their cowardly asses delete the post within mere seconds of posting it, under the disguise that someone told them to be the bigger person and take it down. I literally catch myself sitting in my bed yelling at the computer screen, "Bitch please, ain't nobody told you to take that mess down, your ass is just scared! Which is why you waited to the wee hours of the morning to post that subliminal bullshit anyway...you had all damn day to say what you wanted to say!"

I have my girl Hiri cracking up when I call her to spill the tea about some of the people we know from back home. It's almost like watching soap operas but instead on Facebook, you really know all of the characters personally or by association and boy is it entertaining.

I swear, The Young and The Restless and All My Children ain't got jack shit on The Days of Our Facebook! In fact, it's actually the most entertainment I have in my life at the moment. Sitting in this condo all day, every day, can get extremely lonely and a girl has to find something constructive to do to pass the time while my darling husband is doing God knows what, with God knows who in Miami. "I don't want you to work," he'd said. So, I quit my job. "I want to take care of you," he'd said. But then he left. "I want you to be the mother of my children," he'd said. But after I had two miscarriages, he'd stopped touching me all together.

J'Sat Necolle

Smitten

"When life hands you lemons, you just have to make lemonade," I said as I hurried towards the front door of my condo overlooking downtown Atlanta to get the fifth take-out purchase, I've had already this week... and it's only Tuesday.

Gavin purchased this property for us after he'd gotten his first promotion at the company. Back then our future looked so bright, we thought we had the world at our fingertips and were looking forward to a long and beautiful union. We wanted three kids; twin boys and a baby girl.

I can remember sitting on the terrace our first night overlooking the Atlanta skyline talking about the family we would one day have. Gavin wanted five kids, but I told him he had to compromise because I was too fine to be pregnant that many times. The most pregnancies I could do was two, so he'd said, well at least one of the pregnancies would have to be twins and stupidly I agreed, like our dumb asses really had any control over what God wanted for us.

That night under the brilliant dark sky and the sparkling city lights, my husband made love to me with a sense of urgency that I'd never experienced before. It seemed like the deeper he dove into me, the greater the depth of our love grew and when we finally erupted together in a serenade of our oneness, the stars in the sky seemed to brighten momentarily as we lay there in each other's arm until the sun peeped out from behind the velvet sky and washed over us in calmness. Everything about that night was absolutely magical and two months later when I found out I was pregnant, I wasn't the least bit surprised. Before the doctor could even try to figure out my due date, I told him exactly when I conceived. That night changed my life...in more ways than one.

Chapter 3

"Come on, heifer!" I yelled into the receiver.

"Damn, bitch...hold on. I'm coming!" *Lord, why do I always do this to myself?*

Ever since I've known Yana, she has been slow as hell. And now that her trifling bastard of a husband has taken away her self-confidence, she is even slower. And she knows how inpatient I am, but does that make her put a pep in her step? Hell no, it never did! Our outings always start with the same argument, yet we've been doing this same Cagney and Lacy tango for the last twenty-seven years and honestly, I wouldn't have it any other way. I love my best friend, flaws and all, and there is literally nothing I won't do for her slow ass.

Smitten

As she exited her upscale condo building with her locks curled cutely to one side of her head, rocking a tangerine and gold short maxi dress, with gold sandals tied up her beautifully toned legs and simple gold hoops dangling from her ears, I smiled on the inside. These days you never know which Yana you're going to get. One day she might show up looking like her old flawless self, then other days she might show up looking like someone had just dropped her on her fucking head and ran over her backwards.

"Dammnnn girl, now I see what took you so long!" Smiling from ear to ear, she turned around and gave me her diva-girl twirl. Shoot, even with her extra twenty-five pounds, my girl still had it going on. If you ask me, the added weight actually enhanced her natural sex appeal because it went straight to her butt and her breast. My bestie's body is looking just like Porsha Stewart from Atlanta Housewives, after she dropped Cordell's punk ass. But in her mind, she's fat, because that's what that insecure monster she married wants her to think.

He has had her emotionally and mentally enslaved for years and I am sick and tired of it. But I learned a long time ago to not say anything because when I do, it seems to just drive a wedge through our friendship and losing her or not being able to keep a close eye on her is definitely not worth it. So, I just keep my mouth quiet and pray that she will soon come to her senses. And when she called the other night saying she was ready to get out and have some fun; all I could say was, "Hot damn!"

That was on Tuesday, and I tell you my week went in slow motion after that. Saturday could not get here fast enough. I actually took off on Friday but that's the beauty of owning your own business, you make your own hours, and can't nobody say jack-shit.

I picked Yana up around ten that Friday morning, we headed straight to the Nail Trap on Wesley Chapel and got our favorite Asian, Mitzie, to hook us up with a mani-pedi and an eyebrow wax. Yana has been dying to get some individuals, so we headed back towards Candler Rd. and veered in to South Dekalb Mall and got our eyelashes and makeup done. And honey, let me tell you, our faces were beat to the Gods!

All our bougie friends think we're crazy because we always head right back to the south side when we want to get pampered but what they don't understand is that you get the best service in the hood because they know you'll fuck them up if they mess up your shit.

In Buckhead; however, they think we're all just some rich broads out spending our husband's money and don't know any better. Humph, but me and this ignorant mouth of mine let them know quick, "Don't let these Louboutin 's fool you, because if you mess up my face, I will put them straight up your ass."

J'Sat Necolle

Smitten

My grandma certainly didn't raise a punk and I'll be damned if you're going to take my hard-earned money and not give me quality service. Not on this side of west hell, *oh no mam*! I don't play that!

After we'd gotten pampered, we left the Southside and had lunch at The Fish Market because both Yana and I absolutely love their crab cakes and calamari. I honestly think we've tried everywhere in the metro area and hands down; The Fish Market has everybody beat with those two dishes. It's crazy though, because prior to us leaving Lithonia and going off to college, neither Yana nor I had ever even been to Buckhead and it was only thirty minutes away. Hell, her family was poor and mine was poorer, if that's even a word.

We grew up two apartments down from each other in the projects off Panola Rd. and trust me, we weren't nearly the poorest ones over there. Everybody was struggling back then but it seems like people, especially black people were much nicer to each other back when nobody had a pot to piss in and a window to throw it out of.

If people knew you were struggling or having a rougher patch than usual, they'd give you a few dollars or drop off some food. Shoot, I can't count how many rent parties my grandma went to, just to help someone else out. That was back when people still cared about their neighbors and knew them and their children on a first name basis. If we needed some sugar or an egg or two, my grandma would just send me next door and borrow it and then she would return the favor when the Johnson's needed something. That's how everybody was back then, but once black folks started getting a little something, we got beside ourselves and started thinking we were better than the next.

Yana and I swore that when we came back from college we were going to make a difference in our community and we honestly had good intentions, but life somehow got in the way. *Or were we just like the others*, I thought.

After lunch, we headed straight to our stomping ground, Phipps Plaza and we tore that mall up. Just imagine my shock when Yana exclaimed as she slide inside my sleek convertible Porche 911 that everything was on her today. Normally, Gavin's petty ass had her pinching pennies like we were still waiting on our welfare check at the first of the damn month, while his pretty boy ass was floating around here buying Versace and shit, like he was Usher or somebody, about to perform on the damn Grammys or something. But not today, my girl was paying the cost to be the boss! *Bout damn time.*

As we were loading my trunk with the many designer bags we had scored she looked over at me and softly said, "Thank you."

J'Sat Necolle

Smitten

"What in the world are you thanking me for, shoot you just treated me to the shopping spree of a lifetime!"

Throwing her head back and laughing out loud reminding me of just why I love her, Yana started singing to the top of her lungs, '*Thank you for being a friend, we traveled down the road and back again...your heart is true...*"

With absolute admiration, I joined right in singing the infamous Golden Girls ballad, "*You're a pal and a con-fi-dant.*" We got even louder as we embraced each other under the close scrutiny of all the onlookers passing by, many stopping to stare, "*And if you threw a party-y and invited everyone you knew-w-w, you would see the biggest gift would be from me and the card attached would say...Thank you for being a friend!*"

With tears now streaming down both of our faces, we hugged each other tighter than we had in a long time and remained that way for what seemed like hours. The other mall patrons in the parking lot witnessing our performance were clapping and cheering, some even had tears in their eyes, while they held out their cell phone recording us. *Damn, I hope we don't go viral*, I thought.

Chapter 4

"Oh my God!" Yana yelled, squealing in delight as Luscious Lucius slowly pulled her pinky toe out of his mouth. Looking over at me with a clod of haze covering her smoky grey eyes, my best friend since I was four years old said, "Bitch, when you said you had a surprise for me, I sure as hell didn't think it involved going home jumping in a cold shower!"

"Who says you have to?" I asked innocently, looking around the male strip club at all the chocolate delicacies roaming around the packed space. It had been ages since we'd both attended the Thursday night male review at Club Mirage. This used to be our stomping ground. Every Thursday like clockwork, me, Yana and this whore we used to roll with name Dominique used to roll up in here high as hell. The bouncers never bothered to ask us for ID because word on the street was Dominique had the best head on this side of the Mason-Dixon line.

I ain't never been one to gossip but all I know is, she always came with us, but she never left with us and we never had a thing to worry about. We didn't pay to get it, we didn't pay for parking and we didn't pay for drinks, hell; we even got free lap dances. So, imagine our surprise when we came home from college one Christmas break and found out she had gotten married...and to a preacher nonetheless.

Smitten

I almost felt sorry for Rev. Daniels. Poor thing, but then again, he's not the only preacher I know who's trying to turn a whore into a housewife. As a matter of fact, I know so many of them doing this dumb shit, I'm about to believe they were all told in divinity school to just skip over the entire book of Proverbs; because in chapter thirty-one, God specifically told them to find a virtuous woman.

That's just why I don't take my happy ass all up in the church house with all that fakery and foolery. What the hell do I look like sitting up in there listening to a minister who sins way more than me, and completely ignores the commandment of God by marrying these first ladies that have had more dicks than I've had hiccups. *Oh, no mam!* I'll take my chances of getting into heaven on my own.

As long as I live I'll never forget the last time me, Dominique and Yana had all been together. We were on our way to the clinic, going with Dominique to have her third abortion in two years. While, I was totally against the bullshit and didn't want any part of it or those fake ass tears Dominique was shedding, Yana on the other hand, was playing Mother Theresa, like this whore really deserved forgiveness.

"Would you shut the fuck up?" I yelled from the driver's seat of Yana's mom's Cutlass Supreme. "I don't know how in the hell I let you heifers talk me into this dumb shit, anyway. Your no-good ass ought to be made to have this baby and ten more to go along with it," I spat at the disheveled girl crumpled over in the backseat pleading how sorry she was.

The more I fussed, the louder her sobs got, while Yana just sat her mute ass over there looking out the passenger side window like there wasn't shit going on. *Maybe she's praying that we get her mom's car back before she realizes it's gone*, I thought to myself. Which is highly unlikely because the Yearwood's are the only ones in Building C that has a car, so everybody and their mama always needed a ride somewhere and bless her heart, Mrs. Yearwood was the June Clever of the hood and didn't have the heart to tell anyone no.

"Yana!" I yelled. She didn't answer. "Bitch, what the hell is wrong with you?" I yelled even louder, this time reaching over and grabbing the arm of her prized Members Only jacket.

"What?" she said solemnly, looking at me with tear-soaked eyes.

"Damn Bitch, why you taking this shit so hard?" "Hell, you ought to be used to it by now. But you're sitting over there acting like you the daddy or something," I said laughingly trying to lighten the mood.

In a voice barely above a whisper she said, "No... but my daddy is."

J'Sat Necolle

Smitten

Speechless. This was the first time in my life I had ever been speechless. Not even when my mother dropped me off at my grandmother's apartment one April day when I was only four years old, saying she was going to the store; and didn't come back for five years, was I speechless.

Not even when my mom finally did return with her new husband and his seven-year-old daughter and their five-year-old twins was I speechless.

Not even when I overheard my mother yelling at my grandmother telling her that she didn't want me and that's why she wasn't taking me back with her, even that didn't leave me speechless.

But seeing my best friend hurt so bad, that...now, that shit left me speechless.

Sitting in the waiting room of the sterile clinic, neither of us said a word. Holding tightly to Yana's quivering hand as she gazed at the door where Dominique had vanished over forty-five minutes ago with the stoutly, rude nurse, I couldn't help but to think about how smooth Mr. Yearwood was because he had fooled us all. Hell, he's always acted like he loved the ground his wife walked on. Always kissing and hugging on her, buying her nice gifts. But I guess Betty Wright was right when she said, "*Un, un, honey, some gifts are just to make you feel better while he's on his guilt trip, about the night before.*" You know what I mean! He damn sure had me fooled

Smitten

because I never would have thought he was the cheating type and from the looks of it, neither did Yana.

Suddenly the infamous door swung open and Dominique slowly emerged walking hand in hand with the short, portly nurse. Never looking up from her clipboard, the nurse placed Dominique's hand in Yana's and said that she may be groggy, so she doesn't need to be driving and she will be sore for a couple of days but just get the prescription filled for the pain. With that, she spun on the heels of her well-worn orthopedic shoes and walked away.

I led the way out of the now crowded facility. Looking around for the first time, glad this whole ordeal was finally over; I was surprised by the number of young, lily-white faces filling the waiting room. *Ooh, so that's why the teenaged pregnancy rate is so much higher in the black community.* It all began to make sense. They get pregnant; they just don't have the babies.

Instead they hop their entitled asses into their little Honda Accords and mosey on down to the hood in hopes that they don't run into anyone they know. Then swipes daddy's American Express card and get their little indiscretions sucked right on out. Afterwards, they head right back across town to catch dinner with their friends at their country club like just another ordinary day, all along praying silently no one ever discovers their little secret.

J'Sat Necolle

Smitten

As we walked towards Mrs. Yearwood's car, Yana, still holding Dominique's hand, reached down in her purse and pulled out the car keys and headed towards the driver's side. *Good, because my nerves are way too bad to be driving,* I thought. Hurriedly jumping into the passenger side before Yana changed her mind, I was caught completely off guard when I heard Yana say, "Bitch, where you think you going?"

Stammering, Dominique could barely get anything out, "Pl-pl-please Yana don't." Swinging her toned legs inside of the car, Yana slammed the door with such vengeance that Dominique had no choice but to jump out of the way. "How am I supposed to get home?" she cried out.

"Bitch, that's your problem," Yana said with the coldest voice I'd ever heard. As she squealed off from the curb she threw the paper the nurse had given her along with the remnants of Dominique's purse out the window, without a single glance back.

Chapter 5

Looking around the crowded club, I saw just as many men there to see the show as there were women, then I remembered, this is the reason we stopped coming in the first place. While, I certainly don't have any problem with anyone's sexual preference, I just find it impossible to get turned on by any man after I've just seen him give a lap dance to another man.

I know everything is just an illusion but the whole idea about coming to a strip club is about the fantasy of it all and I damn sure ain't never had two men grinding on each other in any of my damn fantasies. I think I'll pass on that. I'm not saying gay men don't need to see strippers too, but they need their own damn night.

Yana, on the other hand, seemed completely lost in all the male testosterone surrounding us that she barely noticed my complete and utter disgust. I supposed she needed some dick even more than I did. When putting this on tonight's agenda, I'd actually thought it was a good idea but now I'm really second guessing myself.

Just as I was about to get up and head to the ladies' room for the third time in twenty minutes, the scantily clad waiter placed an Amaretto Sour in front of me and pointed to a dark-skinned brother on the other side of the dim club. Making eye contact, I nodded my head and gave him an appreciative smile but hurriedly jumped my ass up and damn near sprinted towards the restroom door before he had the nerve to come over to the table. The last thing I wanted to do was make small talk with some wanna-be player, whose only game was to hang out at a male review hoping to pick up some lonely, broken-hearted sister just gullible enough to fall for his promises of forever. *Child Booh, he can miss me with that.*

I am lonely, and I might even still be a little broken hearted, but I'll be damn if I'm that fucking gullible.

By the time I came back out of the restroom, the club was going full swing. The male review was over and the walls to the large industrial warehouse had been opened and the men from the female review on the other side were now packed in casually amongst all the giddy women. Everyone was just drunk enough and just horny enough to party unsolicited and without fear of who was watching. D.J Herb had the Atlanta vibe going in full effect; first we Bankhead bounced, then we leaned with it and rocked with it, and to round his mix off, he had everyone in the place doing the A-town stomp.

As I looked over at Yana on the dance floor, I changed my earlier thought and was now happy as hell that I'd chose to come here. For the first time in years, I felt like I was finally going to eventually get my friend back to the confident, self-assured woman that she'd been before her marriage. As she slung her heels over to the side of the dance floor and proceeded to twerk her round ass all over the guy she was dancing with, I just threw my head back in pure bliss because from the looks of it her day of reckoning was coming sooner rather than later.

By time we left the club and headed to the Waffle House, just like the good old days, sweat was drenching down the crack of my ass but I'd had the time of my life watching my girl get her sexy back. Even though I've never been half the dancer Yana was, she was giving me so much life from the dance floor that I couldn't help but join her. And when I say...we danced our asses off, we literally danced our asses off!

Once we finally finished our food, the light was just beginning to grace the sky, turning the darkness grey. I headed straight to my house, not wanting to take Yana back to her den of misery and with a silent understanding she laid her head back on the headrest welcoming the calming reprieve.

Chapter 6

"*N*o, absolutely not!" I screamed into the phone before I hurriedly pressed the end button.

The nerve of this bitch to call me and ask me to do something for her ass. The last time I'd seen her trifling ass is when she'd showed up two days after my Grandmother's funeral asking about a damn insurance policy.

The good thing is that some people don't find out until someone dies that their other family members ain't shit; but me on the other hand, I've known all my life that my mama ain't shit.

She's a good-for-nothing, self-serving, money- hungry bitch that ain't never brought me nothing but pain and misery. So, when she showed up looking for money, that was just what I had expected her to do.

I suppose my grandmother must have knew it too, even if she did hate to admit it. I honestly couldn't believe my own eyes when I realized my mother's name was nowhere on any of Grammy's insurance policies. In fact, my grandmother had even written up her wishes for her own obituary, and she didn't have the bitch's name on that either. Left to mourn her memory was only a beloved granddaughter...me.

Smitten

To let Janis tell it, that's the bitch's name, the reason why she had missed the funeral was because she and her twins, Rayne and Storm, were so distraught at how my grandmother had disowned them that they could not muster up the strength to attend. Funny how they seemed strong as hell though when they burst into the attorney's office for the reading of the will. I'll never forget the look on their faces when the attorney disclosed a hand-written letter detailing how all my grandmother's possessions; her home, restaurant and money, were left to her only living heir... me.

My grandmother went on to express in her letter that her only daughter had died the day she walked away from her own flesh-and-blood as if I wasn't hers, then raised her other two biological kids to act as if though I didn't exist, too. By the end of her letter, she had reiterated a lesson she had been telling me my whole life *"...and Hiri, never forget,"* she would say, *"the best way to get revenge on someone that has wronged you is to be successful...and they'll know that they didn't have a damn thing to do with it...then let God handle the rest."*

I honestly thought Janis would keel over and die right then and there. I was laughing so hard at her reaction that I almost pissed on myself. Her creamy complexion turned blood-shot red and just as her two minions jumped up and charged towards me, my girl Yana jumped up and pulled a nine-millimeter hand gun from her

J'Sat Necolle

Gucci purse and said in no uncertain terms, "I don't think you wanna do that."

That was honestly one of the best days of my life; even though, I can't say the same for that attorney. Can you say, he got the hell out of Dodge! I think he forgot we were in his damn office because he hauled ass out that joint like my grandmother had left that bitch to me in the will, too. Every time I think about the irony I call my life, I literally have to laugh to keep from crying.

Now, ten years later, this heifer has the nerve to call me asking me to see if I'm a match for her precious twin. I haven't even been off the phone with her but five minutes but for the life of me I can't even remember which one of them she said needs a kidney. It's probably because I really don't give a damn, cause ain't neither one of them getting mine.

The whole time she was talking, all I could think was that I really had no idea of just what my own mother's voice sounds like. When I first answered the phone, I'd almost hung up on her ass because I thought she was playing on the damn phone. All I could think was that Yana's crazy ass had gotten Rickey Smiley to play a prank phone call on me or something, cause ain't no way this is my mother on the phone. The unfamiliar voice seemed sweet, yet weak and fragile at the same time. It's sad though, because the only memories I have of her speaking are of the times she was yelling at my grandmother

41

about how she didn't want me. I can't remember ever hearing her call my name, it was always 'she' or 'her' and sometimes 'that.'

So, when I heard her say, "Zahiri, it really is me, Janis, your mother," I just knew someone was playing a cruel game. But once she started stammering over her words and telling me how sick her daughter was and how her twin wasn't a match and how her baby was going to die if I didn't help her; I knew it had to be her. She has to be the only individual on this earth that cruel and that selfish. Hell, as funny as Rickey's prank phone calls were, even the funniest comedian in the world couldn't make up that kind of shit.

The sudden ringing of my office phone startled me. I'd obviously been starring out into oblivion for the last twenty minutes, thinking about nothing and everything at the same time. "Yes Julia," I said into the receiver.

Only half listening to my assistant as she ran down my itinerary for the remainder of the day, I stopped her mid-sentence, "Julia, please call Mrs. Calhoun back and reschedule our consultation until next week." Taken aback, she hurried off the phone to carry out my request because I rarely canceled appointments, especially with high-dollar accounts like Mrs. Calhoun; whom just so happen to be the chairman of the board of the most prestigious golf resort in North America.

Smitten

While, Mrs. Calhoun was nice enough, her blatant bigotry was undeniable. She often casually dropped underhanded innuendos about one's 'rightful place' and her love of her president's left-wing policies; and today is just not the day for that bullshit.

With the mood I'm in, I'm liable to tell that racist bitch just what I think of her self-loathing ass. She can sit on as many boards, suck as many dicks and vote Republican for the rest of her natural born life, and that still won't change a damn thing. She was born black and she's going to die black. Just like my fucking mother.

I might be wrong, but it seemed like to me that mixed people would understand more than anyone that if you got 1% of black in you, then you're black. The laws of Jim Crow south hasn't changed and in the eyes of society, it never will. When my mother came back with her white husband, her white step-daughter and her beloved lily-white twins, that sealed my little brown fate forever.

It had taken me years to realize that my mother didn't really hate me, she hated herself. Being black was a burden to her and once I was born, the burden escalated even more. I didn't have the skin tone of my bi-racial mother or her white father, instead I reached into the soul of my ancestry and took the melanin of my grandmother, much to my mother's dismay. The caramel-latte color that gracefully coated my body revealed my African heritage; and my mother's burden.

Now, her wanna-be-white ass has the audacity to expect my black ass to give her precious white child a second chance at life, with my damn kidney. "She must've bumped her fucking head, cause I ain't giving them shit but my ass to kiss," I said aloud, as I slid my chair away from the desk.

Grabbing my Gucci bag and slinging it across my shoulder, I headed out my office door, quickly circling by the receptionist desk, I yelled over my shoulders, "Julia, please go ahead and clear my schedule for the remainder of the week, I have a family emergency." And out the door I went.

Chapter 7

*A*s I swerved in and out of traffic down 85, trying to get as far away from Buckhead as my car could take me, I blasted 104.1 as loud as I could, as blasts from the past filled by vehicle and my heart, taking me on another unsolicited scroll down memory lane after a. When Whitney Houston's powerful vocal cards belted out, *"No o-ther wo-man is gon-na love you more... cause tonight- is- the- night, that I'm feeling all- right. We'll—be- making- love- the- whole- night through-h-h. So, I'm saving all my love...yeah, I'm saving all my love; yes, I'm saving all my love for you-u-u,"* all I could think about was my first love.

As the sweet sounds caressed my heart and made me reminisce on days gone by, the realist in me could not help but see the irony of it all. It's incredible how we as women seem to distort our own reality to make it reflect what we really wanted it to be. Hell, I know that fool didn't love me, but every time I hear these songs, I instantly think of him.

Talk about distorting reality, what a fucking understatement. Shit, I can't even begin to explain what my first heart break felt like, nor would I wish that kind of pain on my worst enemy. I suppose it's a rite of passage though, one that all little girls must eventually go through... but Lord why does it have to hurt so much? If these little fass-ass girls around here knew half of what I know, they would listen to their mamas when they tell them they'll be grown soon enough because heartbreak does not discriminate...it fucks up women from eight to eighty; blind, crippled and crazy!

For many women, like myself, the act of falling in love is one of the most amazing feelings on earth. But I can honestly say I've only been in love one time and that one time was all it took. Event though, I have loved again, I have never allowed myself to be in a place where vulnerability was the catalyst of my existence. Which is what allowed me to fall head over heels in love in the first place. Shit, once I got over Kenyan's ass, I promised myself that I would never allow myself to care that much about anyone else ever again...and I haven't.

In fact, it wasn't until my sophomore year in college that I finally decided to give love another try and for a while it was actually pretty cool. His name was Giovanni, but everyone on campus just called him Vani. He was cute with curly black hair, with the cutest dimple in his chin. He was at Fordham on a full-ride athletic scholarship; he played shooting guard on the basketball team. Ironically enough, we met in an African-American Studies class where me and all the other girls were left completely mesmerized every time he opened his mouth and spoke of the injustices plaguing the African American community. Something about an intelligent and articulate man has always made my blood rise for as long as I could remember. For the most part, every box I had on my check list for the kind of man I wanted to spend my life with was checked off with Vani, with the exception of one thing; he wasn't black.

I don't know if it was because I was bi-racial, or if it had something to do with my own experience with my white heritage, but for whatever reason I had never considered anything other than a black man. While I'll be the first to admit that most of my experiences with men ended on a sour note, when the getting was good, it was real damn good. And for the life of me, I couldn't imagine anyone other than a black man being able to make me feel that way. Hell, I figured if God made anything better than some black dick...he kept that shit on the hush-hush.

So, when I caught myself developing more than a superficial attraction to the tall, muscular French man, with the sexy accent and innocent smile, I was caught off in left field somewhere and didn't know how to function.

It started out innocent enough, we would meet up for discussions and study groups with some of our other classmates. Five or six of us would get together and go to campus protests and rallies to fight for the rights of blacks in America. It was just something about the fact that he was advocating harder for our rights than most of the black men on campus that made him even more attractive than he already was. And it seemed that I wasn't the only sistah on campus that was caught up in his spell, because there wasn't a time when we were out in groups that one of the other sistahs weren't throwing themselves at him. Imagine my surprise when he finally asked me if he could call me some time. To say I was taken aback was an understatement, and at first the whole interracial thing was a bit much, but I soon got with the program.

We'd talk on the phone for hours about any and everything, which had me a little apprehensive because it made me remember a time I wanted to forget. Eventually though, he got the nerve to ask me out on an actual date and I said yes. You talking about weird, that shit was hella weird at first. I felt like everyone was always starring at us, especially other black men.

Then I had this idiotic complex about kissing him; even though, his skin was only about two shades lighter than mine. It honestly took me about two months of dating before I could even tongue kiss him. Oh, but when I did...let's just say, there is a reason why the term "French-kiss" exists.

The night it happened, we were actually at the movies watching New Jack City for the third time and Homeboy tongued me down so hard I came all over myself right then and there. I'm not sure if it was him or because I was really caught up in the scene on the screen when Nino Brown was grinding all up in Unique's goodies. All I know is, "*I wanna sex you up,*" started blasting from the speakers behind the back row where we were sitting, then all of a sudden he reached

J'Sat Necolle

over and grabbed me by the back of my head and when his tongue wrapped around mine, they mingled into an adulterated pleasure that I could not resist.

Sensing my longing, he pulled his tongue out of my mouth and stuck his finger in its vacated crevices and I hastily pulled it in and out of my mouth in pure hunger, as he used his other hand to ease my panties over from under my mini skirt and proceeded to insert first one, then two fingers inside my throbbing abyss, then just as I was about to scream out in ecstasy, he pulled his finger out of my mouth and gently covered my entire mouth with his hand to mask my moan, while he simultaneously removed his gyrating fingers from the walls of my blazing inferno and before I could cry out in protest, he'd replaced his fingers with his mouth.

Oblivious to all the other patrons in the theatre, on the back row of one of the most gangster movies of all time, I came over and over and over again, as I was formally introduced to the immense joys of oral sex.

By the time we walked out that theatre hand in hand, him steadying me because my legs felt like Jell-O; I didn't give two fucks about who was staring or what they had to say. All I knew is that this man walking beside me had given me pleasures I'd never known before and I didn't care if he was white, black, French or Asian! There was no way in the world I was going to deny myself that feeling again, for no damn body.

Smitten

From that night on, we became inseparable. It was something right out of a fairytale and while his actual sex wasn't anything special, especially in comparison to my two other sexual partners; the way he tongue-stroked my insides morning, noon and night...who needed a big dick tearing their insides out. Which is exactly what Tyrique was doing my last year in high school and not just to me, but to the whole female student body.

I'll never forget the first time I brought Vani home from school... my grandma almost shitted bricks. Over the months we'd been dating, I'd told her everything about him, with the exception of his race.

Honestly, a part of me didn't know exactly how she would feel about it but never in my life did I think she would take such an adamant stance against it, especially being that my grandfather was white. I'd never in my life seen her treat someone so badly. From the time he stepped foot in the front door, she treated him like shit. I must say he was a class act though because no matter how insulting she was to him, he responded with only kindness and respect. So much so that it almost had me wondering if he was retarded or something, because if that had been me and his mother...oh, I would have read that bitch.

Later that night when we were getting out the shower in the suite he'd gotten for us

J'Sat Necolle

downtown at the Omni Hotel after my grandmother had told us in no uncertain terms that there was no way on God's green earth he was sleeping under her roof; we held each other closer than we ever had before. It seemed as if we were both feeling that if we could hold each other tight enough, then no outside force could ever come between us.

According to Grammy, "I might can't tell you what to do at that uppity college, but I sure as hell can tell you what you can do in my own damn house, and ain't no way in hell you gon' be laying up with no damn white man up in here."

As soon as she said that, I jumped up and almost ran to the front door because I'd had about enough. Here she was acting a pure fool after she had practically begged me to bring him home to meet her. She acted just like she didn't have a whole damn baby, by a whole damn white man. That was some hypocritical bullshit at its finest.

Instead of him hurrying on out the door behind me, he walked over to my grandmother and looked her straight in the eyes and said, "I'm really sorry you feel this way, but it has been a pleasure to finally meet the woman who raised Zahiri to be the beautiful, bold and courageous woman that she is. Enjoy the rest of your evening." Then with a warm smile and polite nod of his head, he turned and walked over to the door where I impatiently stood, grabbed my hand and led me out the door.

Smitten

Still baffled at my grandmother's behavior, I apologized to him over and over again on her behalf; although, he repeatedly told me that I didn't owe him an apology, nor should I keep making the habit of apologizing for other people's ignorance. Nevertheless, I still felt like shit, though.

My Vani though, in all his infinite wisdom described it like this, "That's like white people today still feeling the need to apologize for slavery. What the hell are they apologizing for? Shit, they didn't do it! All they need to do is acknowledge the fact that it was wrong and raise their children without bigotry and hatred to ensure that dark era in history will never exist again."

In all practicality, I knew he was right, and I certainly understood where he was coming from, but it didn't make me feel any less mortified that someone I love treated another human being that way; an undeserving human being at that.

When I asked him later that night as he stroked my backside with his tongue, how he was able to remain so calm while someone berated him like that. He answered softly, "Because I love you."

J'Sat Necolle

Chapter 8

*V*eering right off I-75, I turned the sleek, luxury vehicle in the direction of my best friend's condo. Since I lost my grandmother more than ten years ago, she has been the one constant in my life. My Grammy used to always say that family ain't just blood and for as long as I could remember, Yana has been family. When I got upstairs to her door, I chastised myself for not calling first because knowing Yana she was probably laying her ass around wallowing in her own self-pity and didn't need my bullshit added to her already unstable piece-of-mind, but I had to tell her about the phone call from Janis. Hell, I needed somebody to help me make some sense of the bullshit
.

As soon as I rang the doorbell, she flung the door open immediately.

The stunned look on my face couldn't even begin to describe the utter shock my heart went into when my girl opened door wearing only a radiant smile, a sheer-black camisole and some six-inch black heels.

"Whatdafuck!" I exclaimed. My mouth dropped wide open. Never in a million years did I expect to roll up on this. Maybe some loose

Smitten

fitting sweat pants and a dingy tank top, but
never this.

Covering her mouth in surprise with her well-
manicured fingers, she let out an exasperated
giggle and said, "Bitch, get your ass in here
before somebody sees all of this!"

I wanted to move. I knew I should move...but
for the life of me, the signal just would not
register with my brain for me to move one
fucking inch. I just stood in the doorway, staring
like an idiot, still uttering, "Whatdafuck!"

Laughing uncontrollably, she grabbed me by
the hand and yanked my stoic ass into the condo
as hard as she could. "Bitch come on!"

Once inside, she literally had to usher me
over to the plush grey sectional filling the room. I
still couldn't move on my own or close my damn
mouth, so she lightly shoved me onto the couch
while she hurried out the room laughing.

She was yelling something from the back
bedroom but as of yet, I still haven't heard a
damn thing she said. The only thing I could
remember is her saying something about chilling
with Netflix or some shit. Then, suddenly the
alarming chimes of the doorbell ringing almost
made me jump straight out of my skin. Yana,
damn near did a 100-yard dash out the bedroom
with a robe barely covering her nearly-naked
body, she hurried around the corner, then looked

J'Sat Necolle

back at me and said, "Bitch, you better not say nothing."

And I remember thinking, *Bitch, I'm fucking mute...what the hell can I say.* When she swung the door open and fell into outstretched arms, I thought, *Damn, this nigga must want something, he's back in town trying to smooze her again.* But when she stepped aside, it wasn't Gavin's punk ass starring back at me. *Oh, my God...I'm in the Twilight Zone.* "Hiri, you remember Brandon, don't you?"

Looking from him to her and back to him, my brain finally strung a complete sentence together, or so I thought, but when I opened my mouth to speak, the only thing that came out was, "Whatdafuck."

They both began laughing hysterically but at that moment I didn't find shit funny. *I think this bitch done broke my fucking brain.* Sensing my anxiety, she casually walked over to me and playfully slapped the side of my face. "Girl, snap out of it."

Brandon walked over to the marble kitchen counter and pulled three wineglasses from the overhead cupboard, then reached inside the wine fridge on the adjacent wall and pulled out a bottle of Moscato and walked over to where Yana and I sat on the couch. Never in a million years did I imagine coming over here and catching my best friend, my ride-or-die, my confidant, playing secret rendezvous with

Smitten

Brandon Lewis, the one man whose heart she'd broken into a million pieces.

When she broke up with him her Senior year at Howard to start dating Gavin's broke ass; I, by far, thought it was one of the dumbest mistakes she'd ever made. But hell, one thing I'd learned about friendship was sometimes it's better to say little, than risk losing a lot. So, I kept my unsolicited opinion to myself.

Once the wine finally registered with my brain and stimulated my vocal sensory, I said, "B, it really is good to see you!" "How have you been?"

Displaying the amazingly genuine smile that I've always adored about him, he said, "I've been good, Hiri. Really good." He came over and gave me a warm embrace and I reciprocated genuinely because I'd always liked B. I absolutely hated it when Yana had abruptly called off their engagement, when she started seeing Gavin.

I was immediately caught in the middle because we'd all been friends our entire lives. For years Brandon had lived behind us in the same housing projects in Building D. His mother used to play cards with my grandma and Yana's parents for as long as I could remember. We'd played on the playground together every day as youngsters, then we chilled together in high school and somehow or another, when they went off to Howard University their familiarity and friendship turned into something much more.

J'Sat Necolle

Smitten

I would say I was shocked when she'd called my dorm late one night freaking out because she'd fucked up and given Brandon some earlier that night after a frat party, when he'd walked her back to her dorm. She wanted to blame it on the alcohol and the fact that she was horny as hell, but I didn't believe that mess one damn bit. But me being me, I just let her kept fooling herself.

Everybody and their mama could always see that those two had some intense chemistry going on, and it was only a matter of time before nature took its course. My Grammy used to always say, 'What don't come out in the wash, will shole' nuff' come out in the rinse.'

So, I just let her go right on believing the bullshit she was feeding herself and sure enough, less than two months later, she called my dorm at 2am one morning, crying her heart out because she'd seen him leaving a party with another girl. Sometimes all it takes is seeing the possibility of losing what has always been available to you, to make you finally see the obvious.

The next day, at my insistence, she walked over to his dorm and when he came to the door, she didn't utter a word, she just handed him a cassette tape like I'd told her to, then turned and walked away. I specifically instructed her not to record a whole playlist of songs, just find one song that mirrored what she was feeling, and then record that baby on repeat. Ever since that day, I've always joked with him about how he'd made it back over to her dorm clear across campus before side A had ever finished playing.

To let him tell it though, it took the same song playing for the third time in a row for him to finally catch the hint that the tape was a love letter to him. Until this very day, no matter where I am or who I am with, every time I hear Xscape's heartfelt jam, *"Do You Want To,"* I remember the night these two officially began.

*Well, I'll be damned...*me and this broke ass brain of mine just registered the fact that ever since I stumbled through the front door, that same song has been playing on the internal speakers this entire time. Forgetting why I was even here, I jumped up like someone had stuck a firecracker up my ass. *I'm a lot of things,* I thought to myself, *but I damn sure ain't no cock-blocker.*

Lightly kissing him on the check, then her, I said, "Oh, Bitch, you got some explaining to do, but right now, I'm out." Throwing up the deuces sign, I almost tripped over my feet trying to get to the front door. As I was hurrying out the door, I could hear them still laughing at my awkwardness.

She's a grown woman, I told myself as I quickly exited her building and entered the garage looking for my car with a newfound happiness in my heart, and Janis the farthest thing from my mind.

Chapter 9

The next few weeks seemed to fly by so fast; working non-stop on all the new contracts I had to get filled before spring came on full blast was taking up all my time. Sometimes I felt like I didn't even have time to sleep. Ever since my company, Tre' Unique had been chosen by Forbes Magazine as one of the premier interior design companies on the east coast, my client log has grown immensely. In just over a year, I have gone from a 1800 square foot office space to a 8,000 square foot show room to accommodate my growing business. I've gone from six full-time employees, to twenty-five, full-time employees.

While, I must admit I welcome the wonderful opportunity that I've been afforded, I do miss the days that I could solely concentrate on doing what I love. Every day I seemed to get pushed farther and farther away from direct contact with my clients, and the planning and executing phrases of beautifully unique designs, to the mundane task of keeping up with management duties. I often wonder if the money is worth the trade-off. While, I have always wanted to be successful, for more reasons than one, I wonder if that success has come with a costly prize. It's during times like this that I miss my grandmother the most.

For someone with little to no education, she was one of the smartest people I've ever had the pleasure of knowing. Just as I was getting lost in thoughts of my Grammy while mulling over the budget reports for the stadium project, Julia came over my intercom, "Excuse me, Ms. James, I have Janis Simpson on line two again. She says it's urgent." *Lord, Grammy, help me, please.*

Sensing my apprehension, Julia said quietly into the intercom, "Zahiri, I know this is none of my business but whatever is so severe that it has this woman calling up here two and three times a day in tears, and is obviously causing you turmoil because you've cancelled more appointments in the last month than the entire five years that I've worked for you...it has to get settled. You have to settle it once and for all, you can't keep running away from it."

What I wanted to tell Julia is that she's absolutely right, it was none of her business, but I couldn't. I know she is coming from a good place. Over the past five years that she's worked for me, her and her husband Joe have become like family to me. Their fifteen-year-old granddaughter, Khloe, thinks the sun rises and falls on me, and I simply adore Jaxson, their 6-year-old grandson, both of whom they have raised since birth because of their daughter's battles with addiction.

With an exasperating sigh, I told Julia to go ahead and schedule a meeting with her in my office tomorrow after all the employees have gone for the day. I couldn't quiet explain the feeling that washed over me at that moment. Suddenly, I felt relieved like a one-hundred-pound weight had been lifted off my back. "Perhaps it's past time for me and good, ol' Mommy Dearest to chop it up. I've got 31 years of build-up shit that she needs to hear," I told myself. *And when I'm done with that, I'll tell her just where she can stick her request for my damn kidney.*

"Hello," I oozed into the phone. I've only seen Yana's ass twice in the last three weeks. Apparently, she's been getting dicked down by Brandon on the regular, so she didn't have time to kick it. "To what do I owe this unexpected surprise?"

"Ahhh, Bitch please," Yana snorted into the receiver. "Don't act like that and bring your ass on over here to scoop me up. I'm hungry."

"Bitch are you stupid?" I said. "I just got out the shower and am not about to take my black ass out this time of night."

"Oh, so it's like that now...a bitch starts getting some outside nookie and her own girl start to disown her!"

Smitten

I know Yana, and this was her way of getting a heat check to see how I really feel about her cheating on her husband. She knows I've always been the poster child for fidelity and all. In fact, one of my best and worst attributes is that I'm loyal beyond belief. But truth be told, I honestly did not give one single fuck about her cheating on Gavin's spineless ass. For the life of me, I can't figure out what took her so fucking long. In my opinion her marriage has been over, she's just the last one to figure the shit out. But again, some things are better left unsaid.

Interrupting my thoughts, the sound of the doorbell jolted me to my feet. "Hold on, Yan, it's probably the delivery guy at the door. As I reached for the door knob, I suddenly heard a familiar voice yelling, "Hurry up, Bitch, I've got to pee." Snapping my head back in a heart-drenching laughter, this heifer never ceased to amaze me. I snatched the door open and pulled her into a warm embrace.

Lord knows, I didn't want to call and wine to her about Janis' trifling ass and ruin the reunion she and Brandon were having, but damn was I happy she was finally here. I really needed help wrapping my mind around this bullshit. Grammy used to always say, "He may not be there when you need him, but he's always there on time." *Want he do it!* I thought to myself as I closed my door, still in disbelief that this heifer showed up once again when I need her most.

J'Sat Necolle

Smitten

"Girl, you must have ESP," I said to her departing backside, as she bypassed the bathroom and headed straight into my kitchen towards the liquor cabinet. She must've sensed I needed something just a little stronger than wine too because she reached down and popped the top on a new bottle of Peach Crown and poured us two straight shots each.

Flopping down lazily on my couch, she passed my goblet over to me as I sat down beside her. "Now, what the fuck is Janis blowing your phone up for?" "Do you need me to handle that?" "All you've got to do is say the word and I'll gladly put my foot right off in her ass!"

I could tell in her eyes she was dead-ass serious too. The last time I'd seen this look in her eyes was the day she'd pulled her piece out on Janis and the twins and before that it was eight years earlier when she left Dominique's trifling ass outside of that abortion clinic. That day was the beginning of the new, more improved, talk shit and back it up, Yana. The sweet, innocent Yana died that very day; right along with her father's unborn fetus.

Even though I don't want to see this fool kill nobody, it is absolutely amazing to see this side of her resurfacing again. This Yana slowly started fading away shortly after her second miscarriage and by the time she'd had the third miscarriage, the only similarity she had to her old self was that she still sat down to pee. She was totally different. Part of me understood but then there was this other part of me that couldn't even understand the fascination of wanting to have a baby so badly, especially given the state of emergency of her marriage.

Personally, I've never wanted children; in fact, that was one of the main reasons why Vani and I split up; besides the fact that my grandmother hated his guts.

I'd told him in no uncertain terms will I be bearing anyone's children and he just could not understand that. I'd told him time and time again that all women don't want children and that's their personal choice and no one; including the man they love, has a right to question what they want to do with their own damn bodies.

It had gotten so bad in our relationship that he used to leave all kinds of hints around the apartment once we moved in together. One day I came home and lying on the sofa was a big ass box of pampers, like they'd came from Sam's Club or Costco's or some shit, so I just assumed he'd brought them for someone as a gift. After they'd taken up space in my small living room for a couple of days, I finally asked, "So, who's shower did you buy these pampers for?"

He jerked his head up so quick from the video game he was playing, I could have sworn he'd heard the voice of Malcolm X or something, then stated matter of factly, "Those are for us, they were on sale."

J'Sat Necolle

"Ohhh, they are," I said, looking at his ass like he had grown a horn in the middle of his fucking forehead. But instead of me being my usual bitchy self, I didn't say another fucking word. I sat that big ass box on the floor and kept on folding my cloths and watching my DVR of the last season of Scandal, thinking, *This Nigga done lost his fucking mind. He better hope, like hell pampers don't have a fucking expiration date.*

Those same damn pampers stayed in the living room for about two months before he finally moved them and put them in the hall closet. But by that time the damage had already been done. Every day that I'd came home from work, tired as hell, with that fucking pampers box glaring at me, I realized even more that if this man didn't even respect my right to fucking choose, he doesn't respect shit else about me.

And before long, everything he did got on my nerves. That sexy ass accent I used to love so much, got on my nerves. The way he stroked my hair, got on my nerves. Even the way he licked my ass crack, got on my damn nerves. It had gotten so bad that I would only let him eat it, and when he thought he was about to get his little wink-wink wet, I'd always jump up with some excuse. Sometimes I used to feel so bad when I saw the look of rejection in his eyes because I know that feeling all too well, but I couldn't help it. I just didn't trust his ass. Mother-fuckers walking around buying baby shit for a non-existent baby are liable to do any damn thing...like put a hole in a condom, or even

Smitten

switch out my birth control pills with a placebo. Hell nawl, me being me, I wasn't taking any chances. *Oh, no mam!*

Finally, it got to the point where I was staying at work as long as I could, just to avoid his ass. Then I'd jump up two hours early just to keep him from rolling over with a hard dick expecting some morning nookie that wasn't happening. At one point, I'd gone three weeks without actually having any type of communication with him whatsoever because I'd get home well after he was sleep and be out the door well before he woke up.

One night though, in the middle of my shift at the Waffle House, two gunmen stormed in and robbed the place. By the time the cops got through questioning us, I was physically and mentally drained, so I headed home. Walking in the door, still somewhat disheveled, I tripped over something in the middle of the floor. When I reached over to turn on the kitchen light in the small apartment, I became instantly pissed when I saw cloths strewn all over the place. *Nasty bastard*, I thought. I suppose I was still pretty shaken up from the robbery because it took me a minute for the entire scene to come into focus.

There on the tiny kitchen table that my grandmother had given me when she updated the décor in her restaurant were two plates; the steak and lobster on either had barely been touched. Two half-empty wine glasses and two fucking candles almost shriveled down to

J'Sat Necolle

nothing, putting out a soft glimmer of light. *Well, I be fucking damn,* I thought to myself. Then I did what any other reasonable girlfriend would do...I sat down and finished off their steaks and lobsters, drank their wine, grabbed his wallet and then I quietly tip-toed to the hall closet and grabbed that big ass box of pampers and left.

When I got inside my room at the Radisson, the most expensive hotel I could find, the first thing I did was call Yana. As I gave her the run-down of my night, she laughed so hard she literally peed on herself. "But Bitch, what made you eat them folk's food?" And I honestly didn't have any logical answer other than the fact that I was hungry, which made her laugh even harder.

"Besides," I said, "I knew damn well that lobster was going to be a helluva lot better than that lil' dick he was giving her, so, shit, I was winning."

Now, laughing hysterically, she was barely able to get it out, "Well, I'm lost...why did you take those pampers and why on earth didn't you cold bust his ass?" She went on ranting about ain't no way in the hell she could've walked out of there without letting him know she was there and how she would have had to have known who it was he'd had in there.

Once she calmed down, because she was way more upset than I was...but that was Yana for you, I finally said, "Well, I didn't try to fuck up his nut because I really didn't give a fuck. He deserved a nut and he damn sure wasn't getting it from me. I gave even less of a fuck about who he was screwing with that itty-bitty winky of his because I already knew it wasn't you and it damn sure wasn't my Grammy, so anyone else was more than welcome to it." She laughed so hard that I couldn't help but to see the humor in it myself.

"And the reason I took his wallet is because as soon as I get off the phone with you, I'm getting on the internet and order all new shit; then first thing in the morning, I'll go put a deposit down on a new apartment."

"Okay, okay," she said. "All of that does make sense but how do you explain that big ass box of pampers?"

"To be honest," I said, "I really don't know what the hell made me grab those damn pampers. I literally said to myself when I was getting those bastards out the closet, *She can have his ass, but I bet she won't get my baby's shit!*"

She laughed so hard that she pissed all over herself right then and there. I heard Brandon's ass in the background jump up and yell, "That shit ain't that funny, you done pissed all over me!"

I doubled over in laughter, I'll never forget that night as long as I live.

J'Sat Necolle

It took Vani about three months before he finally stopped blowing my phone up. That was around the same time I finally mailed his wallet and his maxed-out credit card back to his ass. After that, when I did run into him on campus, he'd just drop his head. I never did find out for sure exactly who it was he had in our apartment that night but word around campus was that he was messing around with Ms. Ingram, our African American Studies professor but I wasn't really sure. But by the next semester, he was gone and so was she.

Chapter 10

Snapping myself out of the closet, filled with the skeletons of my past, I asked, "So, how do you know about Janis calling me?"

"Well... I would like to say God and I have this wonderful connection but that would be a lie. I'm probably so far down God's shit list right now that he has already picked out a special place for me in hell; right between Saddam Hussein and Donald Trump."

We both laughed hysterically. "Julia called you, didn't she?" I asked.

"Technically, no. I actually called the office looking for you and then she told me I need to check on you because you're closing her out, but some chick name Janis keeps calling you and it has you all weirded-out. By the way, you do know she's as bossy as Grammy, don't you?" She asked, looking as serious as a heart attack.

"Child, who you telling?" I said laughing hysterically. "She is a mess and a half and reminds me so much of Grammy. She's forever in my business but the first thing that comes out of her mouth is, '*I don't mean to be in your business or nothing.*' "Yeah right, she lives to be in my business." We both laughed.

I can't believe it, but Yana sat there quietly as I told her about the first time Janis called weeks ago, which was the same day I showed up at her condo unexpectedly and got my brain broken. Then I told her about how she's been blowing up my office phone everyday ever since and just how the weight of it all has my head screwed up.

"The thought of being the reason why any human being dies doesn't sit well with me," I said. "But on the other hand, it's not my responsibility to ensure that a perfect stranger lives."

After sitting there for a moment carefully analyzing the situation, Yana finally spoke up, "Damn man, this is some deep shit. First of all, let me be really clear," she said, using her hands for emphasis, looking me dead in the eyes. "You don't owe anybody a damn thing!" "Whatever decision you make should be yours and yours alone. So, don't you let that bitch, or any other bitch, for that matter, make you feel obligated to do shit." "You hear me?"

With tears streaming down my face, I nodded my head in agreeance. Then she went on, "First of all, you don't even know if you are even a match, so you might be putting unnecessary pressure on yourself about something you probably can't do a damn thing about." I nodded my head because I'd never considered that point.

"Secondly, she went on, "when that bitch called you and asked you to donate your organ, did she even mention how risky this procedure could be for you?" I shook my head '*no*'.

"Lastly, did the ho even attempt to apologize to you at all, or did she act like she always has, like you owe her something?"

"Of course, the heifer didn't even mention any risk for me. Hell, that was the first time I'd ever even heard the ho say my name. And yes, you already know that selfish bitch acted like her asking me such a thing was appropriate, like she had the right to ask me for anything," I said between sobs, as my voice began to crack, and tears blinded my vision.

I think the last time Yana had seen me cry over Janis and her minions was about five years ago around Mother's Day. I'd gone out to my grandmother's grave site and saw a new flower bouquet, when I opened up the envelope it had "Love, Janis, Storm and Rayne inscribed on the card. In one breath I was happy that she'd thought about my Grammy on Mother's Day, but on the other hand, it just made me sad to see the three of their names signed next to one another and my name nowhere to be found, which was symbolic of my life. I left there and headed straight to Yana's and cried my heart out.

In my thirty-two years on earth, I've only discussed my real mom with three people. Grammy, Yana and Kenyan; my first love. After Kenyan broke my heart, I learned then and there to stop being so open and vulnerable with people. That's why I keep my business and my feelings to myself. Grammy always used to say, "*Your business ain't everybody's business,*" but I think it was because she was embarrassed that her daughter was a dead-beat mother.

She'd caught me on the telephone crying one night, telling Kenyan all about my mom, and how she had left me and never came back for me. I had been sitting on the floor by the trashcan because all we had in our apartment was one wall phone and it hung in the kitchen over the trashcan, across from the sink. That night I was supposed to be washing dishes and I really had been for a little while, until I heard my Grammy back in her room praying louder than usual. So, I eased a couple of feet down the hallway, nervously playing with the long phone card. When I peeked inside her bedroom door all I

J'Sat Necolle

could see was her down on her knees holding the picture of Janis that she kept on her night stand, she was just rocking and crying, saying over and over again, "Lord, bless my baby."

I don't know what came over me, but I felt so lonely and so angry in that moment that all I could do was cry. At first, Kenyan didn't have any idea what was going on, he just kept asking what's wrong, was it something he'd done. In between sobs I'd tried to tell him that I was okay but when he finally yelled that he was on his way over there, my words started flowing like the river Jordan.

There wasn't no way in hell I was about to let him come over there. Grammy would have killed us both. She had no idea I called myself had a boyfriend, especially one three years older than me. She thought I was on the phone with my friends every night. When he called me, he would always get one of his girl cousins to ask to speak to me in case Grammy answered the phone. That shit worked for a long time too.

Even though I was embarrassed to let anyone know my own mama didn't want me, I couldn't help myself for breaking down to him because it just hurt so much seeing my Grammy cry over her that night after the way she'd treated us both. I've always felt like she didn't even deserve a mother like my Grammy. I deserved her. I just wished that I was enough for her, but no matter how hard I tried to be perfect for my Grammy, it just never seemed like enough.

Smitten

If I came home with all A's & B's, she would say, *"Your mama used to make all A's."* If I came home and said how Rev. Stanley said I was so pretty today, she'd say, *"Everybody used to tell your mama how pretty she was all the time."* I'm not even sure if she even realized she did that, but every time she did it, it felt like one more piece of my soul got abandoned too.

Kenyan understood though, he said he felt the same way about his dad. We used to spend hour after hour talking on the phone. He'd tell me about his dad and I tell him about my mom. We'd share our war stories where our dead-beat parents were concerned. I used to reassure him all the time that he was at least blessed with one good parent because the way he described his mom, she seemed closer to an angel than anyone I knew, besides Yana's mom, of course. And at least he did know who his dad was, I had no idea what mine looked like, sounded like; hell, I didn't even know the man's name. All I knew was that he was bi-racial, unlike like my granddaddy, who was just plain white...and that's all I knew about his trifling ass, too.

That's when Grammy walked in...before I knew it, she had pressed the thing down on the phone to hang it up and was reaching down to snatch the receiver right out my hand. I dropped that receiver so quick and jumped up from the floor where I had been sitting Indian-style for hours pouring my heart out. "Get your ass up and finish these damn dishes," she yelled. By now I

J'Sat Necolle

was clear on the other side of the room standing by the door huffing and puffing. Grammy was old, but she was still pretty quick, and she'd been known to bust me upside my head a time or two when I started talking back and I wasn't taking no chance. She wasn't about to hit me with that hard ass phone upside my head. *Oh no mam.* I was in high school and thought I was cute too. I didn't have time for bruises.

"You talk too fucking much," she said firmly. "Family business, ain't everybody's business. Your business, ain't everybody's business. And my business, ain't no-fucking-body's business," she yelled at the top of her lungs; right before she unplugged the receiver from the card, then marched back to her room and slammed her damn door.

I didn't see that receiver for another two weeks. Those were the longest two weeks of my life.

Chapter 11

*I*t never failed, Yana swooped in and saved the day yet again. Ever since we were little girls, playing on those raggedy ass sea-saws in our projects, she always had my back and ain't shit changed.

Last night she stayed over, and we ate popcorn, drank liquor and watched old movies on Netflix. She even explained to me what Netflix and Chill meant and that let me know that if I don't get some dick soon I might as well join a convent. Usually, Khloe, Julia's granddaughter, kept me up on shit like that but we really haven't gotten to spend any alone time together since the business has been growing so rapidly. I spit the remnants of the toothpaste out in the wash basin and reached for my I-Phone X, "Siri, remind me today at noon to schedule a spa day for me and Khloe next weekend."

"Yesssss, Bitch!" Siri responded. I absolutely love the new features the new I-phone have. I customized Siri to sound just like a gay BFF and I absolutely love it! When my alarm goes off in the morning, it says, "Biiiittttttchhhhhh," then pauses about three seconds, then it says in a more high-pitched, much sassier tone, "Bitch, I know you hear me!" That is always the highlight of my morning, but today took the cake. When that alarm went off, I thought Yana was going to lose her damn mind. She jumped up and looked around the room, and when it said, "Bitch, I know you hear me!" she sat straight up in the bed and started praying.

"Oh, God. Oh, God, please forgive me!" She pleaded earnestly. I fell out the bed laughing so hard at that fool. She was so fucking serious and really had no idea that it was the phone talking. When I tell you, she put one more cussing out on Siri's ass when I told her that it was just my alarm. I wish I had been recording that shit because she would have certainly gone viral. That's just why you don't keep yourself in a bubble for three fucking years on account of a no-good man. The world has been going on about its business and she's been stuck in Never-Never land.

Even after talking with her last night, I realized she still has about three toes stuck in Never-Never land, because she honestly thinks that her marriage is worth saving. According to her, Brandon knows this is just a fling and she loves her husband.

But according to me, she said B's name one time too many last night, even in her drunken sleep, for this to be just a fling. But, this is nothing new, Yana has always been the last one to see what is sitting right in her face. I just pray it all doesn't blow up in her face. B is a good dude, but she hurt him something serious the first time around.

Smitten

By the time I had finished getting ready for work, she was already on the phone scheduling everything for today. We decided last night to get all my ducks in a row before I agree to sit down and meet with Janis; if I decided to do so at all.

First, Yana called my office and got Janis' cellphone number from Julia. Then she called Janis. I could hear her from the bathroom, "Good morning, Mrs. Simpson. This is Mrs. Smalls; Ms. James' office manager, she will no longer be able to meet with you today; however, she is interested in finding out more information about the procedure, so I need you to send over the physician's contact information this morning so that I can schedule an appointment."

Apparently, Janis' entitled ass must've gotten beside herself and thought I was agreeing to be a donor because I heard Yana say, "No, Bitch! I did not say Hiri was going to donate ya'll shit. What I said was send me the doctor's fucking contact information so that we can find out everything we need without speaking to your trifling ass."

That's my dog! I thought to myself. Grinning from ear to ear I finished enhancing my eyebrows, then reached over and pressed the side of my phone and told Siri to remind me to schedule a trip for just me and my girl.

J'Sat Necolle

Chapter 12

*A*s Yana and I headed inside the medical center off Ashford-Dunwoody and Peachtree, I guess she could sense my apprehension, so she grabbed my hand and held it tight just like she used to do when we were kids. "Don't worry, Buddy," she said. "It can't be that bad if the doctor waited two weeks to schedule a consultation with a potential donor."

How she can always find logic in the most illogical situations is beyond me, but damn if she didn't just do it again. It probably isn't half as bad as Janis' ass is making it out to be. According to Grammy, she always was a damn drama queen. But hell, I wouldn't know because I don't know the bitch.

As we took the elevator up to the sixth floor of the immaculate building, I had to focus on something besides the situation at hand, so I focused on the wood work throughout the building. The intricately carved wood panels that lined the hallways and elevator were absolutely stunning. I believe in my past life, I must have been married to Bob-the-Builder or some shit because I'm a HGTV watching fool. In fact, for my new office and showroom, I got right in there with the contractors and got my hands dirty too, and I loved every minute of it. I think that's what makes me such a talented designer. Not only can I develop creative and unique designs, but I am visually able to structurally maneuver it all in my head while creating the design.

Where this talent comes from, I honestly don't know, but it has made me a very rich woman, I thought to myself as we exited the elevator and entered the huge receptionist area.

Yana set about the business of signing us in as soon as we entered the office. I went and sat at the very back of the semi-crowded office and fixated my eyes on the television.

"I'm not sure who her attending physician is; however, here is the contact information she provided to us," I heard Yana say to the receptionist.

What if she's already dead, I thought to myself. *Does that mean I killed my own damn sister?* "Hiri, snap out it." Yana said as she grabbed my hand. I offered her a weak smile just before glancing around the waiting room. *Oh my God,* I thought as I looked at the suffering human beings all around me. Some were alone, others were with loved ones but one thing that was obvious in each was the effects of kidney failure. *I wonder what Rayne looks like,* I asked myself, just as the nurse called my name to come to the back.

Yana stood first and lightly tugged at my hand, which she was still holding. *I don't know what in the world I would do without her,* I thought as she ushered us to the back. The nurse

J'Sat Necolle

took us to a small conference room in the rear of the building, then she said, "I want to thank you both for coming in today, we know you have a lot of questions and we are here to make sure you understand everything fully, so that we all can provide the best help for your loved one.

Loved one, I thought, *hell, I don't even know the bitch. The last time I saw her, she was trying to beat my ass about some money from the death of someone she barely even knew.*

"Dr. Spivey, Rayne's Nephrologist, was called away on a medical emergency," the kind nurse continued, "but one of his colleagues, who is very familiar with Rayne's case, will be in shortly to explain everything and answer any questions or concerns you may have. Please help yourself to some snacks from our concierge bar if you like."

As soon as she closed the door behind her Yana said, "You damn right, I like," and got up and swished her chunky ass over to the concierge bar in the rear of the room. "This is what you need to add to your conference room for your clients, it says 'class,' and waved her hand in the air. *This is one more fool*, I thought, *but she just might be on to something.* She'd actually been spending more time at my office over the last few weeks and has given me other critiques to help me take my showroom to the next level. She has also been a Godsend when it came to catching up on the budgetary reports I'd gotten behind on since dealing with Janis' sudden intrusion in my life.

Interrupting my thoughts, Yana yelled quietly, "Girl, they got smoked salmon up in this bitch, too," and started jumping up and down for effect.

As I got up from the cushioned high-back chair and walked over to where she was now preparing a Lox-n-Bagel, I just shook my head in amused disgust. "Bitch, if I didn't know no better, I would think your ass was still in the projects. You probably got smoked salmon going to the bad in your refrigerator right damn now, but here you are acting like you had sardines for dinner." We both laughed hysterically.

Laughing at her own foolishness, she couldn't even dispute the fact. "Shit, you can take me out the projects, but you...." the sound of the door opening halted her finish.

"Good morning ladies, I'm Dr. Warner."

Chapter 13

Lord Jesus, please let this be a short, fat, white man from the Bronx, I prayed. But even before I turned around, I already knew...and obviously Yana did too, because she grabbed my hand and squeezed it so fucking tight I felt like I had spandex around my damn neck. "I got you," she whispered, as she ushered both of us around in an about-face position.

There, standing only a mere ten feet away, was the boy who'd turned my whole world upside down. Kenyan Warner.

When he raised his eyes from his clipboard and looked at us, it was obvious it had thrown him for a loop too. He quickly looked back down at his clipboard, then right back up as if he was trying to figure out if he'd seen a ghost or something.

"Zahiri. Yana?" he asked puzzledly, his voice laced with confusion and recognition at the same time. "Oh, my God! What are you all doing here?" He asked while hurrying over to us and wrapping me, then Yana, in a warm embrace.

"Kenyan. Kenyan Warner. Oh, my goodness," Yana gushed. "I can't believe this shit." She was laughing and shit like she was really happy to see him. I wanted to stab her traitorous ass in the fucking side. Then I wanted to reach up and slap the shit out of him for all the nights I sat and waited for my phone to ring but it never did and all the nights I'd cried myself to sleep. But most of all I wanted to hide just how much seeing him was fucking with me by just saying, 'Hi.' But I couldn't. I couldn't move, I couldn't speak. *My fucking brain is broken again. Whatdafuck!*

Sensing everything that was going on inside me, Judas; I meant Yana, spoke up on my behalf, "Sorry Kenyan, you have to excuse Hiri, she's been out of sorts since she found out about Rayne's deteriorating condition. Can you help us understand everything?"

I finally found my voice, "Yes, Kenyan, my apologies. It is great seeing you though, I'm just so worried about my... sister." As the word 'sister' stumbled out of my mouth, I felt like I was going to throw up the remains of my breakfast and last night's dinner.

Thank God, he turned and walked away just in time, right before my knees buckled and Yana had to catch me and push me back up on my feet. She nudged me in my side and pulled me by my hand as we followed him back to the head of the mahogany conference table. *Someone did an excellent job with their interior design,* I thought to myself, right before he pulled out chairs for us to be seated. I was happy as hell she'd taken the first seat that he proffered, which was the one closest to him.

Smitten

As he took his seat, he said "You all just don't know how happy I am to see you both, I just only wish it wasn't under these circumstances." *Fuck you and these circumstances,* I thought to myself.

That was the last thing I heard either of them say. First his lips were moving. They'd move, he'd look down at his notes, then his lips would move some more. He'd move his hand across his bald head, in some sort of gesture, then his lips would move again. Yana's lips would then move. I suppose she was asking a question, then his lips would move again. He would look from, Yana, then to me, then back down at his clipboard, then his lips would move some more. When Yana nodded her head as his lips moved, I nodded my head too. When Yana would ask a question, he'd nod his head, so I'd nod mine too. This went on for what seemed like hours, but in reality, it was only about forty-five minutes. When he stood up, so did Yana; so, I did the same. He smiled, so did Yana; so, I smiled too. He then reached out to hug Yana, then me. He must have said, 'Goodbye,' because I saw Yana wave, so I did the same.

As Yana held my body steady as we exited the conference room, I could still feel his eyes on me. As we waited for the elevator, I could still feel his hands on me. As we got in Yana's truck, the tears broke because I can never forget what he did to me.

"It's okay, baby. It's okay. Let it out." Yana said as she rocked me like a baby on the

Smitten

passenger side of her new Infinity QX80, her anniversary gift to herself.

By the time we'd made it back through the city to my house, I was physically and mentally drained. On the ride home, I had convinced myself that God hates me, that was the only explanation I could find for the way my life was unraveling around me. *Perhaps he's always hated me...I'm just finally figuring it out,* I thought, while trying to climb down from that big ass truck.

"You don't have to stay," I turned to Yana and said.

"Yes, I do," she said rather matter-of-factly. "I'll go to the guest room though and give you your space until you feel like talking," she said, as she got down out of the truck and came around for me to lean on her yet again.

As we walked into the house Yana hummed the words to *I Just Can't Give Up Now,* which just so happened to be Grammy's favorite song and only my girl would have known that.

When I walked into my bedroom, I climbed straight into my Canopy bed and buried myself under the covers. She left out but came back about three minutes later with a can Sprite and some Tylenol and said, "Take these now, that way your head don't hurt so bad later."

J'Sat Necolle

Smitten

"Yes mam," was all I could utter as I laid my head on the pillow trying to drown out the painful pounding going on in there.

Before closing the door, she said, "By the way, I've cleared your calendar for the next two days. Next week you have a busy week, so you got four days to get this shit out your system." "I love you."

I quietly whispered, "Love you too, sis." And that was enough for her.

Chapter 14

*Th*ose four days went by so fast, but my girl Yana stayed by my side the entire time. By Saturday afternoon, she and I were both going stir crazy up in that house. My four-thousand square foot home started feeling like only six hundred after a couple of days. With every memory and flashback that invaded my mind, the walls seemed to get tighter and tighter. Before long, I felt as though I was losing my mind the more my past came back and slapped me in my face. I actually felt like I was suffocating.

Yana waited until we had taken a break from our day of pampering before she explained to me the process that I would have to go through, if I decided to donate one of my kidneys to someone I barely even knew.

"Kenyan said that the first step in the process is to see if you actually are a match and to do that there are a series of test you will have to undergo. The first step; however, is to access your medical history."

Laughing sarcastically, I said, "That should be interesting."

"Why?" Yana asked, looking confused as ever. When I say this has been my girl, she has been my girl. I met her the day my mother dropped

my ass off at my Grammy's and have talked to
her every day since.

"Why," I said. "Why is because I have nothing
to say about my medical history, except the fact
that I had that surgery on my torn ACL my
Freshman year, and I don't even want to speak
on that," I said, throwing my hands up to show
the frustration that little ordeal had brought.

"Man, I want to laugh at your ass so bad right
now because I still say that was the dumbest shit
you'd ever done, but I ain't even gonna do it,"
Yana said while trying to hide her smile. If her
dimples weren't so damn deep, she probably
could have gotten away with it.

Shaking my head at my own stupidity back
then, hell, I couldn't even get mad at her for
laughing because that shit had to be some of the
dumbest shit I'd ever done but hell, it was during
my stuck-on-stupid phase. Trying to veer the
subject away from thoughts of Kenyan, which
had ironically been flooding my head on an
hourly basis since I saw him, I said, "Other than
that, hell, the doctor probably already knows
more about my family's history than I damn do."

Sensing my pain, she reached out and took
my hand as I continued, "I don't know shit about
my mother; and know even less about my father.
Hell, the only thing I do know about my family's
history is that we are obviously fucked up from
generation to generation. Hell, my grandfather
didn't have shit to do with my mother. My

mother didn't have shit to do with me and even worse, she'd turned her back on her own damn mother, too." *Talk about irony.*

"Child Booh," Yana said dismissively, hoping to halt off a full-blown depression, something she has perfected over the years dealing with me. When I say this is my girl, I mean...this is my girl! And she has been since the first day I met her, the day my mother dropped me off at my Grammy's and drove away like I was a Salvation Army donation or something.

Snapping me out of my daydream, Yana said, "Fuck them, but anyway, after that, you'll have to submit to a blood test, which is ultimately the determining factor if you are a match to be a direct donor."

"Shit, I hope that blood test comes back and say that I'm no relation at all to the Wicked Witch of the South, or her fucking minions."

"Well, if it's any chance of that miracle, the next damn test will sure tell it. That thing checks everything; TB, Hepatitis B, your liver, your kidneys, your pancreas and your heart. This mug lets them know if you'd even 'had a touch of VD.'

When she said that, we both died in a fit of laughter. Leave it to this fool to find something to laugh about even in the most intense situations. Hell, she's worse than white folks. I can remember it like it was yesterday, when Dominique finally returned to school after her abortion, word on the street was that she'd had a 'touch of VD.'

According to one of the fellas on the football team, she'd burnt him and his brother. Everybody was talking about it, even the teachers and parents. The boys lived with their grandmother and when she came up to the school raising hell about the situation, she was too nice to say STD or venereal disease, so she just kept telling the school nurse, "Ya'll folks need to get that little fast tail girl checked 'cause she got a touch of something wrong down there."

Low and behold, one of the other students heard the rant and before lunch time, that shit was all over the school. I'm certain no one other than me and Yana knew that the real reason she had been absent so many days was because of the abortion, but hell, we gave two fucks about clearing her name.

And after that, any time the word 'touch' entered a conversation at school, she immediately became the butt of the joke. Hell, I wonder if Yana and I are the only two that still gets a good laugh at that? *Hell, probably not,* I thought. Poor thing, her senior year had to have been one of the worst years of her life.

Chapter 15

The days were turning into weeks and the weeks into months since me, Yana and Julia all sat down and concluded that I should undergo testing to see if I was a match for Rayne. The decision was unanimous from all of us since we each realized that there would be no way I could live with myself if I could keep anyone from dying and not even try to help. It was the toughest decision of my life but one I just had to make, for myself, rather than anyone else.

Yana had been a God-send, she handled my scheduling with my work appointments and my testing. Neither of us was surprised when I came back a match for Rayne, we had already prepared ourselves for that, based on the irony that God had always placed in my life. But just as always, I rose to the occasion because I am the bigger person. Besides, once Yana cursed Janis' ass out and told her to never contact me again, the situation became a lot easier to handle.

I was in my office, the day before we were scheduled to see if I was a match, when I suddenly heard Yana go all the way off, "Bitch, I know you're not stupid. How do I know, you ask? I know because my best friend is too fucking smart for your ass to be plain stupid. Therefore, I know damn well you understood Mrs. Julia the other one-hundred and thirty-thousand times she's asked you not to call here anymore. Well, Bitch...I ain't asking you!"

By this time, I had come out of my office and was standing in the doorway in awe. Mrs. Julia had completely stopped sending the fax she was working on and was now clutching the papers to her chest, like she was in complete shock...knowing damn well she was the one that had orchestrated this little show-down.

Now it's beginning to make sense why Yana has been hanging around here for the last few weeks, when for the past two months she had been spending every hour of every day fassing around with Brandon's ass.

Although, by title, he was still the Executive Chef at his Duluth restaurant, *Devour,* he rarely made any kitchen appearances. His culinary staff had been with him since the opening of the establishment six years ago, and it now runs like a well-oiled machine. Which leaves him and Yana a lot of spare time to do God knows what...and from what she's been telling me, they've been doing it... God knows where.

So, when she walked in a few weeks ago all eager to 'help a sistah out,' I should have known she was up to something. I also should have known that Julia's ass was caught up in the mix somewhere, because nothing goes on in this entire building without her nosey ass finding out about it. Laughing inside at their antics and humbled by their protectiveness, I tried to mask the expression from making it to my face. The last thing I could do in this setting was to let these two know that I was down for the foolery, because I know Yana, she would have really given the broad the business then.

Janis' ass was lucky all she got was cursed out but if they knew I was down, they probably would have set her ass up for the okey-doke. I can see Julia's ol' petty ass now scheduling an appointment for Janis to finally meet with me; only to have Yana's wanna-be-hood ass waiting for her in the parking lot. Thank God, they respected my business just as much as they respect me and knew that a parking lot beat-down would be bad for my bottom line.

The haunting chill in Yana's voice snapped me out of my thoughts and back to the phone lashing taking place in my corporate suite. "And just so you know," Yana said, her voice now barely above a whisper. "Hiri don't give a damn about you, nor does she give a damn about your daughters. It's not her responsibility to make sure if either one of you hoes live or die. That shit is between ya'll and God! Ya'll are not her family. Ya'll have never been her family and let me make myself perfectly clear, ya'll hoes will never be her family. So, don't call here no damn more begging for shit. Not for a kidney, not for any money, not even for a fucking glass of water! Cause if you do, I will be at 4124 Parkway, and a rotten kidney will be the least of your worries. And trust me, this ain't no threat...it's a fucking promise!"

Smitten

Hell, I've known Yana damn near my whole life but I ain't never seen her like this. Shit, I was almost scared to say something. When she placed the phone back on the receiver and turned and looked at me with tears welling around the corners of her eyes, I knew then that I didn't have a thing to worry about because she had my back, because unlike Janis them, we were family and that's what family do!

The next day, I was surprised when she called and told me she was on her way to pick me up to go to the testing appointment we had scheduled. *Shit, I thought she said yesterday that wasn't my responsibility,* I said to myself, while wiping the matter from my eyes. But instead of questioning her, I just pulled myself from under the warm covers and reluctantly told her I'd be ready when she gets here.

As I hurriedly grabbed a pair of cream-colored slacks and a Valentino blouse out my closet and darted to the bathroom, I didn't have time to second guess myself or my hair and makeup. I knew Yana would be pulling up outside in a matter of minutes because here lately she has been spending most nights with Brandon at his Buckhead home, which was only about ten minutes from my place. So, I quickly brushed my teeth, took a quick shower and piled my long, curly hair on top of my head in a messy bun. No time for foundation, I just quickly applied some light gloss to my lips, grabbed my

Prada bag and out the door I went, just as Yana's SUV was pulling up my cobblestone driveway.

Sending air kisses her way, I snatched on my seatbelt, then reached inside my purse to get the gold and diamond studs my grandmother brought for me for my college graduation. As I was putting the one carat diamond in my ear, my mind instantly drifted back to the day I was presented with the extravagant gift. I had honestly never seen my Grammy so happy and I never would have guessed anything could have topped how happy she was the day she opened her restaurant five years earlier, during my senior year of high school. But hands down, my college graduation day made her grand opening look like child's play. She was downright exuberant, which made that day even more special for me.

It was crazy because after the incident with Vani, our relationship had become somewhat strained, even though, we still talked about almost anything, with the exception of him and Janis. If I said something about him, she'd get mad and distant and if she said something about her, I'd get hurt and withdraw. So, at some point it seemed we'd both made a subconscious decision to never mention their names to each other.

Therefore, I was shocked when she showed up that morning all giddy and even seemed excited about seeing him. Hell, I hadn't even realized that I had never even mentioned to her that he and I had broken up two semesters earlier. In fact, it didn't even dawn on me until she asked at breakfast when he would be joining the group because she wanted to apologize to him before everyone got there. All I could remember thinking to myself was, *Oh really, Grammy! Is that what we do now, wait three whole years to apologize to someone for mistreating them because of the color of their skin? Where you do that at? Oh America! I forgot...this is America!*

I just looked at her in amazement, never saying a word. I just put her hand in mine and pulled her back over to mingle with everyone. Yana's parents had drove Grammy up from Georgia and got here before day this morning. They would have flown but you know that grandmother of mine wouldn't hear of it. Yana and Gavin had drove in from Washington last night and a few of my sorority sisters had flown in from their home states to celebrate with me at our Alma Mater, The Fordham University.

Even Brandon had wanted to come to my graduation, but he had called a couple of days before and told me he just wasn't able to handle seeing Yana all happy with someone else yet and no one understood that better than me.

Everyone's spirits were high, especially those few that knew the full-version of my story because I'd learned the hard way to keep my business to myself. Ever since Grammy cursed me out that day, I only told people what they needed to know.

We all enjoyed a quaint breakfast before graduation, then we all went out and at an early dinner after graduation. Myself and my friends enjoyed a drunken night on the town celebrating my accomplishments, while Grammy and the Yearwood's enjoyed their first Broadway play, on me. The next morning before everyone left is when Grammy presented me with these diamond earrings.

I don't think I'll ever forget that moment as long as I live. We were in my living room, now only surrounded by Yana and her parents, when Grammy reached inside her huge shoulder bag and pulled out a burgundy-velvet box. The room suddenly went quiet; you would have thought she was about to propose or something, but the only man in the room was Mr. Yearwood, and we knew from experience that he always preferred his women much younger. Then Grammy cleared her throat and began to tell me how much of a joy it had been to raise me and while I had always taken my mother leaving me there as a curse, she has always taken it as a blessing.

She said she knew the day I was born that I was going to be special, so that day, she'd walked into Helzberg Diamonds with nothing but twenty-five dollars and an honest spirit. She said she'd asked to speak with the manager. She then told the elderly white lady that she wanted to purchase the most expensive pair of diamond earrings that the store had for her brand-new Granddaughter, but she only had a little money and bad credit, on account of a no-good man; but if she let her put the earrings on lay-a-way, she'll give her word that a week won't go by that she won't come pay her for her earrings and for her kindness.

She said that lady looked her in her eyes and said, "Mam, it will be my pleasure to serve you." She said the lady then took her over to the case where the expensive items were housed and told her she can pick out any pair she liked as if she had a million dollars in her purse. She said it had taken her over seventeen years to pay for the earrings, but every week like clockwork, she was there to make her payment and that same white lady later became one of her closest friends, and eventually her business partner.

Yana glanced over at her fiddling with the last earring and probably sensed that her mind was a million miles away because she was afraid, so she reached over and squeezed her hand while she maneuvered the pearl-white SUV out of the cobblestone drive-way and headed towards their destination.

Finally approaching the subject, I said, "Yana, I thought since you told Janis yesterday that I didn't owe them shit and not to contact me again, that I was off the hook with this bullshit."

"Oh, I told that bitch just what she needed to hear, something you've never been strong enough to say. She does not have the right to ask you for shit and I damn sure was not about to keep letting her pressure you like you owe her ass something, because you don't!" Softening her tone, she said, "Besides, I thought we all agreed you were doing this for your peace of mind, not theirs."

"You're right," I said. "Eventhough, I know I don't owe them anything, I don't think I would be able to live with myself if she dies and I could have done something to save her."

"Right, I agree," Yana said. "I don't just think, I know you would not be able to live with yourself. You're too much of a caring person for it not to bother you. Seeming unsure of what she was about to say next, Yana stammered on. "That's why," she said quietly, then cut it off completely.

"That's why, what?" I asked, immediately feeling uneasy about whatever it was that had Yana so uncomfortable. Instead of looking at my cold stare, Yana diverted her eyes out the window and instantaneously began biting her fingernails, a habit she'd had since childhood when she was afraid, or situations were out of her control.

"That's why," she said slowly..." That's why I called Kenyan to see what your rights were, she quickly rattled off."

"You did what?" I screamed in the now suffocating SUV. "Why on earth would you call him and put him in my business like that?

"See...what had happened was..."

"What had happened my ass," I screamed.

Pulling into the already crowded parking lot and quickly whipping into a vacant space, Yana acted just like I wasn't screaming at her from the top of my lungs. Once I finally quieted down, she finally said, "The reason I called Kenyan is I wanted to know if there was any other possible way to save her without you donating?"

"And?" I asked, sounding just as betrayed as I felt, but still hopeful that he knew an alternative solution.

"And," she said, dropping her head as the inevitable fled her lips, "there is no chance in her survival unless she receives a kidney transplant. And," she continued, "because you and she share a very rare blood type, it is highly unlikely that she'll get another donor in time, if you decide not to donate."

Feeling the same sense of dread I'd felt since I'd climbed out of my bed this morning, I glanced out the window at all the people milling about all around me. *When they say everyone has a story,* I thought while staring into the blank faces, *I wonder if any of theirs is as messed up as mine.*

Are any of these people here to save a sister that they never had?

"He did recommend though," she said hesitantly, "if you did choose to donate, that he would recommend that you do so anonymously."

"Anonymously?" "How the hell am I going to do that?" I asked. "Even though their asses have acted like they don't know me my whole life, I still don't think that counts as anonymous."

A strained laugh escaped Yana's lips before she said, "Right!" "But according to Kenyan, their office or any hospital personnel cannot reveal the results of your blood test, nor can they release any donor information if the individual chooses not to reveal his or her identity."

"So, you're saying...or he's saying," I mumbled, unable to say Kenyan's name. "If I am a match, I can donate and not have to worry about faking the funk with Janis or her precious daughters?"

"Yes mam."

"Nor would they know that it was me who'd donated?"

"Yes mam."

"Well hot damn!" Sign me up then!" I said, once again laughing at the irony that I call my life.

J'Sat Necolle

Chapter 16

As Yana and I walked the sterile corridors after we left the testing lab, for some reason I felt better than I had in the past few weeks. I suppose knowing the fact that I can do the right thing without giving those selfish bitches the satisfaction of knowing that I actually gave a damn was liberating.

Just as we rounded the corner near the nurses' station, the hair on the back of my neck stood up and a cold sweat ran down the center of my spine as the familiar tightening of my heart muscle contracted. Kenyan.

Without even looking up, I could feel his eyes on me and although my one desire at this very moment was to just be able to continue this casual conversation with my best friend, but my mouth instantly dried up like I had rolled a million cotton balls around on the tip of my tongue. Then I heard his voice..." Hey ya'll, what's up?"

Yana snapped her head up alarmingly at the sound of his voice. "Oh hey, you," she said, sounding like they were the best of fucking friends. *Look at this shit,* I thought to myself. *One fucking phone call and now they act like they're Batman and Robbin.*

Smitten

Before I could stop myself, I mumbled aloud, "Damn, I feel like I'm in the Twilight Zone." Both Yana and Kenyan quickly looked in my direction but instead of apologizing for my rudeness, I sucked my teeth, then turned and walked away. As I headed towards the elevators, I heard him call after me to stop, which immediately made me quicken my step. "Yana was right about one thing," I mumbled to myself. I don't owe anybody shit, especially his ass."

By the time Yana made it down to the parking garage fifteen whole minutes later, I was absolutely livid. Not only was she conspiring with the enemy, but she made my ass wait in this hot ass garage while she did it. To make matters worse, she jumped her happy ass in the truck like she hadn't done shit. *Really Bitch,* I thought.

The drive back to my house only took about twenty minutes but it seemed like it took two whole years. The air was so thick in the luxury SUV, you could have cut it with a butter knife. I don't know if I was so upset because Yana seemed so chummy with Kenyan, or because I was donating a perfectly good organ to a sister that could care less if I live or die. *It's probably a combination of both,* I thought to myself as I swung my legs out the truck without uttering a word to my ex-best friend.

Slamming the door behind me, without a glance over my shoulder, I walked up the driveway with a vengeance, trying to get as far away from Yana as I possibly could. Just as I was

J'Sat Necolle

deactivating my alarm, my cell phone vibrated, alerting me I had a text awaiting. When I pulled out the phone and looked at the screen, I wasn't even surprised to see that it was from her, it simply said, *'Bye Bitch,'* followed by a bunch of laughing emojis.

"She gets on my fucking nerves," I said out loud, as I laughed at her antics. Long as we've been friends, I never could manage to stay mad at her. She has always been known for always having the last word and usually that last word was so damn funny that you'd forget what you were mad about in the first damn place.

Instead of heading straight upstairs to my treadmill to blow off some steam like I'd been planning to do ever since we pulled out of Emory Hospital's parking lot and headed down Peachtree St., I beelined straight to my sub-zero, black stainless-steel refrigerator and pulled out a half-eaten pint of my decadent pecan-praline ice-cream.

I would love to say this was unusual for me but here lately it seemed like this ice cream and Yana have been the only glue that has been holding me together. First, Janis's trifling ass barges into my life asking me to play God and then in the midst of all that, The Kenyan Warner decides to pop his fine ass back up in my life. It's crazy though cause' he reappeared just as unexpectantly as he'd left; no notice...no nothing. *A regular fucking Houdini.* But, unlike Yana, I can't just act like nothing ever happened.

105

Smitten

Still fuming over Kenyan, I grabbed a tablespoon for the cutlery draw and headed downstairs to the den and quickly turned on my seventy-inch plasma tv. As I scrolled through the channels, I couldn't help but to think what his life was like now and instead of the tv helping to take my mind off him, it just made matters worse.

When I turned to my favorite channel, HGTV, I just knew Chip & Joanna Gaines from the show, *Fixer Upper* were going to take my mind off things, but instead of getting caught up in the drastic home remodels like I normally did, I found myself thinking what it would be like to be married to the love of my life and have such a great relationship. As I was creating my own little fairytale starring me and Kenyan in my head, that damn nasty little monster from that Mucinex commercial suddenly appeared on camera and snapped me back to reality. "Damn," I said aloud, "I ain't never been so happy to see that lil' nasty bastard in my life," and burst out laughing at myself. *How ironic,* I thought, *the one commercial I hate more than anything, ended up saving me from a night of torture.*

Trying desperately to find something neutral to watch on the tube, I quickly turned to my other favorite channel, Food Network. It actually did the trick for a little while but then about thirty minutes into an episode of *Chopped,* I found myself wondering if Kenyan could cook. *Well, I'll be damned,* I thought, as my mind

J'Sat Necolle

quickly recalled a poem I'd written about him back in high school. Even though I hadn't thought about it in years, I was amazed that I still remembered it word for word:

My mind often drifts back, to thoughts of yesterday.
When you loved me so passionately, in every single way.

My mind can never erase the magic, or the joy of your touch.
My body still tingles all over, from that sensation I miss
so much.

There was nothing within reason, that I would not have
given you.
I gave you love, honor, respect and satisfied your passion
too.

Now I have an empty place in my heart, that still bears your
name,
And deep down in my soul, I know my life will never be
the same.

I've tried so hard to forget you, but that's the impossible
part...
For, how can I get you out my mind, when you're forever
engraved in my heart.

"Shit!" I yelled, as I hurled the now empty carton of ice cream into the stone fireplace. Now mad at myself for allowing that bastard to still have this kind of effect on me after all these years, I rushed up the stairs towards the solace of my bed. Shedding my cloths as I took two steps at a time until I reached the landing outside my master bedroom and just as I was about to cross the threshold into my room, I heard my phone vibrate in the distance, signaling I had another text.

Smitten

"Shit!" I screamed yet again, because now I've got to take my out-of-shape behind back down to the den to get the damn phone and after weeks of pigging out on ice cream, that feat was a lot harder than it sounds. Turning my now naked behind around, I sucked in a deep breath and galloped back down the stairs full speed, sprinted into the den, grabbed the phone off the back of the recliner and headed back from whence I'd came, full speed.

By the time I finally reached my bed, I was panting like a dog in heat. I had never been so thankful that I had converted the interior console of my nightstand into a wine cooler when I brought my bedroom suit a few years ago. Pulling an icy cold wine cooler out, I poured a huge gulp of the amber liquid down my throat at once.

As I began climbing into bed, I silently cursed Yana's ass out for making me run back down those stairs in the first place because I knew it couldn't be nobody but her. "She's probably on some more bullshit too," I said out loud as I reached over and picked up the now silent phone from the nightstand.

However, when I looked at the screen, the message wasn't from Yana, but from a 917-area code. Just as I asked myself, "Who could be texting me from a New York...." I cut the word off mid-sentence and my body went numb. After starring at the screen for what felt like hours, my

J'Sat Necolle

trembling fingers finally opened the text message:

> *Hurting you was/is the biggest regret of my life.*
>
> K.

Chapter 17

It has been seven whole days since Kenyan sent that fucked up apology text, and even though I have yet to respond, I also haven't been able to shake away the thoughts of him creeping into my bed with me at night. *Lord, what am I doing, sitting here lusting over another woman's husband?* I thought to myself. My Grammy used to always say, "Baby, God will send you a lot of things, but he won't send you somebody's husband!"

Now, I know my grandmother was a wise woman and everything, and it was very rare that I did not mind my grandmother, but just as show as shit stinks, if Kenyan Warner walked his fine ass up in here right now, I'd say to hell with the way he's hurt me and to hell with his wife and those 2.5 kids he had, the last I heard. It would be a done deal and I would just have to pray about it later.

Laughing aloud at my own antics, I just shook my head and chastised myself, "Calm down, Hiri. The dick ain't worth going to hell over." But in the back of mind, I heard a little voice chime in and say, *'You shitting me!'*

Back in the days, I would have walked through hell with gasoline thongs on to get to his ass. And with that, I picked up my I-phone and quickly scrolled to Kenyan's name that I'd finally saved in my contacts a couple of days ago. Just as I was about to send a text, common sense clicked in and I changed my mind. I'm horny but certainly not stupid. In fact, there's not a damn thing he could say, for me to ever let him smell my coochie again.

The idea of him and my coochie in the same sentence made me immediately start freaking out, just like I did my first day as a freshman at Martin Luther King, Jr. High School, when the upper classman walked over to me as I stood with my friends on the north hall waiting for the bell to ring to head to my third period class. My back was turned away from him as he approached my friends and me, but the sudden silence that overtook the group of gum popping, hormone induced teenage girls alerted me that something out of the ordinary was happening and I was about to miss it.

Eager to find out just what had rendered my friends speechless and had garnered their full attention, I turned quickly on my heels, slinging my red Jan Sport bag over my shoulder. As I did so, only to be met with a hard resistance. Hearing the 'oohs' from my peers, I knew that I had just messed up big time. Slowly looking up from the big, red and black Jordan's my eyes were fixated on, I followed the length of the long legs up to the rock-hard abs peeking through a MLK basketball t-shirt, to a chiseled chest, onto the amazingly handsome face of the finest boy I had ever seen in my entire life. "I'm s-s-so sorry," I managed to get out among the growing snickers from my peers.

"Oh, It's all good, Ma," he said.

Ma? Who in the world calls someone Ma, who is not his mother? I quickly wondered to myself. *But never in a million years have I ever heard the word sound so good!*

"Let me help you with that, Ms. Lady," he said behind beautifully white teeth and a magnetically crooked smile. As he took my book bag off my shoulder and slung it over his, it seemed like something out of a Harlequin romance novel and he was Fabio or somebody.

Nobody was snickering any more, in fact, you could have heard a pin drop in the entire hallway or at least that's the way it felt in my mind. I could literally hear my heart beating outside my chest. As he turned back up the hallway, he eased his huge, muscled hand into mine and eased me into a slow, steady stride alongside his. He walked me to my class never saying another word. Of which I was ecstatic because I couldn't have uttered a single syllable in that moment, even if my life depended on it.

For the rest of that day, I was floating around on autopilot. It wasn't until I got home from school that day and my Grandma started questioning me about how my first day of high school went that I realized I didn't remember a damn thing after second period. The boy was so fine he had literally fucked up my short-term memory!

I didn't remember where my classes were, what my teachers' names were, who all was in my classes, what in the world I had to turn in the next day or how in the world I had gotten home. Hell, it was a wonder I even remembered my own damn name. All I knew was that I was the luckiest girl in the world because The Kenyan Warner had held my hand.

Kenyan, a transfer student from Brooklyn, had moved to Lithonia to live with his aunt and uncle over the summer. Word had quickly made its way throughout the neighboring communities about the fine Brooklyn brother that had all the teenage girls going crazy and all the teen-aged boys that were still battling puberty and low self-esteem, secretly hating.

Word on the street was he had gotten into some trouble up north so his mom sent him down south until things calmed down. That air of mystery and thug appeal surrounding him only boosted his sex appeal even more and had every girl living in the nearby neighborhoods praying to God that when August came around he would still be in Georgia and have his fine ass enrolled in their school district.

Unbeknownst to him, he was already semi-famous with the females in the school; as well as, the teachers and administrators because his reputation proceeded him. However, on the first day of school when the football and basketball coaches at MLK saw the 6'5 Junior walk in the gym and ask, 'Who got next?", his popularity with the fellas went from 0 to 100 real quick.

Chapter 18

$\mathcal{B}$y the time Monday morning had finally rolled around, I was beyond thankful to be going back to my chaotic work schedule. My entire weekend had been filled with mournful glimpses of my past. No matter what I did or where I went, I was haunted by memories of the hurt and resentment I'd suffered at the hands of The Kenyan Warner. And I wanted nothing more than to fill my schedule with work to help take my mind off of things that could only bring me more pain.

Since Yana and Brandon had taken a weekend getaway to Biloxi, I didn't have anyone to distract my miserable existence. So, on Saturday afternoon, desperate to get out of my funk, I had reluctantly agreed to meet this guy, Nigel, I had been seeing off and on, for dinner and a movie.

We met at Atlantic Station because I did not feel comfortable enough to let him know where I live just yet. Even though I've known him for about six months now. I could just hear my Grammy's words echoing in my head when it came to giving out my address, "Child, you think you know somebody...til' you realize you don't know them at all." *Funny how some shit just never leaves your mind,* I thought.

Smitten

I must admit, the movie was good; mainly because it was dark, and Nigel and I couldn't talk, but by the time the bubbly blonde waitress was bringing our dinner out, the only place I wanted to be was at home. Locked away in my own den of misery, being comforted by memories of despair. Normally, Nigel's jokes were pretty funny, and I enjoyed being around him but tonight I just felt completely out of my element in his company. Guessing he could sense things were going horribly wrong, he kept trying to see if I wanted or needed anything. Before long; however, he finally got the point. So, instead of trying to entertain me any further, he became hostile, and told me in no uncertain terms that I could have told him I had someone else before I allowed him to keep wasting his money on me.

In the middle of my favorite dish at Copeland's, I looked at his bitch ass like he'd suddenly grew two heads. "Nigga, what the fuck do you mean.... I made you waste your money?" I was seething. "I can't recall the first fucking time I called and asked you to take me out. In fact, I can't recall the first time I even called to ask how your damn day was going, or if you were feeling well or if you even know how to tie your fucking shoe!"

He started frantically looking around the restaurant hoping no one overheard the insults I was hurling his way. Once he realized everyone was looking in our direction, he signaled for me to shush with his finger. *Lord, what did he do that for.*

Smitten

I began yelling, "Bitch, I ain't no fucking child! You don't shush me. My own mama ain't never shushed me!" And when I said that, the dam broke and all the unshed tears I had bottled up inside came flooding out. Eager to escape the questioning eyes of Nigel and all the other patrons of the establishment, I grabbed my purse and fled the space as fast as my six-inch hills could take me. *I don't think I've even been that embarrassed in my life*, I thought as I gathered my tunic dress inside my small ass car... but then my mind raced back to a day I'll never forget.

It was February 16th, the day after I'd lost my virginity to Kenyan. I will never forget how I felt when I woke up that morning, still wrapped in his arms. The birds were chirping outside, and grandma had the coffee pot simmering in the kitchen, when Kenyan grazed my eyelids with one of his sweet kisses. When I think of that time, I can still feel his breath caress my naked body as he whispered for me to wake up. "I've got to go, my love, before we get caught."

"No-o-o...not yet," I groaned, this morning felt completely different from all the other nights he'd stayed over. For the past four months, ever since the night Grammy had told me not to be telling her business and took the telephone receiver and hid it in her room, Kenyan had been sneaking into my bedroom window. Some nights we'd talk until the sun came up about any and everything; and some nights we'd just lay in each other's arms, lost in our own thoughts until sleep

J'Sat Necolle

overtook us. But never did our kisses and caresses lead to anything more, not because I didn't want it to, but because he said I wasn't ready. But last night...last night was different.

Normally we'd talk on the phone for an hour or two, not wanting a change in pattern to clue Grammy in on our secret. Then a couple hours later, he would lightly tap on my bedroom window for me to let him in. But last night, he never had his cousins to call and ask for me like he normally did. I was walking around the apartment on pins and needles hoping everything was okay. I don't know if it was the Brooklyn in him, but for some reason, he just had a thing for the streets. And no matter how good life was treating him, he just craved a part of that lifestyle. Selling a little weed here and there and occasional gambling was all I knew of, but nevertheless, I was always worried.

After hours of pacing back and forth and fiddling around, hoping the phone would ring, I finally gave up and headed to bed around ten o'clock. Much to my surprise though, when I opened the door to my bedroom, there he was, already sleeping peacefully in my twin bed. As I closed and locked the door behind me, I quietly walked over to where he slept, trying not to disturb him. Pulling back the covers to climb in, I let out a loud gasp that startled him from his sleep.

As his eyes suddenly became focused and transfixed on mine, he followed my gaze down

Smitten

the expanse of his body to the throbbing of his manhood. Almost choking at the sight of his naked body, I'd never seen anything so beautiful and frightening at the same time. Not wanting to scare me I suppose, he didn't move a muscle for the longest time. He just watched me, watch him. Finally, he took his left hand from behind his head, where both his hands had been and slowly ran it down his torso to his still growing membrane. All along, his eyes never left my face. He peered intently as he saw my eyes glaze over in amazement at how the veins in his penis were now throbbing frantically as the blood rushed all the way through to the large head, while the girth of it continued to grow. When his left hand finally encircled his gigantic penis, I understood completely why he kept insisting I wasn't ready.

As he stroked his manhood up and down, then down and up, I could not take my eyes off it. Saliva started to caress the corners of my mouth and a wet sensation oozed into my cotton panties. Sensing my need to explore, he released his mammoth dick and reached his hand out for mine...

Timidly, I allowed him to take my hand in his,
he then slowly took it and placed it...
where his hand had been.

The touch of it felt so foreign to me, it caused heat to gyrate
through my soul.
Never had I seen something so magnificent,
a sight to behold.

He slowly moved my hand up and down inside of his...
his eyes finally leaving mine.

J'Sat Necolle

Smitten

I silently prayed this feeling would not end,
just last a lifetime.

With now closed eyes, he guided me into pleasing him
with discernity;
and with each stroke of my hand I gained a newfound
sense of security.

As he licked his lips in pleasure, I became even more
awakened with desire,
and I knew at this very moment, he had to
put out my quenching fire.

When the soft moans of ecstasy, suddenly
escaped his throat,
something inside made my heart cry, and my soul
immediately broke.

He pulled his other hand from behind his head,
then sat up abruptly.
Pulling me between his legs, sliding up my gown,
he never took his eyes off me.

Snatching off my panties, he softly grazed my mound, with
his awaiting thumb,
and before I could finish gasping, he'd inserted
his other one.

Feeling his finger inside me was much more than
my fragile soul could bear,
but I soon found myself thinking, oh, how I wish
his dick was there.

He must've been reading my mind, like he had been
doing from the start,
cause when he slowly inserted his dick, he engraved himself
permanently into my heart!

Smitten

"Oh my God!" I shrieked. "I can't believe how that poem came back to my memory so easily after all this time."

Shaking my head at the irony, I still remember it like it was yesterday, we made love almost four times that night, and the only reason we didn't go into the fifth round was because we were both too sore. I suppose my tightness had scratched his dick up, so eventually it became too painful for him to bear. But that following morning, when he woke me with his gentle kiss, just as I was protesting his leaving, he slid the soft membrane back inside me one more time, and laid still, while we both felt it grow.

Once it had hardened so ferociously it felt like it was about to come through my flesh, he slowly started grinding against my round ass. As the strokes grew stronger in intensity, he draped his long leg around mine and pulled me into him even closer. Wrapping his hand up in my tousled hair, he yanked my head back until my lips met his in the most captivating kiss we'd ever shared. Suddenly pulling his lips away from mine, he grinded harder and harder and I remember thinking, *How could something hurt so bad, but still feel so good?*

"Whose pussy is this?" he asked roughly in my ear, his sexy Brooklyn accent penetrating

J'Sat Necolle

through to my soul, as he continued his assault on my gushing honeypot.

"It's yours, Kenyan," I cried. Obviously a little too loud though, because he hurried and covered my mouth to make sure my Grammy didn't hear me.

"Is it mine?" he asked roughly, over and over again as he pounded deeper and deeper into the depths of my soul. All I could do was nod my head yes; as he silenced my moans with his large hands, still pounding deeper and deeper into my core. I suddenly felt his entire body start to shake, even more fierce than the night before and before I knew it, I felt the warm sensation filling my insides as he moaned loudly and pulled me closer, drowning me in tender kisses.

"What did you say?" We heard Grammy yell from the kitchen.

"Oh shit!" We both whispered frantically.

"Umm... nothing Grammy. I was singing a song," I stammered quickly. *Shit!* The absolute last thing I needed her to do was come back here and realize my door was locked. Oh, she did not play that shit. To let her tell it, if you don't pay bills...then you don't lock doors. It wasn't until last year when she started fassing around with Deacon Knight that she even allowed me to close the door to my bedroom, and hell, I was thirteen then. To let her tell it, her and the good deacon were having prayer meeting and didn't want to disturb me. She must have thought I was Boo-Boo-the-Fool! Since when did they start having prayer meeting with just two people? *Hmph.*

But I'm just telling ya'll this shit, cause my Grammy would have beat the living shit outta me if I came out my mouth like that to her. Oh, no mam. Her favorite phrase was, "Hmph, I don't play with chillun'!"

Shit, just one time I wanted to get up the nerve to tell her, "And I don't play with grown people," but my balls never got quiet that big.

But anyway...when we didn't hear her making a move in our direction that morning, Kenyan slowly pulled his deflated penis out of my warm, moistness and slapped me playfully on my behind. "I've gotta go and you've got to get ready for school, he said"

"I know, I know," I moaned, while I laid there and watched him get dress, with a newfound joy in my heart. I just knew that day at school was going to be nothing short of amazing. Now, we were going to let the whole world know we're in love. There would be no more secrets, no more hiding, and best of all, no more Christine McCray.

I guess the joke was on me, I thought, as I walked into my plush corner office, ready to take on a new day.

J'Sat Necolle

Chapter 19

By lunchtime, I felt like I had run a marathon. Two of my top designers had called in sick, so not only was I trying to handle my workload, but I was also being forced to take on some of their work. Normally I would be relishing in the idea of being back in the field, working directly with my clients. But, given my present state of mind, I really wasn't sure if I could deal with the indecisiveness of new clients, which is the department that Zara, my top design associate spear headed.

Unlike myself, Zara welcomed the challenge of reeling in the outlandish ideas of our new clients. She was a master at making them adopt her ideas as their own, leaving everyone satisfied, especially me. Unfortunately for me though, she was still out on maternity leave after having her son over three months ago. She was slated to return to work two weeks ago, but it seems that she is having a bit of separation anxiety.

While, I hate she's put me in such an unfortunate position, I do understand how it might be difficult to leave your first born, especially given the complications she'd had carrying her baby to term. This is actually her third attempt, never carrying beyond the first trimester before miscarrying in her previous pregnancies. This time though, because of her high-risk status, her gynecologist had placed her on complete bed rest her entire pregnancy.

Thankfully though, her professionalism is something to be reckoned with. In fact, she has been just as big of an asset to my organization while on bed rest as she was before her pregnancy. She's brought in several high-profile clients just by working her connects from the comfort of her own bedroom. Working remotely with her assistant and video technology, she'd still managed to have the most profitable portfolio in the company.

As I drove towards the address Zara had typed on the top of the design order for her newest client, I made a mental note to send her a monetary token of my appreciation for going over and beyond. I'll have Julia to pick up something for the baby, too. As I came up on the address according to my GPS, I slowed up tremendously, making sure not to pass my turn. *Hopefully, this client won't be as difficult as the last one*, I thought, as I turned back the ignition switch in the company vehicle.

Peering up, I was caught by surprise at the shape of the worn-down stucco house that sat in front of me. Looking around the neighborhood, I was in utter shock that a homeowner's association would allow this kind of neglect, especially given the immaculate lawns and homes that surrounded the unpleasant sight. Grabbing my clipboard and cell phone, I quickly exited my truck because the one thing I hate most is to have someone waiting on me. Noticing there was already a contractor's pickup and a black Navigator parked in the crumbled driveway, so I quickened my pace. As I carefully headed towards the front of the house, I could hear loud laughter from inside. *Great, everyone's in a great mood,* I thought, just as I reached out to press the door-bell, while simultaneously looking down at the design order to locate the customer's name.

"Whatdafuck!" I exclaimed under my breath, just as the door swung open and I came face to face with the one person I hate more than my own mother, Kenyan's wife.

For what seemed like hours, she and I stared each other down. As recognition crossed our eyes, hatred crossed our hearts, causing us both to instantly reflect on another time. Suddenly the sound of laughter stopped from within the house and somewhere in the distance I heard an all too familiar voice call out my name, "Zahiri, oh my God!" "What are you doing here?"

Finally breaking my stare from Christine, I coldly looked up into the eyes of the only man I've ever loved, The Kenyan Warner. It was obvious that Kenyan had no idea what to do. Hurriedly, he headed in our direction as my eyes locked in again on Christine. The last time she and I had been this close to one another was over fifteen years ago, but the words I told her then held even more true today...*Bitch, if you say one word, I will fuck you up.*

Smitten

From the look on her face, I could tell she remembered it and clearly, by the way Kenyan was rushing across the room, he remembered it too. And, by the way my fist was unconsciously balling up by my side, I was never going to forget it.

As Kenyan rushed between us, I didn't feel any sparks or any cold sweats, all I felt was anger and hurt and all I wanted to do was to slap the shit out of them both this very instant. Instead of doing that though, I looked her dead in the eyes and said, "I obviously have the wrong address," then quickly turned to walk away.

Before I could do a complete about-face, Kenyan's hot, sweaty hand grabbed my arm and stopped me dead in my tracks, just as he reached out and grabbed her hand with his other one and quickly pulled her past me. "No!" "Please Hiri, you stay, we'll go!" His eyes finally recognizing the logo on my portfolio, and realized I was Zara's replacement.

Knocking me even more off-guard was the pleading look I saw in his fleeing eyes as he hurriedly pulled her towards the driveway, "I'm so-so sorry," he stammered. "But please don't go."

As he pushed her into the cab of the SUV, I could hear her yelling, "What the hell are you apologizing to that bitch for and get your damn hands off me?"

J'Sat Necolle

Smitten

Starring at the chaotic scene, I felt like I was having an out-of-body experience and certainly could not believe I was a part of this dysfunctional shit; yet, at this very moment, I wanted nothing more than to rush over to the sleek vehicle and kick her ass once and for all, but instead of showing my blackness in this lily-white neighborhood, I simply smirked at the woman that had haunted so many of my dreams and gave her that "fuck you bitch" wave that only us sistahs could do.

Missing the entire exchange as he quickly ran around to the other side of the truck, Kenyan yelled back over his shoulder, "Thank you, Hiri!" "Cleve will fill you in on all the details." And with that he quickly threw the truck in reverse and meandered out the driveway. I could see her arms flaying wildly inside the vehicle and her mouth moving a mile a minute. *Nothing's changed I see, still all talk, no action.* I thought to myself.

Just as I turned to walk back to the gleaming, white, Sprinter van that adorned my company logo, I heard a man's voice yell, "Hey, where are you going?"

"Oh, shit," I said, a little livelier than I felt. I had completely forgotten about Cleve's ass. Whom I assume is the handsome gentleman yelling my name, looking confused as shit.

"What was that all about?" He asked as he walked down the driveway, closing the distance between himself and I. Not waiting for an answer, which was good because I didn't have one to give, he held his hand out for me to shake, "How are you?" "My name is Cleve. Cleve Johnson."

"Hey, Cleve. How are you?" I asked, still somewhat distracted, not feeling at all like myself. "My name is Zahiri. Zahiri James, but everyone calls me Hiri. I'm the owner of Tre-Unique Designs."

"Well, nice to meet you, Ms. Lady" *Oh God, here we go again with that city shit,* I thought at the sound of the distinct New York accent. Before I could apologize for wasting his time and tell him that I wasn't going to be able to take the job he said, "So, how's Zara and lil' man doing?"

Taken aback by his familiarity with my prized employee, I replied, "They are both doing great. Thank you for asking."

"Yeah man, she's had a rough go of it," he said walking back towards the house, shaking his head, "but I respect the way she didn't give up and kept fighting for what she wanted. Kenny and I have both been praying for her; we were so happy when she sent us the picture of her and lil' dude."

Nodding my head, I was amazed at how much I already liked Cleve. He seemed like a real stand-up cat. It was just something about him that said he didn't bite his tongue and his word was his bond, which are two very attractive traits in a man, if you ask me.

Instead of me leaving like I had initially planned to do as soon as Kenyan's vehicle was out of sight, I felt compelled to stay, simply on the strength of Cleve and his fondness of Zara. *Fuck Kenyan...and his skank ass wife too!*

Chapter 20

By the time I made it home that night I was completely exhausted. A preliminary consultation that should have only taken me a couple of hours, ended up lasting about four. Once Cleve and I started with our walk-thru, and he started breaking down all the structural changes he was going to be making on the house and looking at all the different design elements Zara had customized to compliment the construction, I was excited about the transformation.

However, by the time we headed out the disgusting house and sat on the tailgate of his pickup to take a break, and he began passionately telling me about Project Hope, the organization he and Kenyan had started about five years ago, I became completely enthralled.

He passionately told me about how him and his good friend Kenyan decided they were going start making some extra money by flipping houses in their spare time. According to him, everything went really well for the first two years; they'd flipped dozens of houses and had both made tons of money. He was doing very well as a realtor and of course, Kenyan was doing even better as a doctor. But according to him, both their worlds were turned upside down one day when a young lady named Hope Jenkins walked into Kenyan's office. Hope was a single mother with two kids, barely getting by, working as a nursing assistant. That was before she got diagnosed with stage three breast cancer. By the time she'd walked into Kenyan's practice a year later, she was a shell of a person; she had literally lost everything; including her children.

Hope's diagnosis caused a ripple effect in her life that even she didn't see coming. Her repeated absences from work caused her to lose her job; which was the end of her medical insurance. She qualified for Medicaid at that point, but her oncologist didn't take it. The welfare that she began getting was her only source of income; which was nowhere near enough to pay rent anywhere, so soon she found herself and her children living in her car.

And if that wasn't enough, the new baby mama of her baby daddy found out about her misfortune and vengefully reported she had her kids living on the streets to the local DFCS office, just to pay her back for being Baby Mama number one...like that was some kind of esteem honor.

By this time, the untreated cancer had caused her kidneys to begin to fail and Hope had given up the will to live. From what Kenyan had told Cleve, when the young woman came into his office, she could not talk from crying, and as he tried to relay the news about her kidney failure, the sobs became a death-defying wail, but by the time he left the room to get her some more tissue she had quietened down significantly. According to Kenyan, she never uttered another word throughout the rest of the visit, merely starred into space and nodded her understanding.

For the rest of that day, Kenyan said he could still hear the woman's cry ringing in his ear and although he was always surrounded by sadness at work, even the memory of her cry made him cringe in agony. At the time, he didn't know anything about the woman or her life, but he soon realized he wasn't going to be able to rest until he found out if she was okay.

Before he left work that afternoon, he called the social worker that had referred Hope to his office to alert her that the woman did not seem to be in a good place when she left, and he was terribly worried about her. While the talkative social worker had no problem breaking HIPPA violations by telling all the woman's personal business to him; when asked was she going to follow up with a home visit, suddenly her patient's confidentiality became her first priority. *Bitch please,* he'd wanted to say but instead he maintained his professionalism.

Cleve's eyes began to tear up as he relived the memory, "I'll never forget that night when my boy called me about 2:00 in the morning, his voice close to tears. As long as I've known that nigga, I can count the number of times I'd seen him get emotional on one hand, but that night, even his cool ass could not hide his feelings," he said with a slight chuckle.

J'Sat Necolle

Smitten

"At first, I thought something was wrong with him or his family," he said, as a small hint of jealousy pierced my soul. "Nawl man, they straight," he'd said quickly through the phone when he heard the alarm in my voice. "But I do need your help, get up...I'm coming thru."

Slapping me gently on my leg, he chuckled lightly, lost in his thoughts, "That fool had me scared to death!" "I didn't know what was going on or what was about to go on with that fool. If you knew my boy..." he said laughingly, but then looked up at me as he quickly cut off the rest of his sentence, then lowered his head.

Sensing he knew a lot more about me than he was letting on, I simply patted him on the knee for him to finish telling his story, and to let him know that Kenyan's and my bullshit was just that, our bullshit. I wasn't holding that against him.

He continued, "Anyway, by time he got to my girl's house to scoop me up, that nigga was crying real tears and I'd only seen him like that once. He told me about the lady from his office that day and how he'd had a bad feeling ever since he let her leave; so much so, that every time he'd tried to close his eyes to go to sleep, he could hear her cry and see that eerie look in her eyes. He was really afraid that she would hurt herself."

Fighting back tears, he slowly continued on, "That night, we rode and rode; scouring the streets of West End and Cleveland Ave., looking for the car that the social worker had described to my man. When we could never find her, we went and waited outside the DFCS office off Bankhead, until the sun kissed the sky and the caseworkers came filing in one by one."

"After pleading to one supervisor after another, we were finally transferred to one that still possessed enough decency and humanity to help us find out where the woman's kids were, in desperate hope that we'd find her somewhere nearby. Just as we suspected, as soon as we turned on the street where the kids' group home was housed, we saw the cracked taillight on the old, rusty Toyota Corolla. The car had definitely seen better days, just like the frail woman inside."

"When Kenyan lightly tapped on the window, trying not to alarm the woman as he awakened her from a deep sleep, she jumped at the sight of him. Once her eyes finally recognized the handsome face as the doctor she'd seen the day before, she became even more frantic. She immediately started crying out, 'No, God. No. I just need to see them one more time'!"

"Me and Kenyan both started crying right then and there, looking like a bunch of pussies," he chuckled lightly. "Kenyan pleaded with her to let us help her and finally after about an hour, she finally unlocked her door and let us help her out the car. We loaded her into Kenyan's truck, only taking her important paperwork and her personal keepsakes from the car she had been calling her home for the past year."

"First, we went inside the group home and spoke to the dorm resident, who had been expecting us since the supervisor had called her and told her what was going on. The kids were anxiously waiting in the living room when we entered the home and it was obvious how worried they were about their mother. When they saw the frail woman limp through the door, they were overcome with emotion and when we told them who we were and that we were here to help their mother and in turn help them, they became hysterical with joy and appreciation."

"After that," he said, with tears glistening in the corners of his eyes, "Kenyan and I worked on the house that we'd been flipping around the clock. Oftentimes, we would eat and sleep there. Some days missing work all together. We made sure Hope began aggressive chemo treatment for her cancer from the best oncologist in Atlanta, which in turn helped her kidney condition to improve, under Kenyan's watchful eye. And within a six-month span, her health was drastically improving, she was in her own home and her kids had been returned solely to her care. And that's how Hope House began!" he said proudly.

"So now, every year we flip two houses specifically to be donated to a struggling family, that just needs some hope."

Chapter 21

_As_ I climbed into my bed that night, I did something that I haven't did in quite some time; I picked up my bible from the night stand and read the first chapter I came to when I opened the Good Book. _Grammy would be so ashamed,_ I thought. She'd taught me how to give God praise in both good times and bad times, but the better I've been doing, the less I seem to call his name. But listening to Cleve tell me all about Hope's struggles made me realize just how blessed I am. Just, as I reached over to turn my light out, a text lit up my screen. It simply said:

"That's just like a nigga," I said out loud. The thought of him texting me while he was probably lying in bed next to her actually seemed pretty ironic. In fact, after the way that bitch had acted earlier, that shit was downright funny. So, instead of me ignoring his text like I did the other day, I decided to fuck with the bitch:

Smitten

My response must have thrown his ass completely off kilter because for a moment I saw the cursors moving like he was replying, but then it stopped and went away. Then almost an hour later, I got another text that didn't say anything, just had about twenty heart emojis followed by a red one-hundred symbol.

Staring at the screen, I couldn't help but to scoff at the audacity of this nigga. I wonder why men think they can just fuck you over, then throw out a bullshit ass, *'I'm sorry'*, and think shit is just supposed to go back to normal.

Umph, this fool got me fucked all the way up, I thought. But instead of me sending him the bird finger emoji like I wanted to, followed with a quick, *'Boy Bye';* I just rolled my happy ass over smiling on the inside because tonight her man was lying in bed next to her, thinking about me. *Karma is a bitch,* I thought. *Un huh, that's what her ass gets!*

As I dozed off, all I could hear was the song Christine used to walk by my locker singing after word spread throughout Martin Luther King, Jr. High School like wild fire that she was not only pregnant, but she was carrying The Kenyan Warner's baby. *"He might be doing you, but he's thinking about me...... He's mine, you may've had him once, but I got him all the time."*

The following morning, I woke up with an unusual pep in my step, which was unbelievable since I was scheduled to go to the hospital to do some more preliminary work for the procedure, which I'd scheduled a month from today.

Whenever it came to anything concerning Janis or the twins, my anxiety level was always at an all-time high. As I let my garage up getting ready to back out, I wasn't the least bit surprised when I looked up just in time from my driver's seat to see Yana's ass leaning up against her SUV like she was a supermodel or something.

All I could do was burst out laughing. "You are one more fool!" I yelled out my driver's side window. "Your ass better be glad I was paying attention because I'm good for plowing outta here without looking back." Jumping back out the car, I walked up to her and hugged her with all my might.

Even though, it had only been five days since I saw her last, I had really acted an ass and she certainly didn't deserve that. As she affectionately pushed me off her telling me to go on with that mushy shit and headed around her car to get her purse out, I could not help but to think of how blessed I am to have someone like her in my corner. "What are you doing here? I thought you guys were staying for two weeks."

"Now, Fool, you should have known when I said that, that I was just fucking with you," she said laughing uncontrollably. "I was just trying to make your ass feel like shit for treating me like you did, but you know damn well I wasn't letting you go to this doctor appointment alone."

Feeling even more thankful than I already felt, I snuck in another quick hug before she could see it coming, then ran back and jumped in on the driver's side of my Porche. "Come on, chick, let's ride then!" I yelled back at where she was still standing in the same spot. She just shook her head in disbelief and headed to the car.

When we pulled into the hospital's parking deck, we both gave each other a puzzled look because neither of us could remember the drive there. She had been so excited to tell me about all the escapades she and Brandon had pulled while on their romantic getaway and I could not have been happier for her.

Then, I had her dying laughing about how I had to pull my Black Card on Nigel's ass up in Copeland's. But when I told her about the overdue stand-off between me and Christine, she acted a pure-d-fool.

"Oh, I know that bitch didn't!" flew out her mouth so fast, I almost lost control of the steering wheel laughing at her. By the time we parked, she was ready to go to war for me, which endeared her to my heart even more. I said a quick prayer, *"Thank you Jesus for bringing her back to me."*

Smitten

I don't know if Brandon's loving was just that good, or if Gavin's shit had just run its course, but whatever it was, I was happy as hell to see my girl happy again!

The appointment went very well, I actually felt really comfortable with Dr. Spivey. He took his time to explain everything really well and he was easy to talk to, not to mention, he wasn't bad on the eyes either. "I know the nurses in this practice love their jobs," Yana said playfully as we exited the building, "Shit, as fine as Dr. Sprivey and Kenyan are, who needs benefits! No wonder these heifers walk around here smiling from ear to ear. Hell, I'll be smiling too!" she exclaimed.

J'Sat Necolle

Chapter 22

*N*ow that Yana was back in town, my world seemed to be getting back to normal, apart from an occasional naked Kenyan running thru my mind at night, life was good. Once I was finally able to pry her ass off Brandon's dick for a hot minute, I finally convinced her to join me at my firm part-time.

While, I really needed her as a full-time office manager, I knew I would be pushing my luck asking for that. Hell, I couldn't expect someone that had not worked in over four years to just up and start putting in forty hours a week; especially when they are getting some good "D" too. Nope, I didn't even press my luck.

Having her around was everything and then some, not only was she taking so much stress off my plate by handling the day-to-day operations at the firm, she was also good for popping her head in cracking some funny, ass jokes throughout the day, too. On Mondays, Wednesdays and Fridays, the vibe at the firm went from somber to straight up Lit...and everyone loved it; including me.

"I'm headed out now, I said to Yana as I peeked in her office door. She was bent over her desk, thumbing through some reports. Looking up, she offered a dazzling smile. *My Girl is glowing,* I thought.

"Oh, I had completely forgot you're working on site today." "How is that going, by the way?"

"It's going great! I can't wait to see the finished product. It's been so long since I've had the pleasure of working on a project like this. It's really making me fall back in love with what I do."

"Are you sure that's the only thing you're falling back in love with?" she asked, looking at me puzzlingly.

"Girl, Bye." I said dismissively. "True to his word, Kenyan has not graced the grass of said property while I've been there. I'm not sure when he and Cleve do their walk-thru, but he is a non-fucking factor to me. The only thing I want from him is a few more of those fat ass checks with his name on it!" And with that I turned and sashayed away, leaving her in a fit of laughter.

As I pulled up in front of the Dawson St. address, I slammed on breaks. *Damn, I spoke too soon.* Heading towards Cleve's truck, wearing a sweat-stained, white-t and carrying a can of paint was non-other than The Kenyan Warner.

"Whatdafuck!" I sighed to myself, putting the van in park. *I got a good mind to haul ass,* I thought to myself, as I shuffled through everything within my reach; trying to do anything but acknowledge his presence.

J'Sat Necolle

Smitten

Finally, I reached inside my purse and picked up my cell and dialed the office, never looking in his direction. Once I got Yana on the phone, I cussed her jinxy ass out for everything I could. "I have been working on this site, on this project, three days a week for three weeks now and no Kenyan Warner. But the very day, you want to get all up in my business...

> *I pull up on this site...*
> *and what da hell do I see...*
> *The Kenyan Warner.... looking like a juicy snack to me!"*

She hollered at my ill-attempt to rap. She already knows that when I get nervous, I get corny as hell. Usually breaking out with some kind of crazy poem or rap. I'll never forget the first time she saw Issa Rae's show, *Insecure,* she called me screaming in the phone, talking about, "Girl-l-l-l, somebody has been recording you!" I was lost as hell, but she was laughing so hard that I had to join in too.

This was shortly after her last miscarriage, so I was just happy to hear she had some joy left somewhere deep in her spirit.

She went on to instruct me to turn my tv to HBO and watch as the sistah on the scene reenact the same kind of bathroom scenes that I have been doing since we were kids. And when I saw Issa's ass rapping in that bathroom mirror, I hollered too, that shit was me to a T. In fact, our weekly ritual became sitting on the phone at our respective homes, watching *Insecure* and laughing our asses off.

143

Smitten

"Girl, you are a fool!" she yelled into the phone. I swear sometimes she forgets she's in an office, instead she acts like we're in the backyard of those housing projects where we grew up. "You just made me think about *Insecure,* with your ol' corny ass!"

"Child, that's exactly what I was thinking about, too. But for real, for real," I said into the receiver, "if Issa's ass don't hurry up with season 4, I'm gonna have to do her ass the same way I'm 'bout to do ol' boy right here."

She laughed so hard, I could hear her snorting through the phone. "Bitch, you're about to make me pee on myself!" she yelled into the phone. She always thought it was funny when I turn on my Decatur-Where It's Greater slang.

"So, what you gonna do to him, Hiri? What you gonna do?" She asked as animated as a child on Christmas morning.

Not one to ever back down from a challenge, I stressed every word as it came out my mouth, "Imma ghost his ass!" I yelled and hung up the phone in her face for emphasis. I know she was in that office cracking up and I'm sure she had a viewing audience by now. As I finally glanced out the window, it appeared I did too.

"*Thank you, God! I needed that.*" I said under my breath as I exited the vehicle, feeling

J'Sat Necolle

somewhat calmer than I had when I initially pulled up.

By now, Cleve had joined Kenyan at the bed of the truck, putting away painting supplies. "Damn, somebody's got you all glowing today," Cleve admonished as I approached the handsome duo.

"Yeah, yeah," I responded teasingly. "It feels good to have somebody that knows how to make you smile," I said as I reached over and gave him a big hug, which had quickly become our customary greeting.

"Hey, Kenyan," I said, as I finally glanced casually in his direction, offering him a quick head nod, my face adorned with a pleasant smile. *Stay focused, bitch,* I scolded inside my head. I was determined not to give him the pleasure of seeing how much his presence still get to me.

Refusing to even wait for a response, I turned with my hand still around Cleve's waist and headed towards the house, leaving him standing there like the non-factor he was, "Come on Hun, let me see what you fellas have accomplished today," I said to Cleve, in the most sensual voice I could muster. Smiling like crazy on the inside, I was so fucking proud of myself, I suddenly felt like Beyoncé, knowing I had his ass looking so crazy right now.

Cleve and I chatted it up as we walked through the job site, Kenyan was far more reserved than I remembered; not really saying much at all unless Cleve asked him something directly. Then, as I began going over some of the changes Zara and I had agreed would make the project even better, he did get a little more vocal. He asked me to explain a couple of things, which I did. And, I must admit, he was rather polite when telling me the things he did like and those he did not particularly care for. *We're both professionals,* I thought, *this is not going to be a problem at all.* And it wasn't...right up until I asked them to look at some swatches and pick out which ones they liked best.

As I walked over to my satchel to retrieve the samples, I could feel eyes boring into my flesh and I certainly knew they didn't belong to Cleve. He and I have been working together for weeks and he's been nothing less than a perfect gentleman, treating me like the little sister he never had.

However, I'm not so sure Kenyan saw it that way because I'd noticed several times when Cleve and I were teasing one another, Kenyan seemed to look away, then become even more withdrawn. So, when I turned my attention back to them, holding the swatches, I was shocked to see that they were engrossed in a silent; yet verbal spat.

"Is there something wrong?" I asked. Clearly able to see that there was some type of issue but not close enough to hear what they were arguing about.

J'Sat Necolle

Smitten

They both looked at me abruptly, realizing they'd been caught. They looked like two brats having just been caught with their hands in the cookie jar. And now, they are actually passing licks back and forth, down by their side, one trying to get the other to come up with an excuse. After a few minutes, Kenyan finally spoke first, stammering across his words, "It's no-nothing, we were..."

"Oh, it wasn't no 'we'! Cleve blurted out jokingly, looking up at his best friend that stood about three inches taller than his elite 6'2 frame. "Ya boy here," he said, then stared directly at Kenyan, who was now looking down at the floor, scratching his head like a scared little boy in trouble with his mama. "Ya' boy here's mad because he thinks I'm flirting with you," Cleve exclaimed, flinging both his arms in the air for added effect.

"What!" I was completely dumbfounded by the allegation. I looked back and forth between the two of them twice, then for the first time in almost twenty years, I stared directly into the eyes of The Kenyan Warner! *Jesus, take the wheel.*

Now, if we were white and this was a movie, silence would envelop us as we stared at each other across the dimly lit room with unmasked passion until we implode into a tantalizing kiss.

But this wasn't a movie and we damn sure wasn't white, because Cleve was literally killing his self laughing, drowning out any romantic mood that could have been in the air. In fact, he was laughing so hard at Kenyan's apparent discomfort, tears were streaming down his face.

"Man fuck you!" Kenyan blurted, hitting Cleve playfully in his arm, but was still sulking like a little kid, kicking the carpet and whatnot. I was caught completely off guard by his behavior; this was so not him...not Mr. Brooklyn-Smooth himself, acting like this. Not the way he used to call all the country brothas a bunch of pussies back in the day when they would start tripping about a girl.

In fact, I can remember him clowning Brandon for days because he didn't want to kick it with us after school anymore because he couldn't stand the sight of Yana talking to other cats. "Mannn, she ain't even your girl," he'd teased Brandon from outside Brandon's bedroom window. Then, as serious as a heart attack he'd told him, "Man, B... hoes come a dime a dozen, and you got a whole dollar."

That shit really should have told me something then, but nooo...not me. I was so stuck on stupid I could have ate a piece of his shit. *But God! And when you know better, you do better,* I exclaimed to myself.

I was still stuck though, starring back and forth at both of them. "He's lying, Hiri." "I swear, he's lying!" Kenyan said in between chuckles, still

Smitten

unable to make direct eye-contact with me.
Awww, he's embarrassed. That's so cute.

"Man, you play too much," he said, as he
playfully punched Cleve in the arm two more
times, each lick getting harder and harder, while
they both laughed uncontrollably.

Ready to get the hell out of dodge as fast as I
could, I said, sounding like a whining twelve-
year-old myself, "Mannn, ya'll come on and stop
playing!" Holding out the swatches in their
direction, I jammed them in Cleve's chest as they
both came near.

As he snatched the swatches out my hand, he
placed one of his muscled arms around Kenyan's
neck and led him over to the old work table in
the middle of the room. Looking back over at me
with a lingering glint of humor in his eyes, he
said, "Besides, I already told this fool, I'm the one
he gotta worry about, you got a man!" And with
that, Kenyan's head snapped up from the table so
fast it made my head spin.

"Bye, yawl." I said and grabbed my satchel
and almost ran out of there. "Cleve call me with
your decision, "I yelled back over my shoulder as
I rounded the corner leading to the massive
entryway.

I could still hear Cleve laughing and talking
trash as I reached the front door, "I'm sorry,
Dawg!" "Shit, you needed to know. Who the hell
did you think she was talking to earlier... giggling

and shit?" And just when I thought it couldn't get any worse, Cleve broke out singing, "Z*ahiri's Got A Man At Home.*" I couldn't help but to let out a soft giggle, but that's when I heard the loud clash of glass hitting a wall, followed by Cleve shouting, "Damn Nigga, you almost hit me!" I knew that was my clue to get the hell out of Dodge.

Cleve is one more fool, I thought as I finally exited the door, having heard enough. *And he knows damn well I don't have a man.* As a matter of fact, I ain't had no man since a man had me, as my Grammy used to say. But I loved the fact that he was taking my side over his boy's, who certainly didn't have any right to be possessive where I'm concerned. Not now...not ever again. *The audacity.*

Chapter 23

That night I slept like a baby. When I awoke the following morning, I had five missed calls and a text. Of course, all of them were from Yana's crazy ass. At first, I thought something was wrong when I saw all the missed calls, each about thirty minutes apart. My nerves instantly got bad, but as soon as I opened the text message, I laughed uncontrollably. It said...

Bitch, you ghosting me too???

I literally died. Like died-died, for real! Between this fool and my new-found friendship with Cleve's petty ass, I knew without a doubt I would get thru Kenyan's brief intrusion in my life. Besides, it seems to me that he's the one living with a shit-load of regret.

Then, as if on que, my phone vibrated signaling I had a new text message. When I picked up the phone and saw that it was from Kenyan, I started looking around my bedroom to see if Big Brother was watching or some shit, and when I read the message, that simply said, "*Sorry about last night.*" I dropped the whole damn phone. "Now that's some creepy shit!" I said out loud.

Smitten

Determined to enjoy myself this weekend though, I just laughed at the irony of it all. I quickly sent Yana back a text with a ghost and bunch of hearts, then I rolled over to the cold side of my king bed and closed my eyes.

When I first purchased this bed with Vani's credit card, I had such high hopes for it. I just knew once I jumped back on some black dick, my love life would pick up dramatically and I would put these massive bed posters to some good use. Swearing to reach ho status within six months of our break-up. Child Booh, I can count how many times I'd came on these mattresses on one hand. And sad to say, most of them came after I'd sent the sorry fucks home.

I don't know what it is about these new-skool brothas. They think they can just jump on top of you and just do their business, like Mister in *The Color Purple. Spsshh...nigga please.*

According to one of my homegirls, these fools don't even know what foreplay is anymore. She said...and I won't call her name, because she's got a man now, instead of them taking the time to kiss and caress you in the right places to get you wet, these new-skool fools have the nerve to spit in their hands and rub it on their junk to lubricate their entry that way.

I was seriously like, "Whatdafuck!" "You've got to be fucking kidding me!" I can't believe these tricks are that damn nasty that they are allowing these idiots to put their fucking spit in

J'Sat Necolle

them, without their tongues being attached. That's right; the only time a nigga's spit is going inside of me is when he is eating this full-course meal. *I wonder if Kenyan eats coochie,* I thought, as I began drifting off into a deep sleep. *Ain't nothing like NyQuil in the daytime.*

When I finally awoke, I felt as refreshed as the first day of spring. My day was still on track. I had planned on sleeping all day, then going to Lenox Square to pick up my dry-cleaning before heading over to the mall to pick out some new boots before heading to Dinner and a Movie in Atlantic Station.

The hot water from the shower vanished the last little bit of grogginess from my body and rejuvenated my soul. Careful not to get my hair wet, I let the droplets make love to me as the multi-shower-head caressed every crevice of my body. Now, I ain't never been into sex toys, but my shower-head was welcome to play with me any time.

I am so thankful the sistah at the Neiman Marcus wasn't as bougie as she'd looked. When I initially inquired about the Golden Vantage Shower Panel System, it was only because I was intrigued by a shower head that cost so damn much. So, after she threw out her best sales pitch, I was like, "Oh, okay. That sounds cool. But not today."

And when she hit me with that customary rebuttal, "Are you sure?"

Smitten

I politely declined, telling her that the shower pressure in my home was pretty good, so I don't see the need in spending three-hundred dollars for something that wasn't going to get me any cleaner.

We both laughed at my joke; then I suppose she saw that I wasn't as bougie as I looked either, so she looked around the store to see if anyone was within ear-shot, then she leaned across the counter and whispered, "It might not get you any cleaner, but it will damn sure make you have to wash down there twice!"

When I looked up into her face with blatant shock, she had folded her arms across her body, cocked her head to one side, and was nodding up and down; looking at me with that sistah-girl smirk, which I interpreted as her saying, *"Yasssssss, Bitch. Yasssssss."*

Not only did I buy me one, I got my girl, Yana, one too. What can I say...shit, that's what friends are for. Hell, when Snoop Dog said *"Ain't no fun if the homies can't have none,"* I felt that shit! That thing had me cumming so much, I know I was bathing at least four times a day. And Yana's stupid ass had the nerve to say all those jets and that little hand-held wand almost made her swear off men forever. It was so good in fact, that two-weeks after I'd purchased them, we went back to the store and gave Cheryl, the sistah girl sales clerk, a fifty-dollar tip and an Amazon gift certificate, who, by the way, now carries that

J'Sat Necolle

same brand for a hundred dollars less. But hell, I honestly didn't give two fucks, I'd pay top dollar all over again if I had to, it was worth every damn penny.

As I walked out my front door heading to my mailbox, I was alarmed by the sleek Mercedes blocking my driveway. "Excuse the fuck outta me!" I mumbled to myself as I stopped dead in my tracks, enraged at the audacity of someone to block my entire driveway. Looking at my neighbor's home on the right, it didn't look like the person could be at their home because their driveway was empty, but just as I was about to take my cell out and call my other neighbor, I saw some slight movement behind the darkly tinted windows and a glow from a cell-phone. *Oh, okay. They're probably lost and using the cul-de-sac to turn around and re-route their GPS.*

Always eager to help those in need, I was almost about to approach the car to see if they needed any help, but something said, *"Fool, mind your damn business. You see missing women on the news every day for being just that stupid."* And with that thought, I bee-lined to my mailbox and just as I opened it, I could hear someone opening the car door on the opposite side of the curb. Remembering to mind my own damn business, I proceeded to thumb through the mail, not bothering to look up...not until I heard someone clear their throat.

"Hi-Hiri," Even as he stammered over my name, I recognized the sound of his voice and couldn't believe that he was actually here. The Kenyan Warner was at my house. The place where I pay bills. The place where I lay my head. And the only place I can go to hide out from the outside world. *Whatdafuck!*

Still in shock, I just stared at him. *He did this shit on purpose.* He wanted to catch me off-guard, so I wouldn't have anything or anyone to buffer between us. No Yana. No Cleve. And hell, even no Christine. Just Me and Kenyan plus air and opportunity.
Whatdafuck!

After staring for what seemed like hours, I finally asked, sounding more angry than necessary, "What are you doing here?"

"W-well," he stuttered, while ringing his hands together in nervous anxiety. "I was going to call first, but I knew if I did, you weren't going to agree to let me come."

"So, if you already know I don't want you here, why would you still come?" I asked, my voice sounding much stronger than I felt.

"Because I had to take a chance," he practically yelled across the yard. "Something, I should have done a long time ago," he said, his voice now barely above a whisper as he closed the distance between us on the plush lawn.

"Stop right there," I said. There was no way I would allow him to get any closer to me. My knees were already shaking, my palms were sweating and I'm pretty sure my heart was going to beat right out of my chest at any moment.

Trying to sound tough; yet unbothered at the same time, "Kenyan, you didn't have to come way out here. There's nothing we have to talk about...we're cool."

"Well, you don't have to talk, but please let me say what I need to say." He took two long strides and was right up on me, "Can we please go inside and talk?"

He was now so close I could feel his breath caress the side of my face while he awaited my answer. Just as I was about to give in, I looked up hesitantly, right into his handsome caramel-latte face. The piercing hazel eyes, the soft pink lips with the crooked smile...he must think I'm Booh-Booh-da-fool...ain't no way in the hell I'm about to let him up in my shit just like that. He obviously thinks I'm still that naive fourteen-year-old girl he left behind.

Taking a defiant step back, I looked him dead in the eyes and said, "Nawl man, we definitely can't go in there and talk." Stressing the word 'there' for extra emphasis. I could see his jaw line twitch, which let me know I had struck a nerve. Fifteen years later, some things still hadn't changed, I knew exactly what he was thinking.

"So, that's it?" He said, his voice rose about three decibels. "You're worried about your man coming home and catching me here?" *Look at this shit.* I thought to myself. *This fool is just as jealous as all those other 'pussies' he used to talk about.*

"Really, Kenyan?" I asked, not even waiting for a response. "First of all, I ain't worried about shit. Secondly, my man and what we have going on up in there ain't none of your damn business. And lastly, you've got some fucking nerve showing up at my home, demanding a courtesy you forfeited years ago!"

"Nigga, please," I mumbled under my breath as I brushed passed him headed in the direction of my garage.

"You're right, Hiri. I'm sorry," he said as he reached out and grabbed my arm, slinging me around to face him. "Everything you just said was the absolute truth and I'm sorry. Could you please just hear me out?" he asked, pleadingly, the octaves in his voice decreasing with every word.

Damn, his fine ass still got that puppy dog thing down to a T, I thought. "Look, I'm sorry, I've got shit to do. You can't just pop up on a sistah and just think she got time for you." I said as I pulled my arm out his grip, hoping that would relieve the tingling sensation I felt deep in my soul.

Playfully he sucked his teeth, then teased, "Girl, where you got to go?" "You know that shit can wait." *Damn, this nigga makes me sick,* I thought to myself, trying desperately not to laugh at his antics. *He always did know how to make me smile.*

"Whatever man." I said and tried to quickly turn away before he saw the crimson blush stain my cheeks.

"Shit, you probably weren't going nowhere but Whole Foods," he said, still teasing; knowing fool well his comedic antics were helping him get my guard down. *Two can play this game,* I thought.

Licking my lips seductively, I looked at him with what the old-folks called 'bedroom-eyes' and said, "Now, do I look like I was only going to Whole Foods?"

And with that single question, the air outside became thicker than the smog encircling the Empire State Building in the middle of winter. Kenyan finally took his time to take the site of me in from head to toe. In that very moment, I was so glad I chose the silk, plunged-neckline blouse by Anne Taylor to accentuate the fitted, distressed Bodycon jeans. Yes honey, I love to pair a little classy with a little ho, in my personal style aesthetic. When I checked the ensemble out in my floor-length mirror, I was thoroughly pleased, but when I slid on the pair of caramel, Michael Kors stacked-wedge sandals, my ass and my hips immediately stood in attention. And now seeing the way Kenyan is responding to me...*Girl, want he do it!* God sends blessings our way and

159

we don't even see them coming until they are staring you in the face...literally. Just like Kenyan's ass is doing right now. *Nawl, who's laughing now, Nigga?*

I obviously threw him completely off guard, because Mr. Confident started stumbling over his words like Elmer Fudd. Who could blame him though because the body that he couldn't seem to take his eyes off was certainly not that of the fourteen-year-old virgin he knew all those years ago. *Joke's on you, Booh.*

"N-no, Zahiri, you certainly don't look like you're going to get grocery." His voice was so soft and sensual, he almost made me cum right then and there, but true to his jealous nature, I could see his eyes cloud over as the thought penetrated his head. "So, you've got a date?" He asked, his voice barely above a whisper.

Switching my weight from one foot to the other one, to not only draw out my response. I knew his mannish ass couldn't resist the rise in my thighs or the way the jeans caressed my curves as I shifted positions. Then I looked up at him and said, "Yes, Kenyan...I do have a date."

Somehow, I thought it would be funnier to see this kind of reaction from him, especially after waiting almost two decades for some pay back, but he looked so pitiful. I almost felt sorry for him. *Almost.* When he finally let out the breath he was holding and turned to retreat, I

J'Sat Necolle

grabbed him by his hand and said, "Today... I was dating me."

Man, I shole hope my cameras are catching this shit cause Yana ain't gonna believe me when I tell her, I thought. He actually looked like I had made him the happiest man in the world. The normally cool and chill, Kenyan Warner, threw all that macho bullshit out the window then and there.

"Please, Hiri. Please, let me take you!" He grabbed my hand and was looking dead in my eyes as he hopped up and down anxiously, like he was about to pee on his self. "I promise, Hiri, I'll be on my best behavior. I won't even talk, unless you want to be talked to...just let me escort you on your date with you. Please, Zahiri. Please. I just want to be with you...."

Listening to his voice crack as the last words trailed off, hell, I didn't know what to do. I had never seen him like that and I must admit, a part of me was pleased. It felt good to know that he never stopped caring. Then, I thought about his wife, who was probably at home, washing his dirty draws and cleaning up behind their bad ass kids...and that was all I needed. "Ok, Kenyan. You can escort me on my date with me." *Fuck that ho! Karma is a bitch.*

Chapter 24

Somewhere between buying my groceries at Whole Foods and running my errands at Lennox Square, Kenyan's charisma had beckoned me to drop my guard and we were having a really great time. He was actually even funnier than I remembered, and I was so surprised that I was able to be myself with him. Shit, I even dropped a bar or two, straight Issa Rae'd his ass. He didn't even see it coming.

For the life of me, I can't even remember the last time I went shopping for myself with a man in tow. That was almost like taking Charlie Brown to pick out Christmas trees.

My soul purpose of taking this weekend to myself was to mark shit off my list, but the list seems to be getting longer and longer. If only my hair would grow that fast, you couldn't tell me shit.

As we walked around the crowded mall, weaving in and out of the pedestrian traffic, Kenyan was very protective, which I thought was really sweet. Whenever we came upon a large group, he'd put his arm out a little just to shield everyone off me. I noticed he was also very kind to everyone we were in close proximity to, a trait I really admire in anyone, but was quite surprised to see it in him. Back in high school, he was kind of stand-offish until he got to know you. I suppose because of the rumors that emerged when he got to Georgia, he always felt like people thought he was just another hood nigga; so, it was nice to see that he'd came out of his shell and was more trusting of people.

Hell, I've always thought life was too short to walk around angry all the time. Shoot, I talk to everybody and when I say everybody, I mean every-damn-body! Yana is always joking with me every time we go somewhere. She swears there must be an imaginary stamp across my forehead that says. *"talk to her...she'll talk back,"* because people everywhere just walk up and start full-fledged conversations with me. No lie.

I can be in a group of ten people, but I'll be the only one that strangers approach and ask, *"What's the occasion?"* or *"Can you take our picture?"* or *"Where are you all from?"* It never fails...and it's always been this way. Grammy used to say it was because I have an old soul, and other good people can sense that. So, I just embrace the gifts God gave me...even if it's funny to everyone else.

While we were shopping, our conversation stayed pretty casual and the vibe between us was pretty chill. Just by looking at us, you would never know that he had just accidentally re-appeared in my life after nearly fifteen years. That he'd been the man on my dreams that sadly turned into the man of my nightmares after he took my virginity; then left me without ever saying goodbye.

In fact, we ran into several couples that he knew and some of his single friends. He didn't seem the least bit nervous or anything, introducing me to some as a really good friend, and to a couple of the fellas as the one that got away. I was utterly dumbfounded. Because me on the other hand, when I saw a couple of my colleagues, I grabbed his hand and hauled ass in the other direction. Damn if I was going to be introducing his ass to my peers. Besides, what the hell would I say, 'Oh, this Kenyan, he picked his wife over me' or 'meet Kenyan, the one that got away...after he got my booty though.' *Oh, no mam! They can miss me with that bullshit.*

Snapping me out of my thoughts as we walked thru the crowded mall, now hand-in-hand, he said, "Do you still like ice cream?" *My God, this cat is smooth as shit.* I didn't even realize he was still holding my hand after he'd rubbed the massage oil on it back at that kiosk. Now here I am strolling around all willy-nilly, like we're Bobby and Whitney or something. *I just be damned!*

Surprised that he remembered my ice cream addiction, I nodded my head slowly in an up and down motion and with that he led the way over to the Haagen Dazs store. I ordered me a Pecan Praline and he ordered a Double Chocolate Chip. I waited as he paid for it, noticing how the young sales clerk was checking him out and how badly

J'Sat Necolle

she was trying to get her homegirl's attention, so she could check him out too. *Child, Booh, been there...done that.*

I was behind his back starring at that heifer so hard, my eyes had to be burning a hole in that nametag on her shirt. And when Little Miss. Shelly did finally give in to my stares, I gave her that sistah-girl smirk that only a sistah could give, and she knew just what the fuck I meant because she didn't look up for the rest of that transaction. And neither did her little cross-eyed friend. *Trifling trolls.*

As we walked out of the ice-cream shop, I just could not help but to think about the damn audacity of some women. The same shit used to happen when Vani and I went out around campus, but at least those were women of age. When the hell did teen-aged girls get bold enough to come on to grown-ass men, while they had their women by their sides. *Well...I'm not his woman, but hell, they didn't know that. Disrespectful asses! Who the hell raising these hoes?*

When I started telling him what had happened, he laughed so hard. "Really, Hiri?" "You actually mean-mugged a child about me?" Still a little pissed, I didn't think the shit was funny...at least not as funny as he was making it. "Sooo... you still think I'm cute, huh?" He teased, while tickling me in the stomach, smack dab in the middle of Lenox Mall. I was trying to make him stop without dropping my ice-cream. People started coming by 'ooh-ing' and 'ahh-ing' about how sweet we were. *If they only knew,* I thought.

Faking like I was getting mad; hoping to make him stop, I said, more forcefully this time, "Get your hands off me, Boy!"

He stopped tickling me immediately, then walked right up to me, never taking his eyes off mine, "Boy...Oh, I got your boy." And then took a lick of his ice cream. In that instant, I didn't know what had happened. I wasn't sure if it was the elements, the tickling exploits, or the way he looked at me with those doe-like hazel eyes, but I swear to God, those six words were the sexiest things I'd ever heard in my life.

I stood there comatose for what seemed like hours, staring at his mouth as he continued to slowly and seductively devour the ice-cream. Without uttering one single word; his eyes burned a fire through my flesh as he memorized every line in my face. His breathing got heavier and heavier as he erotically licked his lips and around the sides of his mouth between bites. Finally, I said, "Boy, get the hell away from me!" Pushing him playfully in his chest to give myself a reprieve from the torch he'd ignited in my thong, I hurriedly turned to escape the inferno as fast as I could. *Bittttccchhhh, what the hell were you thinking?* I scolded myself quietly.

My common sense wasn't common when I agreed to let him accompany me on my date, but now that shit was kicking in full-force. *I know I knew better, but I did the stupid shit anyway,* I thought as I took even longer strides trying to create some distance between us. Hell, even if we didn't have history, when you looked at his fine ass, you immediately thought of the Trey Songz lyric... *"this right here's a panty dropper."*

He is most definitely too damn fine to be playing games with, unless you plan on losing. "Was that my plan?" I asked myself subconsciously. Hell, even those babies back there recognized how undeniably sexy he was, and he's damn near old enough to be their daddies. *"Oooh Daddy,"* I mumbled, as visions of ice-cream foreplay with Kenyan entered my mind.

"What did you say?" I heard his deep, baritone voice penetrate my thoughts.

"Oh, my bad. I was just going over my list in my head."

Grabbing my hand, he pulled me on towards the Apple Store, like nothing had ever happened. So, I just followed suit and the rest of our mall excursion went quite well.

As we headed out the mall, I could hear my stomach growling and wondered if by chance he'd heard it too because I saw his head jerk around. But as I followed his eyes, I realized it wasn't my damn stomach he heard, it was my best friend. *Damnnn*

Chapter 25

"*L*ord, please help me. Help me, Lord!" I prayed over and over again while Kenyan looked on, toppling over in pure laughter. When he tried pulling my hands from over my eyes, I closed them even tighter like a frightened child. There scurrying across the crowded parking lot was my girl, Yana Yearwood-Smalls, looking like Sofia in *The Color Purple.* And from the scowl on her face and the look of shock on Brandon's face as she dragged him along, it looked like she was two minutes from saying, *"You told Harpo to beat me."*

By the time they finally made it over to where we were, Kenyan was almost down on his knees crying with laughter. If I wasn't so afraid of Yana's reaction to seeing me with him, I would be laughing too, because I know this was some priceless shit. Out of all the malls in Atlanta, how in the world did we all end up here at the same damn time. Again, I'm convinced that the universe hates my guts.

As recognition transpired between Brandon and Kenyan, they embraced each other and picked right up where they'd left off fifteen years earlier. *Why can't women be more like men,* I thought, as I watched how genuinely happy they were to see one another. But women can't do that. Hell, I talked to Sofia...I meant, Yana, just yesterday and texted her this morning, but here she is gazing at me like she's never met me in her fucking life.

Despite the distinct humor in the air among the fellas, her deafening silence eventually became awkward for them too. As I lowered my head even more under her scrutinizing gaze, Kenyan spoke up, trying to explain to her like she was my mama or something. "Yana, I can explain," he said, but before he could utter another word, she reached up with her left hand and shushed his ass.

Both, his and Brandon's mouth dropped at the same damn time. Neither could believe she'd done that disrespectful shit. I was the only one that wasn't surprised and just as I was about to go off on her ass for that dumb shit, she said, "What's up, Ghost?" And burst out laughing.

Everybody let out a sigh of relief and joined her in her antics. She gave Kenyan a tight hug and then began bashing him about how his face had dropped a few moments ago when she'd shushed his ass. After standing in the parking lot talking for about fifteen minutes, we all changed our plans and headed over to Brandon's new restaurant with them.

I must say, now in retrospect, I'm glad we ran into them. That was the best time I'd had in a long time. It seems we all were enjoying each other's company, reliving stories of the past. Brandon was also a huge part of our hook-up team back in the day. Him and Kenyan used to hang pretty tight, just so the project gossipers would have no idea Kenyan was really over there to get next to me. All it would have taken was for one word to make it back to Grammy and I would have never seen the light of day again.

In fact, knowing Grammy, she probably would have tried to home-school my ass, and she could barely read her damn self. No mam, my Grammy did not play and everybody and they mama knew it. Since the day I'd gotten my first visit from Aunt Flow, she'd vowed that I was not getting pregnant on her watch, and she meant that shit.

As it got later and later into the night, I leaned in and told Kenyan that I was ready to go whenever he was, not wanting to get him in that much trouble. I realized that although what had happened between us was messed up, we were kids, and shit happens. He seemed to be a good guy and I didn't want to get him in serious trouble with his wife and jeopardize the peace in his family. That wouldn't be right.

But hell, he just kept on talking and carrying on with Brandon and Yana like he wasn't in any hurry, so I kept rolling with the punches too and before we knew it, it was 3:00 in the morning and we were all tipsy as hell. Tim, the restaurant's manager came over to the table and asked if he could get us one last round before everyone left. "No, absolutely not," I said. "We have kept you guys here too late as it is."

J'Sat Necolle

Smitten

Looking at Kenyan, I said, "You, get up and go bring the car around."

Then I looked at Yana and said, "And, you, you get up and help me clear this table."

Lastly, I looked over at Brandon and said, "And you, you go handle your business," pointing at the tired-eyed servers waiting for their boss's dismissal.

No one moved immediately, they all just stared at me in awe, but by the time my hands made it to my hips with a puff of my lips, they had all scrambled to their feet and were getting to the tasks at hand.

"Damnnnn, Grammy!" Kenyan yelled over the now empty restaurant as he walked out the front door. Both Yana and Brandon stopped dead in their tracks and laughed uncontrollably, both agreeing they were thinking the same thing but just didn't have the nerve to say it.

Once Kenyan pulled up out front with the car, Yana came and gave me a quick hug and whispered in my ear, "Just do you."

Touched by her genuineness, we walked arm in arm to the door where Brandon and Kenyan were gathered making plans to get together later in the week. As we approached them, Kenyan walked over to Yana and gave her a great, big hug and then mushed her dead in face and told her she better not ever shush him again, which brought on even more laughter.

As we waved our good-byes, he led me out the front door, with his hand draped lightly around my waist. "We have got to do that again," he said as he was opening my door and helping me into his car.

Whatdafuck. I hope he don't think we finna be besties, I thought to myself. *If he does, he damn sure better think again.* But I didn't say anything. I decided to just enjoy the night for what it was, there was no point in spoiling the best day I've had in a long time just to state the obvious.

As we pulled away from the hilltop restaurant, the lights from the city below welcomed us, beckoning us back to reality. And, I'm not sure if it was the heated leather seats in the car or the four glasses of wine after dinner or the tender way The Kenyan Warner kept looking at me, but it seemed like a fuel had been lit somewhere deep within. *Lord, help me.*

As he meandered the city streets, I realized he was taking the long way to my home. Unsure if it was intentionally, I asked, "Do you need directions?"

"Nah," he said softly. Then with misty eyes he looked over at me and said, "I just really hate for this night to end." Understanding exactly how he was feeling, I slowly turned my gaze back out my window, leaving us each to our own thoughts.

J'Sat Necolle

An hour later, we finally pulled into my driveway. My house was completely dark because I'd forgotten to leave the light on, not expecting to be gone so long. Before I could reach for the door, he caught my hand and said, "Can we talk, now?"

Looking down at my lap, I carefully aligned my words. "Seriously, Kenyan, there really is nothing to talk about. The past is the past and there's nothing either of us can do to change it." Giving my words time to sink in to both him and I, I finally looked up at him and said softly, "Besides, we've had a great day. Something I didn't expect, as I'm sure neither did you, and I don't want to see it end on a sour note by dredging up ancient history."

As the words were flowing from my mouth, I could not believe how mature I sounded. For years, I'd waited for this very day, where I could tell him everything I've ever wanted to say to him. But now that it's here, it's nothing like I had imagined it would be.

"I hear what you're saying, Hiri, and I honestly think the world of you for that, but I owe you an apology and I will be less than a man if I don't take this opportunity to give you at least that." As I slowly looked up into the depths of his eyes, my entire body quivered to the core.

He then took my hands in his, touched me lightly on my face to turn me towards him, "Hiri,

Smitten

I am so sorry for hurting you and there has not
been one day in my life that has gone by that I
haven't regretted how I treated you. You didn't
deserve that, and I'm sorry, Hiri. I will always be
sorry."

"Shush," I said, putting my finger to his lips as
his voice began to crack. "Thank you," solemnly
left my lips as I pulled him into a warm embrace.
Closure...Finally.

J'Sat Necolle

Chapter 26

The days seemed to be trickling by so fast since that magical day I'd spent with Kenyan. He'd tried calling and texting me a few times, but I reluctantly declined his calls and ghosted his texts. While, I was grateful that I now had closure, I was still not in a place where we could just kick it like old friends. I'd even changed my ringtone on my phone to *"We Can't Be Friends,"* so I wouldn't be tempted to answer it.

Besides, the way he'd smelled that night when we hugged already had me up at night wishing I had been the one he'd chose...and Lord knows I've been down that lonely road enough to last a lifetime. I can't tell you how many restless nights I'd dreamt of rushing through the chapel doors just as he said, 'I do,' to her, and instead of Vesta Williams singing *Congratulations,* it was always my stupid ass.

Oh, no mam! I thought to myself, those days are finally behind me and I'll be a monkey's ass before I go back down that road again.

Three days before the surgery and it still feels like I have so much to do. According to Yana's infinite wisdom though, I am intentionally adding shit to my to-do-list in order to avoid thoughts of Kenyan; as well as, thoughts of Janis and her two minions. "Listen Bitch, if you don't want to do it, it's not too late. You don't owe anyone anything."

"Yeah, I know, but I'm not doing it for them, I'm doing it for me," I said, my voice barely above a whisper. While flipping through the floor lay-outs for the interior space that Zara and I were finally wrapping up on The Hope House project, I felt an instant pang in my heart when I said the words. Looking up into the eyes of my best friend I said, "Even you don't know how long I have wanted them to want me. Loving someone who doesn't deserve your love is the worst pain in the world," I started to sob.

Throwing down the expense reports in her hand, Yana rushed around the side of the desk and pulled me into her warm embrace. "There, there, now. Don't cry," she said, as she rocked me back and forth, wiping the tears away from my eyes.

"Hiri," she said softly. "You're wrong, I do know what it feels like to love someone knowing they don't love you back." And when I heard her say those words as her voice began to quiver, I felt like the worst, most selfish friend in the world.

"Now, that I've been spending time with Brandon, I can't remember what I ever saw in Gavin in the first place," she continued while she stared out of my office window absently stroking my hair. "Hell, if I'm completely honest with myself, he didn't just get selfish, he was always selfish. But as sick as it sounds, I think that's what turned me on." She had now stopped stroking my head and walked over and threw herself on the chaise lounge in the corner of my office.

I watched intently as she placed her hands behind her head and stared up at the ceiling for a few minutes, lost in her own thoughts. "When we first met on campus, it was something mysterious; yet, intriguing about him at the same time. He was always laid-back and pretty chill, which everyone loved...including all the girls. Every time I saw him he was with a different girl and for that moment, that girl thought she had the best thing in the world. I used to sit in the frat house and watch as he strolled them in and out the front door like they were disposable plastic, and they seemed okay with it. At first, I thought he was a piece of shit for treating women like that but after a while, something about that...and the fact that he always ignored my ass, started completely turning me on. So, I made it my mission to get his attention, by any means necessary. "

She chuckled a little at the irony of it all before she continued. "Poor Brandon, he didn't have a clue. Sometimes I would leave Brandon's suite in the frat house and head straight down to Gavin's room on the second floor and wait my turn. The first time I'd gone down there, I knew that he wouldn't be able to resist all this ass up close and personal, but when I told him what I was there for, he'd looked at me disgustingly and told me to get the fuck out; which made me want him even more."

"I started stalking him between classes, all around campus; even when I had Brandon with me. If he went to the game, we went to the game. If he went to the step show, we went to the step show...and no matter where we were, I made it my business to make sure I pranced this ass all up in his face. But he just wasn't interested, and I couldn't take that shit."

"That shit went on for months, then finally one night when I was leaving the frat house, he was coming in with this white girl name Macy hanging all over him. When I spotted them coming up the walkway, I instantly felt a ping of jealousy and bumped his shoulder as hard as I could as I walked passed. He let out a sarcastic chuckle and kept on his way, but just as he reached the door, I heard him say, "Hey, you," and I turned around to see who he was talking to, "come on."

"At first, I looked from side to side but there was no one else he could be talking to, so I did what any well-respected fiancé of the president of the Kappa Phi Alpha Fraternity could do…. I followed him and Macy's trashy ass up to his bedroom amidst the stares and whispers of all the other brothers and their skanky midnight snacks, still chilling in the common room.

J'Sat Necolle

Smitten

"That night was the beginning of the end for me," she said in a more sorrowful tone than ever before.

Unable to hold my tongue any longer, I yelled across the room, "Oh, no, Heifer, don't stop now!" Sensing that she was about to shut-down, just like she always did when it came to his trifling ass. "So, did ya'll have a threesome or what?" I asked anxiously, now sitting up on my desk with my ears tuned in attention, like I watching *The Young and the Restless* or some shit,

Giggling and shaking her head at my intense absorption in her story, she said, "Sorta-kinda; but not really."

"Biiitttcchh, it can't be no, 'sorta-kinda; but not really. Either you did, or you didn't!" *Lord, please don't let her sneaky ass clam up now,* I thought. I couldn't believe that after all these years she was finally spilling the tea.

"Damn," she laughed sarcastically while shaking her head absently. "I have never said this stupid shit out loud." With a heavy sigh, she said, "No, we technically didn't have a threesome but all three of us engaged in sexual acts that night."

"Explain," I said, now sitting up intently in my chair, anticipation having wiped all my tears away.

"Well, first, when we got to the door of his bedroom, he sent white-girl Macy on in, then turned to me and roughly asked, *"Are you sure you want to come in?"* Hell, that should have been my first clue to get the hell out of dodge, but I was determined to show him I was down. So, I said I was damn sure."

"Girlll," she exclaimed, "when I say, in the one minute that it took for us to get inside the room, white-girl Macy had already taken her clothes off and was lying naked as hell in the middle of his full-sized bed, playing with herself. I was completely taken aback. I didn't quite know what I was expecting, but it sure as hell wasn't baby Martha Stewart in there fingering herself." I laughed so hard at Yana's candidness, but was still in complete shock that she was finally telling this crap.

"I guess Macy was determined she wasn't going to let some big booty sistah come in and steal her magic stick, so she was going to do anything within her power to keep that dick to herself. Little did I know, that was just who she was...ol' trashy ass."

Laughing at the mere thought of it, she continued on, "After watching Macy's performance for what seemed like hours, the air in the room was thick and musky. He walked over to his desk and pulled out the chair and told me to sit down. He then walked over to the bed and told Macy to get up. When she did so immediately, something about that tuned me on even more because I thought he was about to kick her trashy ass out but instead, he started tongue-kissing her."

"Shit, first I was mad, and then I was jealous, but by the time they had finished though, I was horny as hell...no matter how much a part of me told me to get up and get the hell out that room, I just couldn't. I couldn't take my eyes off them. He never said another word to me the rest of the night and my stupid ass just sat there and watched as she did things to him I'd only seen in porn. Things that made me want to touch myself all over...and that's what I did," she uttered softly.

Staring off into space as if she was reliving that night, she continued on, "Once they were finally finished, he went into the bathroom and turned on the water, while she laid in bed staring at me but never saying a word. Once he came out the bathroom, he looked her straight in the eyes and said quietly, *"Goodnight."*

Completely mesmerized, I asked, "What happened next?" Just knowing my girl was about to tell me how his freaky ass fucked the shit outta her for the rest of the night.

"Well," she quietly said, completely lost in thoughts of her own, "when he told her goodnight, she reluctantly got up from the soiled bed and slowly put back on her cloths and walked out the room without uttering a word."

Smitten

Damn, that was cold, I thought, *he could've walked her home.*

Obviously reading my mind, Yana said, "Shit it gets worst."

I starred at her like she had two fucking heads. *Damn, how much worse could it get,* I wondered.

She said, "After White-girl Macy closed the door, the bastard had the audacity to look over from the bathroom door in my direction and say, *"That goes for you, too."*

She laughed sarcastically, trying to keep from crying. Then continued, "Again, I didn't know what to expect, but it damn sure wasn't that. Brandon had never treated me so harshly and degradingly and even when I showed back up to his suite at four o' clock that morning smelling like sex and musk, he opened his door and let me in, never questioning my love or where I had been."

"So, is that when you started cheating with Gavin?"

"Child, Booh!" "That fool acted like he didn't even know me that next day and every day after that for the next six months."

"Dang, Sis. For real?"

J'Sat Necolle

Smitten

Staring into space, she nodded her head up and down to signal just how stupid she had been for Gavin's ass from day one; even though I never knew any of this. I suppose it's not easy calling up your homegirl and telling her you know you are making a damn fool of yourself, but you can't even help it. As if she was reading my mind, she said softly, "Yeah, that bastard didn't just start treating me like shit, he's always treated me like shit."

I looked up just in time to see her wipe a stray tear off her beautiful face. "So, how could you fall in love with someone like that, Yana?" I asked as thoughtfully as I could.

"Girl, I wish I knew," she said softly, more of an afterthought than anything else. Then she suddenly jumped up from the chaise and walked over to my desk and picked up next month's sales projections and headed towards the door and tossed back over her shoulder, "Anyway...bye bitch, you are not Iyanla and you damn sure can't fix my life." Leaving me with my mouth wide open in awe...

Later that night as I stepped out the shower, I could not help but to think about all the things Yana had shared with me earlier and was still completely baffled. *I suppose that explains a lot,* I thought as I toweled off. Eventhough I wanted to ask her so much more, earlier, I knew she was stepping outside her comfort zone by telling me that much; besides, I was just happy she was finally waking up and realizing she deserved so much better. I suppose I can thank Brandon for that.

Just as I was about to reach down and pull the lotion out of my bathroom cabinet, I heard the vibrator go off on my cellphone that was lying by the toilet where I was now sitting. Reaching down, I picked it up, careful not to get lotion on the screen or to turn off my Pandora station. When I saw Kenyan's name on the screen, my breath caught in my chest, and I let out a small gasp. For some strange reason, whenever, I saw his name appear on my phone screen, my reaction was always the same...surprise, mixed with anticipation.

When I opened the text, it simply read:

> I just NEED to hear your voice...
>
> K.

What the hell, I thought...

> What's stopping u...

But before I could finish sending my text good, my cellphone was already ringing. Still giggling when I answered, "How may I help you, Sir?"

Silence engulfed the line for what seemed like minutes, then I finally heard his rich, baritone voice whisper, "You already have."

At that very moment, the walls of my va-jay-jay yelled all the way up to brain, *"Girl, what the fuck are you doing?"*

As I heard his faint breath vibrate through the speaker phone, the clenching in my lower region tightened even more and I knew right then that finally taking his call was probably a really, big mistake. But instead of ending the conversation before it began, something inside of me had to indulge just a little while longer. "Why did you need to hear my voice?" I asked, placing a bunch of emphasis on the word 'need'.

"Because I never want to forget what it sounds like again." For the third time in less than two minutes, this man had succeeded in making my heart skip a beat, so I quickly diverted the subject.

"I'm glad you called though, because I wanted to ask you what I can expect after my surgery on Friday." And just like that he changed from The Kenyan Warner, my first love; to highly regarded, Chief of Nephrology, Dr. Kenyan Warner.

Smitten

He gave me the complete run down about how I should feel, to how my body will heal. He also told me what type of pain medications I can take, what I'll be prescribed to fight off infection and how much time I will need to recuperate. While Dr. Spivey had already did an excellent job relaying all this information to me prior to now, hearing it come out Kenyan's mouth made me feel a lot more reassured with the entire process.

After the medical consultation was over, our conversation moved from topic to topic. We discussed everything from music, to politics, to police brutality, to discrimination. There were times in the conversation where we both laughed hysterically and then there were other times, mainly when talking about the Netflix docu-series, *When They See Us*, I could tell we were both trying hard to fight off tears. Talking to him was so easy; a call that I thought would only last a few minutes, was now going on three hours later. *Where the hell is his wife?* I thought to myself, as I was curling up in my oversized bed laughing at something silly he had just said.

I honestly could not believe he had held my attention this long. Typically, I prefer face to face communication. But with him, I almost felt like we were face-to- face, minus the dazzling smile, hard abs and pussy-caressing eyes.

Nowadays, brothas think they can send you a couple of texts and swear that suffices for spending time together. *Boy, please.* I am a grown ass woman, that needs a grown ass man who can

J'Sat Necolle

stimulate my mind, just as well as my body. In fact, those "WYD" and "TTYL" text messages at my age are a total turn-off.

I always want to ask what the hell do they think I'm doing in the middle of the damn day. Nigel's ass was notorious for doing that dumb shit. I should have texted his ass back just one time: *Fool, I'm working! That's what the fuck grown people do in the middle of the damn day.* That would have gotten rid of his simple ass a long time ago.

I wondered if Kenyan was that type of man. Did he sit up and play Fortnight all night, while his wife took care of the kids; or did they just let the kids raise themselves, like so many millennium parents today. Just as my mind was envisioning him sitting on the floor bonding with his wife and kids, his husky voice derailed my thoughts, "Hiri, I can't stop thinking about you."

Lost in the abyss of those simple words, that it seems I have waited a lifetime to hear, I didn't know what to say. At that very moment, all I could hear was my grandmother's voice echoing in my head again, *"Baby, God will send you a lot of things, but he won't send you someone else's husband."*

"Goodnight, Kenyan Shahid," I whispered softly into the receiver, as the longing in my soul resonated in my heart, just as the sunlight kissed the sky welcoming a new day.

Chapter 27

*F*or the next two days, it took a shit-load of effort to ignore Kenyan's calls and texts. Something deep inside me wanted nothing more than to sit on the phone and talk to him all night, but something at the cusp of my heart told me that I would only be setting myself up for failure by doing so.

Since Cleve and I had worked so closely on the Hope House project before Zara's return, he and I had become really good friends. That afternoon though, when I stopped by to see how Zara and her crew were coming along on the project, Cleve suggested he and I get together after work to talk about some mutual acquaintances.

Of course, I knew exactly who he was talking about, but Zara, on the other hand, was looking so confused it was downright funny. Knowing Zara, she probably thought Cleve and I had made a romantic connection...which in another world, would have been very possible. He was tall, handsome, funny and personable, and he has that sexy ass New York accent that I love so much; but most of all, he was kind and loyal.

I knew Cleve was only trying to look out for me, so I promised him that after I have the surgery, he was the next scheduled appointment on my list. *Besides,* I thought, *it will be nice to be*

*able to talk to a man about my reluctance to let
Kenyan back in my life on a friendship level, just to
hear a male's perspective.* Eventhough, I know
Cleve's loyalty lies with Kenyan, he doesn't strike
me as the kind of man that would down-right lie
to me, even to help a friend.

That night I laid restlessly across my bed
trying to decide if I was really going through
with this shit. While, I honestly felt sorry for my
sister, was I really willing to put myself in danger
just to save the life of a complete stranger. *Who
am I kidding?* I thought to myself, knowing damn
well I didn't have any choice but to help her. My
grandmother would literally raise from the dead
if I didn't help her. In fact, the Ghost of Grammy
would never let me sleep another peaceful night
in my life if I didn't help my own damn sister. I
could hear her now, *"Child, I raised you better
than that!"*

Just as I was about to reach over and turn the
light on my nightstand off to try and get some
rest, my cellphone vibrated, alerting me that I
had received a new text. Figuring it was Yana,
letting me know that she wasn't coming over
tonight as originally planned, I timidly reached
over and grabbed the phone. To my surprise,
there was a lone text from Kenyan...

> Open your door.
> K.

Smitten

"Oh, Shit!" I said, jumping straight up out my bed, rushing to the mirror to check my hair. Snatching the bonnet off my head and wiping the remnants of smeared eyeliner from under my eyes, I turning around in circles like a dog chasing his tail.

"Calm down, Hiri," I scolded myself, clearly nervous as hell. My heart palpitated so hard in my chest I thought it was going to pop straight through my gown. *What the hell is he doing here?* I thought as I quickly grabbed the silk rob on my night stand and headed towards the stairs. The closer I got to the front door, the more I contemplated running back up the stairs and acting as though I had never opened the text. *Nah, Hiri, that would be messed up...even for you,* I thought.

Reaching for the knob, he must've felt my reluctance from outside the door. His deep voice broke into my solace, "Hiri, I know you're there. I just want to make sure you're okay."

I wanted to speak, I really did; but my words could not escape my head or my mouth. After what seemed like hours he spoke again with such masculinity in his voice that it caused my knees to go weak, "I know you don't want me...here. But, I'm here...and I'm not leaving until I see that you're okay."

Hearing the compassion and determination in his sultry drawl, I slowly pressed the code on

J'Sat Necolle

my key pad and the lock clicked. Before I could second-guess myself, he'd open the door himself and quickly pulled me into a tender embrace. We stood in the foyer holding each other for what felt like hours, before I finally pulled away.

Looking up into his handsome face, the features I once fell in love with and had memorized in my sleep were starring back at me with as much longing as what I was feeling in my heart, and at that moment nothing else mattered but he and I.

No words left his lips, no words left mine. Gazing deep into my eyes as if he were trying to etch my being into his soul, he slid his hand down my spine. Slowly he pulled my body into the close confines of his chiseled chest and never before had I seen two puzzle pieces fit together so perfectly, and when he slowly rubbed his thumb across my lips, I lost control of all reckless abandon and released myself to him utterly and completely.

Pools of sweet nectar gathered around the entryway of my womanhood, beckoning to feel him just one more time. No longer able to deny himself, he pressed my back roughly up against the wall, as his mouth hungrily devoured every crevice of my own. As he suckled my tongue, his hands slowly grazed up my inner thighs causing my nightgown to gather in pools around my waist. In that very moment, I could not think of anything other than feeling the throbbing sensation of him inside of me.

191

Smitten

My head began spinning completely out of control when in one swift motion, he lifted my body up against the wall and threw my legs across his shoulders, then abruptly pulled his tongue from the depths of my mouth and plunged it into the folds of my being. *The Kenyan Warner does eat pussy*, I thought.

Letting out a loud grasp, I cried out in ecstasy with each thrust. His big, strong hands caressed my ass tightly as he maneuvered my body around and around on the tip of his tongue. With every flick of his tongue, my body experienced a different sensation and after what seemed like hours, he began suckling on my clitoris like it was his last life-line to the world, sending my body into a spontaneous combustion "Oh my God, oh my God, I'm cuming!" I moaned as the sweet nectar of ecstasy rolled out of my honey pot onto the onslaught of his mouth.

My body fell completely limp as he mined every ounce of fluids from every crevice inside me. Never in life can I recall such a feeling of pleasure as I did in this moment. Gone were thoughts of our past, the hurt he'd caused, and the wife he had at home...the only thing that mattered in this moment is how he's making me feel.

As he slowly removed his face from the confines of my vaginal walls, my equilibrium was still in chaos, so he held me body tight as he allowed me to slide down every length of his masculine, 6'5 frame. As the bulge of his

J'Sat Necolle

manhood accosted my flesh on the excursion down, my soul cried out in anticipation. Subconsciously my tongue escaped my mouth and licked my lips as the thought of what was about to come next assaulted my senses.

Reaching down, he picked my petit frame back up from the floor and planted my feet on top of his own, then tilted my head up so that my eyes reached his gaze and kissed me with the gentleness and desperation of a dying man. Lost in the moment, our mouths intertwined in a dance that belonged to only us...in a moment that belonged to only us.

Suddenly he pulled his mouth away, gazed in my face for what seemed like an eternity before planting a light kiss on each of my eyelids, then guided my body off of his feet, then turned and walked out the door, without uttering a single word. *Whatdafuck!*

Chapter 28

The ride to the hospital the next morning was funny to say the least, which was sort of ironic being that this was the most frightened I've ever been in my life. When, I heard Yana come in last night, I knew her ass had ran into Kenyan as he was leaving and was not going to let me hear the end of it.

I should have known locking her out of my room last night and ignoring her pleas to let her in and spill the tea was not going to be enough to get her off my ass. When she gets her drawers in a bunch and can't get her questions answered, she's like a pit bull...been that way ever since we were kids. But I assumed that because of how early we had to get up and the anxiety she knows I'm feeling with my looming surgery, that would be enough to keep me in the clear this morning though, but no-o-o-o...not my bestie. Guess who commanded Alexa to play, *Rock Me Tonight,"* as soon as she heard my feet hit the floor.

All I could do was laugh, besides I could hear her crazy behind outside my bedroom door crying because she was laughing so hard; especially when she sang out *"for old-time sake."* Hell, if I didn't know any better, I'd swear Alexa's petty ass was laughing at me, too. I must say though, I don't know what I would do without her and this morning, laughter was just what my soul needed, as fear gripped my mind...even if the joke was on me.

Trying to put the memories of last night as far from my mind as I could muster, I joined Yana in meaningless conversation about office gossip, her and Brandon, and God knows what else...anything to keep my mind off Kenyan.

The closer we got to the hospital, the butterflies circling around in my stomach became even more distracting. Suddenly I could feel my head begin to swim as my breaths became more and more labored, and just as I was about to exit the vehicle, the nausea I had been feeling became even more obtrusive. I could not stop the bile as it arose from the pit of my stomach and hurled out at once. I could hear Yana yelling, "Oh, shit!" "Are you okay?" But before I could even answer, another erosion came bubbling up.

Suddenly, I felt a strong, masculine hand rubbing the back of my neck, "Babe, it's okay. I got you." *Damn, what's he doing here?* I thought to myself, just as my body betrayed me once again and relentlessly fell right into his embrace.

He gently ushered me down into the wheelchair he had obviously been pushing and handed me a small, white tablet and a bottled water, then commanded me to take it for the nausea. "Damn, Nigga, you must be a psychic or something?" Yana teased.

He let out a light chuckle, "Did you forget, I'm trained to know these things."

"Shit-t-t...okay then, Dr. Feel-Good, do your thang!" Yana responded between giggles as she ushered her hand in front of her, directing him to lead the way.

As he pushed the wheelchair at a slow pace, he and Yana made small talk; while I rested my head in my hand that was propped up on the arm of the chair. I'm not sure if I was afraid to lift my head up because of the nausea or because of the summersaults vibrating against my pussy walls from just being this close to him again.

What the hell was I thinking? I chastised myself in my head. *I know, I know better!* In all my years, I have never slept with someone else's husband and when I laid in my bed last night, I could hear the Ghost of Grammy loud and clear, *"Child, what you do in the dark will come to the light."*

But at that moment, cum was still oozing out of crevices I didn't even know I had; and even the voice of my dead grandmother couldn't stop the tingling sensation that came along with that. So, I just rolled my happy ass on over and drifted off into the best sleep I've had in years.

As he rolled us pass the registration desk, straight to my room, I could feel the eyes of some of the nurses boring into our backs. *I'm sure hospital gossip is just like any other job,* I thought, *and by lunch time who knows what kind of rumors they'll have out on Kenyan.* Refusing to let that be my problem, I said, "Thank you, Kenyan. I feel better now, I'm sure Yana can take it from here." But before he could refuse my obvious dismissal, Dr. Spivey entered the room right on cue.

"Good morning, Miles," Kenyan greeted his colleague.

"Hey, Kenny," the attractive doctor said, with a small chuckle. "I would say I'm surprised to see you here, but not really," he teasingly confessed.

Oh my God, what the hell has he been telling these people about me. I dropped my head back into my hands in pure disbelief. *And look at Yana's traitorous ass, she has the nerve to think this shit is funny too,* I seethed silently to myself. I'm sure I was probably rolling my eyes ninety to nothing, just like my grandmother's sister, Auntie Shelia. Now, that was a character!

Let somebody say one word she didn't like, she would roll her eyes and start mumbling under her breath so fast that even she didn't know she was doing it. And when we would tell her she was doing it, all she could do was laugh. But unlike my auntie, I knew I was doing it and I couldn't control it. I wanted to scream at all three of their asses, "Ain't shit funny!" But instead, I just rocked back and forth in that wheel chair like Ms. Celie, trying to keep from making an even bigger fool of myself.

As the nurse came in and helped me onto the hospital bed, I did not utter a word. I let the trio carry on as if I wasn't even there. The nurse set about taking my vitals, asking me pre-opt questions and having me sign the last of the consent forms; and the three of them were still chatting it up non-stop.

When the nurse finally announced they were going to give me some privacy, so I can get undressed, I wanted to jump up and hug the elderly woman so tight. *"Thank you, Jesus!"* I whispered under my breath, then looked at Yana and Kenyan and shot daggers in their directions that could have slayed Goliath.

It took a complete stranger to realize how distressed and uncomfortable I was with their presence and my best friend didn't have any idea. *Or the bitch just didn't care*, I thought. *Knowing her, she thinks this shit is still funny because I wouldn't spill the beans about last night.* "Bitch," I mouthed to Yana as the nurse was ushering her out the room too, with her new BFF's.

J'Sat Necolle

Chapter 29

*T*trying to relieve the dryness in my throat, I moved my parched lips slightly apart. I could not muster up a trickle of salvia to coat my throat, so I tried to speak and a gruff sound, unrecognizable to my own ears partially escaped.

"Yana, Yana!" I heard a man's voice yell from a distance. "She's waking up!"

"Oh, my God, Hiri!" "Hiri, can you hear me?" I could faintly hear my best friend, but she didn't sound like herself. *She's been crying.*

I tried opening my eyes to make sure Yana was okay, but it felt like a twenty-five-pound weight was dancing on my eyelids. Then I tried to speak again, but nothing came out. *Yana, I'm dying...the universe hates me*, I thought as I slipped back into oblivion, as Yana's screams became more and more distant.

"Zahiri, I'm so sorry, dear. I'm just so sorry." I heard a voice sobbing in the distance. Trying even more desperately to open my eyes and put a face with the voice, I strained, and I strained, but they would not budge. *I forgot I had died.*

As I listened to the agony in the woman's voice, I wanted to reach out and comfort her so badly. It's so hard to hear someone in such distress and not be able to do anything about it. *Is that Julia? No, that's not Julia's voice,* I thought absently. *Maybe it's one of my clients...yeah, that's probably it,* I thought, as I laid there listening to the emotions of the woman flow from deep down in her soul.

My God. I hate she's taking it so hard. Why don't someone help her, I wondered. *Where's Yana? Lord, let Yana be okay! Oh snap, that's probably Mrs. Yearwood. She's probably taking this real hard, she was like a mother to me...*

Oh, my God, someone please help her, I was crying inside. The woman sounded like a wounded animal, I could barely stand her cries. *Oh, my God, someone help her!*

"It's okay, it's okay," I heard a deep, baritone voice say in efforts to comfort the mourner. Her sobs became a little more muffled, but they continued.

When will this be over, I wondered. I'd given Yana strict instructions to only keep me out for three days. The way I figured, hell, Jesus had died and rose again in three days, the least they could do was have me in the ground by then. I'd told Yana not to be frying no fish or grilling no chicken while I'm still laying cold on a slab. Get me in the ground and then they can do whatever they wanna do after that.

J'Sat Necolle

Smitten

"Ohhh, Zahiri," I heard the woman moan between sobs. *Oh, God! I can't take hearing her cry like that.*

"Mama, it's okay. It's okay, Mama, she knows you love her. She forgives you mama." I heard a small, fragile voice say from over on the other side of the room. *Poor Yana,* I thought. *She doesn't even sound like herself. I know this must be killing her...*

Forgive you. I don't have anything to forgive you for, Mrs. Yearwood, you were always good to me, I was trying to yell from deep within my soul. If she only knew how much her kindness and unconditional love has always meant to me.

I heard the fragile voice getting even closer, "Mama, Zahiri forgives you. She knows you loved her. She knows you wanted to keep her..."

Whatdafuck! Did she say what I thought she said? Is this... who I think it is?

Even in this casket I could feel myself rolling my eyes hard as hell, just like my Auntie Shelia. I know damn well this is not Janis' trifling ass with all this fuss over my dead body. *Man-n-n...if somebody don't get this bitch right damn now, talking about I forgive that bitch. No, the fuck I don't! That bitch can fall dead right here beside me, and that shit won't hurt my feelings one damn bit. That ho got me fucked up!*

And where the fuck is Yana? Just like she knows to bury my ass in three days, she knows not to let this bitch nowhere near me...dead or alive.

"Yana, Yana," I cried out desperately.

Chapter 30

"*H*iri, Hiri!" I heard Yana's tear-stricken voice yell from across the room. Not able to move my neck, my slightly opened eyes darted around the room frantically in search of my best friend. All the other faces in the room were a blur, until my eyes met the teary-faced man who was guiding Yana to my bedside. *The Kenyan Warner*

Unable to get anything coherent out, Yana cried uncontrollably. Kenyan's eyes were bloodshot red, but he managed to let, "Hey, Beautiful," escape his lips. Releasing Kenyan's body, Yana frantically climbed in bed with me and began a soliloquy of "Thank you Jesus…. Oh, thank you Lord."

Kenyan leaned in and gave me a light peck on each of my eye lids, and in that moment, I didn't feel any shame or regret. I was just happy to be alive.

He slowly started feeding me ice cubes, which served as instant gratification to my parched throat. As I looked around the room, my eyes began to come into focus. Now, standing back away from my bed in a corner nestled together was Janis, her husband and Stormy; one of the twins. Julia and Mrs. Yearwood were on the side of the bed opposite of Kenyan, who had Cleve holding on to his shoulder in support. Seated to my right on a couch was Mr. Yearwood,

Zara and Brandon. And standing next to an empty chair over by the door was Gavin's ass. *Oh, snap. Shit just got real.*

Chapter 31

"You don't have any idea how happy I am to finally be going home," I said to Yana, who was putting the rest of my toiletries in the overnight bag I had not seen since I was wheeled into Emory Hospital almost two months ago. If I had known then that the removal of that one kidney, to donate to a sister I don't even know; would cause my blood pressure to sky rocket so high that I'd have a massive stroke on the operating table, nearly costing me my life...I would've said to hell with that kidney and my stranger-danger ass sister, too.

"Child, who you telling? "Those six weeks you were in a coma were the longest six weeks of my life. I couldn't eat, I couldn't sleep; hell, all I could do was pray."

As she spoke, I could hear her voice begin to crack, just as it did every time the subject was brought up. Listening to all of them talk about my ordeal, made me realize just how blessed I am to be alive, even if I don't remember any of it.

Smitten

Just as I was reaching over to grab my ice chips, Kenyan and one of the morning nurses walked through the door. "Good morning, Beautiful," he said, dazzling us all with the most amazing smile.

"Hey," I said, trying to sound more aloof than I was actually feeling. I remembered being worried about rumors on the day he rolled me in here months ago; but I'm sure by now the rumor mill has been working over-time since according to Yana, he'd spent every night that I was in a coma by my side. She said he would get up in the mornings, make a couple of telephone calls, then go to the on-call room and take a shower. He'd then make his rounds and was back by my side by lunch time. According to Yana, he had stopped doing any office visits and was only attending to the patients he already had admitted.

I was very touched that he cared so much but once I came out of the coma and could get my equilibrium back about myself, I demanded he go back to his regularly scheduled life, that I would be fine. Yana stayed by my side, day in and day out. I tried to tell her to go home and get some rest, but she refused. I know she was worried about me, but I also think she was avoiding having to deal with Gavin. Who, by the way, was suddenly playing husband of the year.

According to Yana, three days into my coma, he happened to call her out the blue asking about some paperwork he had misplaced, but when he heard her tear-strained voice, he asked what was wrong and she'd broke down in tears telling him about the swelling on my brain and that it wasn't looking good. The next thing she knew, he was walking into my hospital room a few hours later; he'd caught a red-eye. According to Yana though, that wasn't the only thing he'd caught...he'd caught her lying in Brandon's arms, both sound asleep on the couch.

To let her tell it though, Kenyan was the real MVP because when he saw Gavin come in, he immediately knew he had to be Yana's husband, and immediately sprang into action. First, he introduced himself loudly, which instantly alerted the love-birds. Then, she said he'd made Gavin feel special by telling him how much he'd heard about him and how glad he was that he was finally here. Saying maybe now he could convince Yana that she must take care of herself, too. He then began explaining to him that Yana was pretty out of it now because he had slipped her a sedative to help her sleep because she had not slept in days. He went on to say how Brandon had showed up right on time because as soon as the sedative he'd put in her sweet tea kicked in, she'd passed out and Brandon walked through the door just in time to help him catch her.

Yana said it took everything in her power to keep from laughing at the web of lies Kenyan so eloquently weaved together in a moment's notice. According to her, if it wasn't for the bones twitching in Brandon's jaw and erratic beat of his heart underneath her head, she would have believed the lie herself. She knew Brandon was hurt and all she could do to assure him of how she felt about him was to fall back asleep in his arms, like Gavin wasn't even there.

She said when she finally awoke the next morning, Brandon was gone, and Gavin had taken his place. She said she'd feigned surprise at the sight of her husband and told him how happy she was to see him...acting completely oblivious that he'd had to watch her sleep in the arms of another man. To let her and Kenyan tell it, they both deserved Emmy's for their performances.

A few days ago, after one of Gavin's daily visits, Yana and Kenyan got a good laugh at his expense as they told me how crazy that night was. I'm glad they saw the humor in it, because I didn't see shit funny. And the fact that Kenyan was an expert liar, certainly didn't make my heart feel any better. In fact, it just let me know that he hadn't changed at all since high-school. He was a cheater and liar then, and he's a cheater and a liar now. The only difference is, this time...I'm the other woman.

I was glad they'd told me what had happened though because it explained a lot. Although Brandon was there when I regained consciousness, he's only been back twice since then. He'd sent me a few text messages here and there, asking about my progress, and then explained that things were really hectic at the restaurants but promised he'd be by to see me soon. I felt sorry for my boy. *But hell, I felt sorry for me too... because we were in the same damn boat.*

Chapter 32

"Yana, someone's at the door," I yelled, with still a slight slur to my speech. According to the doctors, I've made a remarkable recovery but I'm so ready to be fully independent. I know Yana loves me, but I've never wanted to be a burden on anyone.

"I'm coming," she yelled from the kitchen, where she had been sitting on the stool talking to Gavin for the last half-hour. I can't front, I can't stand the asshole, but I must admit, he has been there for her during this ordeal. In fact, I haven't seen him show her this much attention since their first year of marriage. He left and went back to Miami a couple of days after I came out of the coma but returned a couple of days later, to both of our surprise. I suppose it had surprised the shit out of Brandon too, because we haven't seen him again since then. And Yana says every time she calls his phone, it goes straight to voicemail.

Smitten

As Yana walked past the sofa where she had me comfortably seated, she patted me on the shoulder in reassurance that everything would be okay. While, I've been trying not to show it, my best friend knows that not being able to do for myself is driving me crazy. I can say though, I am in much better spirits than I was when I first woke up from the coma and realized I could not walk, talk or control either of my arms.

While, Dr. Spivey wanted to wait to begin my speech and physical therapy until after I had been out of the coma for at least five days, Kenyan would not have that. When I heard those words come out the doctor's mouth, I began screaming in my head, but the words never escaped my mouth. As tears welled up in the corners of my eyes, Kenyan recognized my pain and spoke up on my behalf. He told his friend and colleague in no way was that acceptable, while he understood his apprehensions; unless the cat scan revealed that neurologically I was still in danger, he wanted someone from the PT team and speech therapy team in my room within an hour.

I was so happy I could have shitted bricks. While, Kenyan is certainly one of the most attractive men I've ever seen in my life, he'd never been more attractive than he was in that moment. And while, every time he walked in the room a part of me cringed because I knew he was the property of another woman, at this juncture of my life, he was my knight in shining honor; and wife or not, I wasn't going to be

apologetic about that. "What's got you blushing?"
Kenyan's rich voice invaded my thoughts.
Startled I looked up and graced him with a light
chuckle. I suppose I was so deep in thought, I
didn't even realize who was at the door.

"What are you doing here?" I asked as he
came around and sat next to my feet on the
oversized sectional.

"Damn, it's like that?" He teased. "You haven't
been out the hospital five hours yet and I'm
already back to being the bad guy." Now
brandishing me with the most dazzling white
smile, glistening up against his cocoa-caramel
complexion.

I loved how bright his eyes twinkled when he
laughed, and his dimples were always my alkalis
heel. Even when we were teenagers, I would
know he was lying to me, but his playful smile
could always manage to make me forget how
pissed I was. That kind of charm could not be
brought...either you had it, or you didn't. And
The Kenyan Warner certainly had it...then and
now!

"Why Mr. Warner, how could you say such a
thing?" I said, putting on my best southern belle
accent, sounding just like Scarlett O'Hara in *Gone
With the Wind*. As the husky sounds of joy
escaped his mouth, I remembered just how
surprisingly easy it was to talk to him. *That's how
I feel in love with him the first time.* Just as that

J'Sat Necolle

thought entered my head, my common sense kicked in, so I quickly changed the subject.

"Thank you again for getting the therapists set up."

Winking his eye and nodding his head, "No problem. I got you, Ma."

Damn, Not Ma...that's how I feel in love with his sexy ass in the first place, I thought for the second time in less than two minutes. *Is any subject safe to discuss with his ass?*

As if he were reading my mind, he immediately started calling out my appointment itinerary for my in-home physical and speech therapy appointments; as well as, my follow-up appointment with the neurologist for next Friday.

Just the thought of my situation immediately caused my anxiety to flare up. I try to be optimistic that I will make a full recovery, but the idea of not being fully functional at only thirty-three years old is scary as hell. I don't know what I would do if I could no longer physically design homes; or even walk up the stairs in my own home for that matter. I was suddenly overcome with a relentless sadness.

"Earth to Hiri, earth to Hiri," I heard Yana say, breaking into the darkness of my soul. When I looked up, both she and Kenyan were staring at me nervously.

Kenyan spoke up first, "It's okay, babe, don't worry. You're going to beat this thing, I just know it."

"That's right, Bitch-h-h!" Yana said, sounding like she'd just walked off the set of *BAPS*, *as* if her full-fledge Decatur where its greater accent was not enough, this heifer broke out in one of our many childish mantras from back in the day, *"Cause you' s a bad bad bitch, from a bad bad town...it'll take a bad bad bitch just to bring you down."* Hearing her stupid ass brought back so many memories that I just had to join in on the fun..."*so, when you come to Dekalb County don't fuck with me, cause I'm the baddest ass bitch that you ever will see!"* Yana fell back on the chaise lounge laughing her ass off at our antics, while Kenyan had actually fallen off the sectional laughing so hard. Like us, he was probably also reminiscing on our days growing up in the projects, coming up with this ghetto ass shit. Even Gavin came out the kitchen just in time to see what all the commotion was about.

Walking around to where Yana was, he scooped her up off the chaise and sat her on his lap, to both of our surprise. I instantly rolled my eyes and turned my nose up at his pretentious ass, while Yana's gullible ass was soaking that shit up... over there smiling from ear to ear like she'd just won the damn Lotto or something. *Girl stop!* And poor Kenyan's ass was looking back and forth, lost as hell. If he only knew that this was Gavin's first time staying in town this long in almost three years and was more likely to be calling her a fat slob than showing her any affection, he would be rolling his eyes at the bastard, too.

Sensing my tension, he spoke up mildly, "Why don't you Love Birds call it a night, I can see you'll need some alone time. I got it from here."

When I heard those words, I almost choked on my own spit. "Wh-What?" "You-u, You can't stay here." I was stuttering even worse now than when I first came out of the coma.

"Oh, Kenyan, that's so sweet, but I can't ask you to do that," Yana said, finally rolling her ass up out of *"La La Land."* *Oh, Lord, thank you,* I thought to myself. Yana continued, "Gavin and I are going to stay here and take care of my girl, she's our responsibility."

When the last of her words touched my ears, my mind instantly started racing a mile a minute. *Whatdafuck! I ain't nobody's responsibility and least of all, Gavin's trifling ass. Oh, hell nawl!* And in that moment, all rationale went out the window.

"I don't need anyone to stay with me, I can take care of myself!" I proclaimed adamantly, causing everyone in the room to stop.

Everyone stopped and stared for a moment, then Yana chided, "Child, Booh...You must be

outta your mind, ain't nobody leaving you here
by yourself. Hell, you can't even walk...

Instinctively, Kenyan put his huge palm in the
air to hush Yana's next insensitive remark, then
leaned in and kissed me lightly on the lips, before
venturing in on my ear lobes. Whispering
seductively, he said, "Look Ma...it's either me or
Gavin, your choice. But you will not be staying
here alone." With one suck of my ear lobe, he
pulled away, knowing damn well I would choose
him over Gavin any day.

"It's settled, you guys go on, get out of here,"
he ordered.

"Really?" Yana asked, her voice rising three
octaves, revealing her unmasked surprise,
looking anxiously at me for confirmation.
Reluctantly, I nodded my head in agreement, just
as I was pushing Kenyan's playful hand off my
upper thigh. "You get on my damn nerves," I
mumbled under my breath, rolling my eyes in his
direction. He threw his head back in laughter as a
response to my intense discomfort.

After about ten more minutes of small talk
and scheduling coordination between Yana,
Kenyan and myself, I'd had about enough of
watching Gavin's ass play touchy-feely all over
Yana, so I finally told them to get the fuck out, I
was ready to go to bed.

Smitten

"That's right, ya'll...we're ready to go to bed," Kenyan drawled playfully, imitating us country bumpkins, which he loved to call us.

"Ughh," I grunted, flinging the throw pillow, right upside his head with my left hand, as laughter filled the room.

As Kenyan walked Yana and Gavin to the door, my entire mind was spinning. "I don't know how I got here, but I don't plan on being in this situation long," I said adamantly to myself, as I slowly tried to swing my legs off the couch. Since the rigorous therapy over the past three weeks, my left hand had gained a great deal of motor function back. The problem is though, I'm right handed, so things were still rather difficult to navigate. It took a lot of coaxing, but by the time Kenyan came back inside, I had managed to get myself in a standing position and was holding on to the couch for support.

Startled by my presence when he rounded the corner and saw me leaning there, he admonished, "Oh snap...look at you!" His voice brimming with pride.

His reaction made me swell up with pride also. Shit, three weeks ago I could not move anything, and now look at me. I started grinning from ear to ear, blessed to be making progress. As he came closer, he draped his strong arm around my waist and looked me straight on, "I know you're determined to get better, but you've got to be smart, though. The last thing we need is for you to injure yourself more because that could be detrimental to your recovery. Do you understand?"

His serious tone made me focus on the magnitude of his words, "Yes. I understand completely."

"But in the meantime," he said, "I promise you, we're going to take every opportunity for you to work this body back in shape," then playfully slapped me on my butt with a hearty laugh.

If the daggers my eyes shot him could talk, what a horrid story they would tell. "You are really enjoying this, aren't you?" Brandishing that dazzling smile again, he gathered my right arm and placed it around his waist, then clamped his right arm down on top of it to hold my hand in place, since I was not yet able to grip anything on my own.

"Real talk," he said, rather solemnly, "I enjoy any time I get to spend with you, I just wish it didn't have to be like this."

"I feel you..." was all I could muster.

Sensing my mood change, he coached, "Okay, what I want you to do is take your time, just like they taught you in therapy. Remember to pick up your leg and plant it solidly before going on. It's a slow process, but you've got to be patient and put in the work. Okay?"

Smitten

"Okay."

He held me up tightly as I slowly took awkward baby steps, trying to regain some semblance of mobility. "You're doing great, just don't try to rush. Step... and... plant, step...and...plant." The only sounds in the room was his calming voice and my labored breathing, but it all sounded like music to my ears. "Now, when we get to the stairs, I want you to stop. Got it."

Concentrating massively on each step, I simply nodded my head in acknowledgement. "Step...and...plant, I began to chant; along with his rich, baritone voice. "Step...and...plant."

Sensing my fatigue from my labored breaths, his voice lovingly coaxed my ears, "You got this, Babe. Just a few more steps. Come on, you can do this." The excitement in his rising voice fueled my determination even more, and with each step I was feeling more and more sure of myself.

Unexpectedly, I felt my body being swept up off my feet and swiftly being turned around in the air, "Great job, Baby! You did it, you did it!" His boisterous joy was contagious; I felt completely exhilarated. My heart beat wildly in my chest as the adrenaline pumped through my veins.

"Thank you, Kenyan. Thank you so much," I hugged him even tighter as he slid me down the length of his body, stopping me once we were eye to eye.

"You're very welcome, Sweetheart," he said in a hushed whisper, as his eyes pierced straight through mine, right down through to my tortured soul. As we stared at each other, I felt something deep in my heart begin to stir and I knew I was in trouble. The current pulling us together was stronger than either of us could deny and before I knew it, his mouth had captured mine and was intertwining it into a captivating abyss. *I can't do this*, I thought, and reluctantly pulled my mouth away. Looking into the depths of my eyes, he saw the fear that gripped me. Slowly, he allowed my final descendent down the rest of his hard body, until he had my feet planted firmly on solid ground.

Reaching down, he lightly touched my chin and tilted my head upwards, "Listen, Hiri," he said softly, "as much as I wish you and I were a thing, I know we're not. But I am going to be here for you no matter what. I promise I will respect your wishes and your boundaries and be on my best behavior." Sticking his hand out, he said, "Friends."

Limply shaking his extended hand with my left hand, "Friends." I said with a shy smile. Right before he swept me off my feet, yet again, but this time he slung my petit, 5ft. 4-inch frame across his shoulders like a bag of potatoes and up the stairs we went.

Smitten

"Damn, you can warn a sister first, I giggled as he galloped up the winding staircase. We both laughed easily. As we approached the top of the landing, he asked which direction and I yelled from perched behind his back, "To the left, to the left."

"Oh shit, you know that was my jam!" He yelled. And before I knew it, he was in the middle of the hallway singing and doing the Tootsie Roll, with me still dangling across his shoulder. Laughing wholeheartedly, he chanted, " *To the left, to the left. To the right, to the right. To the front, to the front. To the back, to the back. Cotton candy, sweet and gold, let me see you tootsie roll."* When he did that dip with me draped over his back, I just knew we would both be toppling over to the floor at any moment, but impressively he dipped and came right back up, on rhythm, nonetheless; never missing a beat.

"Why, Mr. Warner," I exclaimed gleefully, "I see you've still got it." We both laughed, as we entered the door to my master bedroom. He reached over and flipped the switch as the luminous light transitioned the room from midnight black to a soft golden hue. Having always had my dimmer set on a soft glow, I'd never realized before just how romantic my bedroom was until now, with The Kenyan Warner's presence filling up the space.

Walking languidly over to the middle of the room, he carefully placed me on top of the massive, four-poster bed. Looking around, taking

219

it all in," So, this is where the magic happens?" His voice sounded half teasing, but serious at the same time. Unsure of how I should answer, I elected to change the subject instead.

"There's another master bedroom at the opposite end of the hall, I think you'll be more than comfortable in there tonight."

"Yes, I'm sure it will be more than fine, but what's wrong with that bedroom next door?"

"Oh, nothing's wrong with it, just substantially smaller and doesn't have a private restroom. I just thought you'd be more comfortable in a larger space."

"Shit, I can sleep in a matchbox, if it has a comfortable pillow. I don't need much, besides, the reason for my being here is to help you, and I may not hear you if you need me and I'm all the way down there," he said, still looking around, clearly fond of all the antique furniture pieces adorning the room.

"I suppose that makes a lot of sense. The room's all yours."

"I wish something else was all mine," he said playfully. "But I promised to be on my best behavior, so that's what I'm going to do." Reaching over, he tousled my curly mane, "Don't worry, I got you, Ma."

That's just what I'm afraid of.

J'Sat Necolle

Chapter 33

The smell of fresh coffee assaulted my nose as I lay lazily on the bed. Last night was quite traumatic to say the least. First of all, falling asleep knowing that The Kenyan Warner was lying in the bedroom next to me, with nothing standing between us but air and opportunity, was problem number one.

Secondly, getting up during the night to pee has never been an issue, until last night. It seemed every two hours or so, my bladder was reincarnated into the Niagara Falls. After the first three times of waking Kenyan from a sound sleep to help me go relieve myself, I began to feel even more guilty than I already felt for keeping him away from his family.

As soon as Yana gets here this morning, the first thing I'm going to do is contact an agency to see about getting someone to come sit with me around-the-clock. The next thing I'm going to do is let her ass know that I'd rather die than be Gavin's responsibility. And lastly, but certainly not least, the last thing I'm going to have her do is find some kind of way to keep Kenyan's fine ass away from me. Shit, the universe already hates me enough as it is, I sure as hell can't add home-wrecker to my resume...I'll certainly wake up dead then.

Smitten

I heard Kenyan lightly knock at my bedroom door, "Come on it," I said quietly. "You didn't have to knock," I said as he came on into the room and sat the tray down onto the bed.

"Well, I wasn't sure if you were appropriate or not."

"Really, dude...you must've forgotten that I can't even wipe my own ass without help from you?" He casually dropped his head, not meaning to have upset me. Looking over at the spread, I was thoroughly surprised. There was bacon, pancakes and syrup on one plate, and on the other plate he had cheese grits, eggs and sausage. "Damn dude, I didn't know you could cook!"

Tickled by my comment, he mischievously said, "Shit, that ain't the only thing I can do, but you don't wanna talk about that, though."

Taken aback, I almost spit the orange juice he was giving me right in his face. The laugh lines around his eyes even crinkled up in response to my reactions. "Ooh, you make me sick," I said, once I finally swallowed the amber liquid without getting chocked.

"Yeah, yeah," he said, as he slowly guided my left hand to pick up some meat off my plate. As we shared our breakfast, he was so patient with me. He helped me with how to reach out and grab the food that I could with both my left and right hands, but items he knew I could not get on my own, he fed them to me. He reassured me

J'Sat Necolle

when I needed it and motivated me when I began getting frustrated with myself.

"As much as I hate to admit it, it is probably better that you stayed last night instead of Yana,"

He snapped his head up in amazement, "Really! I can't believe you said that!"

"Well, first of all...that bitch can't cook." He threw his head back and let out a hearty laugh. "But secondly," I continued more serious this time, "she would have just done everything for me, and not allowed me to even try to lift a finger. And I know that's the last thing I need right now..." letting my words trail off as I slowly reached for another piece of bacon on my own.

"Well, you are absolutely right, the worst thing you can do right now is nothing. You have got to continuously work every muscle in your body, however you can, if you want to get back to 100%."

"That's all I want," I said resiliently, my heart feeling every word.

We sat on the bed chatting like old friends, until everything on both plates were gone. I must admit, he really was a damn good cook, especially for a city boy. Then, he suddenly just burst out laughing non-stop.

"What the hell is wrong with you?" I asked, puzzledly.

He couldn't stop laughing long enough to get it out, while I just sat there starring at him stupidly. Finally, he said, "I don't mean to be insensitive, but...."

"But what?"

"But you forgot the last reason you're happy I stayed instead of Yana."

"And what would that be, Mr. Warner?" I just knew his mannish ass had some kind of sexual innuendo up his sleeve, so I got ready for it.

"Well, if Yana had stayed instead of me...it would've been Gavin carrying you up those stairs last night. And helping your beautifully round ass to the potty!"

Ugh...I immediately got sick to my stomach, the thought of that made bile instantly build up in my throat and my esophagus began to swell. Then I got mad, because my brain was telling me to knock the hell out of Kenyan for thinking that shit was funny, but because of the stroke, the message from my brain, could not transfer down to my crippled arms. All I could do was roll my eyes, and I did...hard as hell. *Ugh...he makes me sick.*

Once he finally stopped seeing the humor in my situation, he begged me to tell him why I detested Gavin so much. At first, I was reluctant to get into it with him, girl code and all; but when he said he thought Gavin seemed like a real cool cat and that he seemed to love Yana very much, that was where I drew the line.

I let him know that in no uncertain terms did cool cats stay away from their wives for months at a time. Neither did cool cats call their wives out of their names and treat them like shit. And cool cats definitely don't ridicule their wives following a miscarriage, that she can't do shit right.

The look on Kenyan's face after I finished my little tirade said it all. Just in time too, we heard Yana's big mouth yelling up the staircase, "I hope ya'll ain't naked, cause I'm on my way up."

Shaking his head and chuckling lightly, he said, "Ya girl got some problems." All I could do was nod and agree, because something really was wrong with that fool.

When Yana stuck her head through the door, her childish ass was making all kind of kissy faces. "Girl, you're stupid," Kenyan said, while I just shook my head, not the least bit surprised.

Finally coming all the way into the room, she climbed up into my California King bed, right along with Kenyan and I. She asked a million and one questions about how last night had gone. So, Kenyan filled her in on how well I did last night but also pointed out areas that she sill needed to help me in today while he was gone. He told her in no uncertain terms was she supposed to do everything for me, explaining that I need to move my arms and legs as much as possible. He informed us that he was about to get me out of bed and help me into the bathroom, while Yana bathed me and helped me into a loose dress, with no panties.

"No panties!" Yana and I both shouted in unison.

"Damn-n-n, Dawg!" "So, you a freak-freak!" Yana howled as she threw her hands up for him to give her a high-five.

Shaking his head casually, staring up at her hand in the air, he was in pure disbelief. As hard as he was trying, he couldn't contain the laughter from erupting from his throat any longer. "Nawl, fool," he smushed Yana upside her head. "That will make it easier for her to get to the restroom without peeing on herself. She needs to use her left hand to pull up her own dress, then you and the nurse help sit her down on the toilet. Then you roll off some tissue and hand it to her, she can wipe her own ass," he said, then looked at me with that devilish smirk, both of us recalling how uncomfortable I was last night when he had to wipe me. Eventhough I'd made him close his eyes and walked him through how to reach my pubic area, I had never been so humiliated in my life.

"Umm, it's funny how you have all the right answers now about how I can do it by myself, but last night you were anxious as hell to wipe my ass for me."

"Hey, what can I say?" He laughed. "My best ideas come to me in my dreams."

Yana laughed. I didn't see shit funny. "I bet they damn do," I said, rolling my eyes hard as hell just thinking about how helpless that shit made me feel.

"Ahh, lighten up, it's not like I ain't never seen that thang before," he teased, causing me to roll my eyes so hard this time, my head began to hurt, while Yana's ol' extra ass rolled around in my bed laughing her ass off. *That shit wasn't even that funny,* I thought, as he stood and lifted me off the bed, then began helping me to walk towards the bathroom. *Step...and...plant. Step...and...plant.*

Chapter 34

Yana was completely ecstatic when she saw just how much I'd improved in just one night. "Oh, shit!" "Dude is the real deal," she exclaimed. "Hell, we should have let his ass took over the physical therapy sessions weeks ago. Shit, your ass would've been running like Forrest Gump by now if we had."

I laughed so hard at that fool, but she was right, though. He was much better than the therapist that had been working with me at the hospital. Now, I'm wishing like hell I had not denied him access to my therapy sessions. If I had not done so, he would have known by now that they weren't doing shit.

Yana's ass had even more jokes than Kenyan as she helped me wash myself. She had been going at it non-stop since Kenyan had exited the bathroom, after planting a kiss on each of my eyelids. "Just one more question," she said.

Sighing loudly, I motioned for her to go on, because I knew it was going to be some bullshit, so I just braced myself.

"Okay...so, when he was wiping you last night...did you get wet?"

"What!" I exclaimed. Even I wasn't expecting that shit.

J'Sat Necolle

"Well, I me-mean," she stammered. "Shit, the stroke fucked up your legs, I didn't know if it fucked up your pussy, too."

Staring into her beautiful heart-shaped face, I so wanted to be mad at her, but the look in her saddened eyes told me that she wasn't even playing this time. She really was worried that my coochie might not work anymore either. Honestly, that thought had never entered my mind, either; and I'm really not sure if that's even possible. But the look on my face told my best friend everything she needed to know. *No, I didn't feel anything down there, and I don't know if I ever will again.*

The mood in the bathroom changed drastically as we each became lost in thoughts of my fate. The spacious two-hundred square foot, custom spa restroom, which had once been one of my favorite rooms in the house, now seemed to be the size of a matchbox. I suddenly felt as though the walls were caving in on us.

I slowly felt myself get light-headed, then my heart started beating so fast in my chest that it felt like it was about to burst through my skin, I began grasping for air, but Yana was still lost in thought, and did not see me struggling. Yet, as the last of my oxygen supply was escaping my lungs, I found the will to move my right foot slowly in her direction. I just knew I was going to die because I could not make my leg move any faster and my chest was getting tighter and tighter.

The beating in my ears felt like death drums approaching, but I kept trying. Finally, the light tap on her foot was just enough to alert her that I was in distress. Looking down where I was still perched on the toilet seat, she saw the life draining out of my face and started screaming, "Help, help!" "Kenyan, help me!"

Before she could finish getting 'me' out of her mouth, Kenyan was bursting through the bathroom door with water dripping down his bare chest, wearing nothing but a pair of canary yellow boxers. Looking down at me, alarm quickly registered on his face.

He rushed over to me and quickly scooped my breathless body up off the toilet and quickly laid me on the cold, tiled floor. He told Yana to put cold water on the wash cloth that she was still holding in her hand, but she was completely frozen.

So, he jumped up in one swift motion, grabbed the rag with one hand while his other long arm turned the cold water on at the same time. Wetting the cloth quickly, he hurriedly kneeled back down by my side and placed the coldness on my forehead, then started rubbing it gently down my naked body. "Look at me, baby. Take a deep breath. Slowly, come on...suck in. 1-2-3-4-5, now let it out. Good job. Do it again. Suck in...1-2-3-4-5-, now let it out." As he repeated his chant several more times, my heart finally began to slow down and sweat stopped trickling off my back. Finally getting off his knees, he sat flat on the floor beside me and continued to stroke my body with the cold rag, while coaching my breathing.

After about fifteen minutes or so, he looked up at Yana, who was still frozen in the same spot with tears visibly streaming down her face. "Yana, she's okay. I promise, she's okay." Yana just starred at him blankly. "Yana, I need you to go downstairs and make her some Chamomile tea, you got it."

"Yana!" he shouted loudly, as her eyes were still transfixed on me, her body still frozen in place. "Yana. Get the tea. Now!"

Suddenly startled, she scrambled to follow Kenyan's orders, quickly wiping her face, she exited the bathroom in pursuit of the requested beverage.

Slowly Kenyan got up from where he was perched by my side. He grabbed the plush towel hanging on the back of the door, then rolled it up and lifted my head and placed it back down onto the towel. He then turned towards the linen closet at the far end of the restroom and retrieved another towel. This time, he got on one knee and gently dried the cold moisture from my skin. *If only my pussy worked,* I thought, *I would give him some right here. Wife or not.*

Smitten

Once I was completely dry; coochie, butt-crack and all, he gently lifted me up from the floor and slowly carried me back to my bed. Pulling the covers back with one hand, he placed me back down on the cool sheets. He then turned and headed back towards the bathroom, only to return with the linen dress and bra Yana had carried in with us earlier. "Do you really want this on?" he held up the black lace bra and the cute tangerine sundress Yana had picked out, like I was actually going somewhere.

I turned my nose up and shook my head 'no,' still afraid to speak.

"I didn't think so, shit looks uncomfortable as hell, he said with a soft chuckle. "Do you have any loose dresses or gowns?" With my left hand, I slowly pointed to the armoire over next to the bay window. Walking over to the armoire, he pulled out the top drawer inside and immediately found one of my favorite night gowns...it had a picture of President Obama on the front, seductively licking his lips, and the caption read... "Oh, Yes He Can..."

He looked at the gown, then looked at me, and just started shaking his head. As he walked back over to the bed where I sat naked, I didn't feel the least bit embarrassed, or the least bit vulnerable. All I felt was thankful.

As he slowly pulled the gown over my head, he was still shaking his head in laughter. "Oh, yes he can...what, Hiri?"

J'Sat Necolle

Giggling lightly, I finally said, "You obviously didn't read the back."

"No," he said, looking even more puzzled. Gently bending down my frame to see the caption. "Oh, I see. I see," He said, nodding his head rather defeatedly. "Oh, so Obama can get it, but I can't."

I laughed so hard that I almost choked, and considering what had just happened, that little hiccup scared the shit out of me. Very intuitively, he quickly knew it frightened me. "Don't be scared, Love. You're going to be absolutely fine, that was just a panic attack."

"Damn, that's what a panic attack looks like?" Yana said as she came in carrying two cups of steaming out tea. "I just knew you were having a heart attack," she said, looking frantically in my direction. Then more of a threat than an afterthought, she quickly stressed, "And bitch, you better not ever scare me like that again."

Both Kenyan and I laughed so hard as she came around and sat both hot mugs down on the nightstand before reaching down and hugging me so tightly I thought she would bring on another attack. When she finally let me go, she stopped momentarily and looked at me, then said, "Bitch, you still got that old ass gown I brought you?"

Immediately throwing both hands up in the air, and shaking his head from side to side, he exclaimed, "I should've known." Then he and I both laughed in amusement, while Yana looked to and fro trying to figure out what she'd missed.

"I'll be right back," he announced, as he jumped his bare chest down off the bed and headed towards the door. Both Yana and I starred openly as the chiseled abs, ripped back muscles and round backside glided to the door. Both Yana's and my mouth were stuck wide open. Although we'd both seen him when he first came into the bathroom half naked; we didn't see him at the same time. But now, *'I once was blind, but now I see,'* was the only thought that came to mind.

Looking over at Yana, I tried to stop her before she said something, but like always…I was too late. I just dropped my head because the ignorance was already spilling out her mouth.

"Yo, Dr. McSteamy, hold up!" I just shook my head, as he peeked his head back around the corner of the door.

"Yes, Mrs. Yearwood-Smalls." He answered sarcastically, knowing her well enough to already know she was with the shits, too.

"I've got to give it to you, man; you really surprised the shit out of me," she said, sounded as serious as a heart attack.

J'Sat Necolle

"You must've forgotten I'm a real doctor, fool. I'm trained to handle these types of situations."

"Huh?" She stared confusingly in his direction. "Hell, I ain't talking about no damn CPR..."

"What then?" He asked worriedly.

"Shit... I'm just surprised you chose boxers over briefs!"

Laughter rose up from the pit of my stomach and erupted out loudly enough to vibrate off every wall in my room, while Yana's ass snickered like crazy at her own silly antics. And poor Kenyan hurried down the hall yelling, "Man, get ya girl. Please, get ya girl!"

Chapter 35

Later that evening Kenyan carried me down stairs when a few of my employees showed up unexpectedly to check on me, led by Julia, of course. He and I were upstairs in my room playing Gin-Rummy when they rang the doorbell. When Yana answered the door, the lively crew came trampling in carrying food, presents, balloons, flowers and all kinds of other well-wishes that had obviously been pouring into the office since the news of my coma had gotten out.

I looked around the room in astonishment at all the trinkets filling the space as Kenyan descended the spiral staircase carrying me like I weighed only fifty pounds. But as I looked at my staff in amazement, they were starring back at me in amazement. Initially, their gazes made me paranoid but then I realized that most of them had visited with me in the ICU, while I was in that traumatic state and were probably just in awe to see me looking like myself again. But I soon realized once Kenyan headed back upstairs to retrieve my blanket, that the stares were not about me at all. Those heifers were starring at my man. *Bitch, that's not your man,* I scolded myself under my breath, shocked at how easy my mind went there.

They were firing off question after question about who he was and how long I'd known him and where did we meet. I was so thankful that the questions were coming so rapidly that they were not even allowing me the chance to answer. I looked over at Yana in pure desperation, but she was getting such a kick out of it, she just kept snickering as she lifted the wine glass she was holding in a mock toast to me. I just rolled my eyes and let out a deep breath and mouthed the words, *"I hate you"* in her direction.

I don't know why I did that because that little bit of disdain made her laugh even harder, and the heifer still did not make zero effort to stop the dreadful inquisition. *Man, I don't know why I fuck with this bitch,* I thought to myself, as I noted how much fun she was having at my expense.

Little did she know, she was about half a minute away from me pulling a NeNe Leakes on her ass. That shit was fresh on my brain too, because she, Kenyan and myself had just finished watching that episode where NeNe's drunk ass was going off on Marlo and the other ladies saying they should be there for her, and support her, with all that fake ass crying.

I suppose her dumb ass finally recognized the turmoil that was etched on my face and realized she was going too far, "Alright, alright, ya'll. Leave Hiri alone. Ya'll act like ya'll ain't never seen a man before. Hell, he ain't even all that," she said, looking in Kenyan's direction just as he reached the bottom of the stairs, causing every woman in the room and the one gay guy to look dead at his unsuspecting ass. Looking completely baffled, he just laughed, not having heard

237

everything, but enough to know that Yana was fucking with him again. "Man, stop hating," he fired cleverly in her direction, leaving the whole room in laughter, including me.

"Real talk, though. Everyone, this is The-Kenyan-Warner," she said, stressing each word, and then looked directly at me and him, and winked her eye before continuing on. I just dropped my fucking head, while he laughed hard as hell, both of us recalling that day so long ago, as we sat in the parking lot of our projects with Kenyan and his friends, when she put me on blast and told him how me and the rest of our crew had been crushing on him so hard that we referred to him as, The Kenyan Warner, when he was not around. Looking back now, that bitch been clowning on me forever. *She makes me fucking sick.*

I zoned back in just in time to hear her finish her introduction of my first love to this crowd of horny women. "Kenyan is our homeboy. He went to high school with Hiri and I, and just so happens to be a kidney specialist at the hospital where Hiri had the procedure. There's nothing going on between them, we're all just really good friends, he's just doing what friends do…"

I looked around as she spoke; those heifers were tuned in like she was the first, black, female president and this was her inaugural address. *Ain't this some shit,* I thought. If we were in the office going over our monthly meeting, these hoes would be do everything but listening. But all it takes is a well-hung piece of dick to get everyone's attention. *Damn shame I tell you!*

Kenyan draped the blanket across my legs and then waved at everyone, "Hey, Ladies."

"Heyyyy, Kenyan!" All the ladies rang out in sing-song unison, even Mrs. Julia's old ass. *Well, damn,* was all I could say.

"Oh, by the way ladies... and you, too, Dante'," Yana yelled, diverting the attention back on herself. "Word on the street is that The Kenyan Warner is now a single man, so ya'll have at it!" Kenyan's and my mouth dropped open simultaneously, while Yana was laughing her ass off. *No, this bitch didn't.*

The women started clapping and high-fiving each other like she'd just announced they were handing out good dick and EBT at the nearest grocery store. "Ok, Yana. Pay back is a mug," Kenyan said, his voice full of laughter. "Ya'll, don't pay that fool no mind. She's so full of shit." *Whatdafuck...I know that negro ain't blushing.*

It was Monique's trifling ass that became the spokesperson for the horny hecklers Yana had set off. "So-o-o... are you saying that we can't have at it?"

The room suddenly went completely quiet as everyone, including me, anxiously awaited his answer. Astonished, he looked around the room, then shot a quick birdie in Yana's direction,

Smitten

"Sorry ladies...and you, too, Dante', but I'm taken."

    Moans of disappointment and laughter filled the room. Leave it to Yana to cause all this commotion. If she wasn't good for anything else, she was always good for a laugh or two. I just wish I could find the humor in hearing him say the words that in my heart I already knew, that he belonged to someone else.

Chapter 36

*A*fter a couple of hours of catching up with everyone, feasting on all the delicious food they'd brought over and watching them down one glass of wine after another, I was completely spent. Remembering the look on their faces once they'd finally realized my fate, had left me more drained than the actual visit itself.

When Kenyan called out the array of food for me to choose what I wanted, then fixed my plate, I think they thought that it was just a thoughtful gesture among friends. And when he pulled his chair up close to me and placed my glass to my lips so I could coat my parched throat with the cool liquid, I think they thought just how sweet he was. And even when he picked up my fork and started casually feeding me my food, I think they thought that the two of us were just really cute. But, when they saw the sudden tears roll down my face, I think it was then that they finally realized that I couldn't do any of these things for myself.

The mood in the room suddenly went dismal, but not for long. Yana swept in and saved the day. In a matter of minutes, she'd managed to turn the rumor of one sordid office affair and two cleverly distasteful jokes into a two-hour bitch fest; thus, taking all of the attention off of me.

And I couldn't have been more pleased, but now I am tired as hell.

Noticing my grimacing on the couch, Kenyan announced jokingly, "Ladies, I'm sorry to shut this shit show down, and may God help me to never piss neither one of ya'll off, cause ya'll are ruthless, but, Yana and I need to get Hiri upstairs and back in bed." Laughter, moans and groans filled the room.

"Ah, shut the hell up and get the hell out," Yana teased. "Ya'll heard the man, now do what the doctor ordered." Everyone, including me, laughed at her relentless antics.

As everyone came over hugging and kissing me, I heard the door bell ring. Yana left the group and went to answer the door and came back in shortly with a tall, thick older women walking closely on her footsteps. "Hiri, this is Mrs. Lois, she's the home health nurse the agency sent over to stay with you."

I nodded my head towards the lady in greeting, but then Kenyan chimed in and firmly asked, "When did you order a nurse?"

All the movement in the room ceased immediately, and all eyes were on us.

"I had Yana to call the agency this morning as soon as she got here," I said, looking him dead in the eyes. "I can't expect ya'll to put your lives on hold trying to take care of me every minute of the day. You need to get back to your fa..."

Cutting my words off, he stood abruptly and directed his words to the nurse, "Mrs. Lois, how much are they paying you an hour?"

The stoutly women looked as confused as everyone else in the room, "I-I only make ten dollars an hour, sir," she stammered.

Reaching into the pocket of his jeans, he pulled out a large wad of cash. With his eyes never leaving the lady's face, "Mam, I am so sorry for the inconvenience, but your services are no longer needed here. This should be more than enough for your troubles," he said, as he finally looked down and peeled off ten one-hundred-dollar bills and wrapped them in the palm of her hand. Then he turned his head away from her and looked sternly between Yana and me and continued his speech, "Don't worry, I will also call the agency first thing in the morning and let them know that this mix-up was none of your doing, but a miscommunication on our end."

As his eyes bore into my skin, my mouth fell open at his audacity. But Yana swooped down and pushed my chin up to gently close my mouth, "Shit-t-t...Bitch, you heard McSteamy." Everyone laughed...with the exception of Kenyan, that is, whose jaw bone was still twitching non-stop.

Ignoring Kenyan's penetrating glances from my corner spot of the sectional, I began bidding everyone farewell again as they finished gathering their things. I thanked Mrs. Lois again and apologized to her for the inconvenience while she waited on the to-go plate that Kenyan offered and was preparing for her in the adjacent dining room. All the ladies... and Dante', flirted with Kenyan on their way out the door. He playfully flirted back in good nature as he told them how nice it was to meet them and for them to get home safely.

Kenyan walked back into the room before Yana did and immediately commenced to cleaning up the mess, without saying a word or even glancing in my direction. *Fuck you, too,* I thought.

Then Yana's ass came back in, peeping around the corner first, trying to see where he was. "Ooh, you in trouble!" She whispered, then burst out laughing.

"Me! Hell, you were the one that called them."

"Bitch, you told me to," she said accusingly.

Unable to refute her accusation, I sucked my teeth and mumbled, "Man, ain't nobody studdin' Kenyan's ass. He ain't my damn daddy."

Yana's laugh cut off abruptly when she saw Kenyan come back in through the dining room.

J'Sat Necolle

"Do either one of ya'll want any more of this food before I put it up?"

"Nawl, I'm good, K," Yana chimed, like she wasn't just acting like he was the big, bad wolf. I didn't open my mouth and say a word. *Fuck him.*

When he turned and walked away, ignoring my little attitude, it pissed me off even more. Yana laughed so hard at us as she began straightening up the gifts and placing the beautiful potted plants around the room strategically. "Girl, them white folks must've thought you were dead."

"Now, why they had to be white?"

"Now bitch," she said rather matter-of-factly, putting her hands on her hips, "You know good and damn well 'we' ain't brought these big ass plants, in these fancy ass pots and had them delivered to no office, while the person is still alive. Oh, no mam!"

Then she pointed back over to the table where the other gifts were, "Now, you see those 'Get Well,' Dollar tree balloons over there...now, that's us. We sent 'that' shit." All I could do was laugh because even in her silliest moments, most of the time she was absolutely right.

"As a matter of fact," she continued, as she tidied up the den, "even if your black ass had died, the most you were gonna get from us was a couple of Peace Lilly's, in those cheap-ass wicker baskets, with that little straw shit falling out. Point blank." That fool had my side hurting from laughing so hard.

"Girl, you can get a check." I said rather adamantly. "Real talk, though, I thought I was dead."

"Word?" She asked seriously.

"Word."

I went on to tell her the horrid ordeal I went through while I was in the coma but could still vaguely hear some of the things around me. "Shit, it's a wonder my ass didn't die, from thinking I was dead," I said, laughing at the irony of it all.

"Both of ya'll can get a check," Kenyan said, sarcastically, jarring us from the depths of my horrific revelation.

We all chuckled lightly, trying to brush the gravity of what I'd been through to the back of our minds.

"You ready to go to bed?" He asked softly, looking down at me.

Deciding to call a truce, I smiled and nodded my head in agreeance.

"Ooh, ya'll just made up. That's so cute."

"Man get your messy ass up outta here," Kenyan blurted in her direction. "I can't wait to pay your petty ass back for today." We all laughed, because she really had been giving him the business all day.

"Are you staying here tonight, or are you going home?" I asked, secretly hoping she was staying because that would mean Gavin's ass had swiveled back to the rock he had climbed from under.

"I can stay if you need me to," she said, looking from me to Kenyan, who was crouched down over me.

"I'm straight," Kenyan said, and then a huge smile curved her lips.

"I'm good, too," I said, never wanting to stand in the way of what semblance of happiness she thought she had.

She hurried and grabbed her purse, kissed us both on the cheek and headed towards the door, singing *"Chante's got a man at home..."* and out the door she went. Both our minds momentarily flooded with memories of Cleve's petty ass messing with Kenyan that day at The Hope House. But thoughts of what I'd confided in him earlier that day about Gavin seemed to invade both our minds at the same damn time.

Exchanging worried glances at one another, "Well, she's grown," he said, as he casually walked over and put the deadbolt on the door and told Alexa to set the alarm. "No matter how much we want better for her, she has to want it for herself." Shaking my head, I agreed with him wholeheartedly.

"You're right. So, if she likes, I love it..." but the pain I felt deep in my heart was telling an entirely different story indeed.

Sensing my turmoil, he reached down and scooped me up, "Let's go beautiful, I won't make you walk tonight, I know you're tired."

"Boy, am I." I said as I snuggled my head into the familiar nook of his neck as he carried me tenderly back up the winding staircase. *He's taken, Hiri.* I gave myself an internal reminder.

As we set about getting me ready for bed, neither of us said much, both clearly lost in our own thoughts. He placed me on the bed and helped me get comfortable, then turned to leave the room, still clearly feeling some kind of way because he didn't bother to even give my eyelids a kiss.

"Yo. McSteamy," I called after him.

Coming back to the doorway, he raised his eyebrows asking me what's up.

"So, you're mad-mad?"

J'Sat Necolle

Smitten

He looked at me like I had two heads and was the seed of Medusa, then shrugged his shoulders and nonchalantly said, "Nawl. Like you said... I ain't your daddy." Then turned and walked away.

"Alexa...turn my fucking light off." *Fuck him too, then,*

Chapter 37

*L*ast night was probably one of the longest nights of my natural born life. I had so many emotions going through my mind that it made it almost impossible to sleep. Not to mention, I've been holding my piss all damn night because I'll be damned if I let that bastard know I need him any more than I have to. And having his ass sleeping so peacefully next door had only pissed me off even more.

In fact, I don't know how he could even be over there snoring like his life wasn't just as fucked up as mine, or more, for that matter. In fact, while he's over here playing super save-a-ho with me, who's taking care of his wife and kids. And he has the audacity to get mad at me because I won't let him take complete control of my life.... *Oh no mam!* He's got life all fucked up, and me too, for that matter.

I don't know what kind of marriage slash arrangement him and Christine got worked out but there's no way in west hell any husband of mine, would not be coming home to me and my kids every night. And he damn sure wouldn't be missing work...the way we pay our bills, to go play Dr. Feelgood with some other broad. *Oh, no mam!*

The one thing his betrayal taught me all those years ago is that I don't need a man to validate me. I can pay my own bills, I can buy my own gifts and if push come to shove, I can scratch my own damn itch if I need to. Maybe Christine's co-dependent ass is okay with a man being a man, just for the sake of having a man, but to hell with that. He can miss me with that bullshit. Friends is all we are, and all we ever will be.

Almost as if he was reading my mind or something, I heard him tap lightly on the door. "Is it okay to come in?"

"Sure," *Be casual, Hiri. Be courteous, Hiri,* I warned myself as he was opening the door. "Did you sleep well?" *Shit, I already know the answer to that, I heard you all damn night.*

"Not really." *Could've fooled me,* I admonished inside my head and hoped my facial expression was not saying otherwise. I know my face has a way of contradicting what my mouth is saying...something I really need to work on for both personal and professional reasons. My Grammy used to always say, *"Baby, you can't always let your left hand know what your right hand is doing, but your face tells it every time."*

"Oh, I'm sorry to hear that. Is it anything I can do to help?" *Yeah, Booh, two can play this game. I* looked him dead in the eyes, making sure he saw that I was truly concerned.

"Well, there is something you can do," he said, somewhat mysterious, walking over to the massive bed and taking a seat next to me.

Intrigue got the best of me, so I said, "Sure, anything."

"Zahiri, what you can do to help me is to stop pushing me away."

After a minute or two of pondering on the weight of his words, I finally spoke up, "Well, Kenyan, that's certainly not what I expected to hear, but let me tell you some..." *Be casual, Hiri. Be courteous, Hiri.* I heard my own voice creep back inside my head, cutting me off from what I was about to say next.

Calming down, I said, "See Kenyan, what you don't realize is that I was completely independent before all of this, and I don't plan on losing that independence. Now, I don't mean to sound ungrateful because I really appreciate everything that you have done for me; and I certainly don't take it for granted because I know you don't have to do this."

Cutting me off, he said, "See, that's where you're wrong, Hiri. I do have to do this. The man that I am won't allow me to do anything but this. You see, where I come from, you take care of the people you care about and there's no way I could have gone on with life as usual while you were over here going through your own personal hell. I'm sorry, but I'm just not wired that way," his words trailed off but the enormity of them hit me in my chest like a ton of bricks.

Damn, he's good. Struggling to move my left hand, I was determined to show him that his kindness has not gone unnoticed. What would have normally taken me two seconds to do, now took me two minutes, but finally my hand touched his cheek, "Thank you, Kenyan."

Like the weight of his words struck a chord in my heart, the enormity of my gesture seemed to have struck a chord in his soul, because he reached up and placed the palm of his hand on top of mine and held it there for any eternity while tears escaped his eyes, and in that moment, I saw him in a way that I'd never seen him before. The young boy who had broken my heart all those years ago, was now replaced by a genuinely compassionate man. I slowly closed my eyes and thanked God for bringing him back into my life when he did.

We were still sitting there ten minutes later holding each other when Yana peeked her head inside the bedroom door and broke our spell. "Um, Umm," she cleared her throat, causing us both to look up startled. Looking from side to side at both Kenyan and I with a huge smile on her face, like the cat that swallowed the canary, she finally said," Real talk, I've got so much I could say right now, but hell, it's even too early for my shit." Laughing at her own self, she went around on the other side of the bed and climbed right under the covers and snuggled up next to me.

"For real though," she said, "are ya'll really smooching early this morning or are ya'll just making up from last night?"

Damn, she makes me sick. We both laughed at her accuracy but Kenyan spoke up and informed her that it was neither, that we were just gaining a mutual understanding, that's all.

"Fine, don't tell me then!" She said and grabbed a piece of the bacon off the breakfast tray that I'd let get cold. *She really missed her calling,* I thought. *She would be hell on the Psychic Network.*

The rest of the day went as smoothly as it could considering I can't walk, and I have no muscle control of my right arms. Kenyan and Yana had scheduled back to back appointments; including two physical therapy sessions being that he'd cancelled yesterday's appointments after my anxiety attack.

I don't think I've ever been so physically or mentally exhausted. This entire process is so frustrating because I feel the same as before, and part of me thinks that my body is the same as before, but every time my body fails to respond to my brain's command, it just takes a little more out of me.

J'Sat Necolle

Smitten

Yana has always been an expert at recognizing the warning signs of when my feelings were getting the best of me, having been the one that helped me through my mommy issues all these years. Now, though, Kenyan is starting to pick up on the clues just as well, so I can't seem to hide anything from either of them anymore, which is so frustrating. If one doesn't catch it, then the other Sherlock Holmes swoops in and find the clue. Neither of them seem to understand that sometimes you just want to be inside your own head, without it becoming a big deal. But I don't get that luxury, not with these two always sniffing around like they're the mental health police.

"Hiri, you've got tell me what's going on inside that beautiful head of yours," he urged a few nights later as he tucked me in bed.

I shook my head from side to side indicating for the thousandth time that nothing was wrong, but what I really wanted to tell him is that if he really wants to make sure I'm in a healthy mental state, then tell that bitch, Janis, and her gullible ass daughters to leave me the fuck alone. I've only been home from the hospital a week and already, they've sent three flower arrangements and left eight different voicemails. I just don't know what part of, 'I don't want anything to do with you' they don't understand, but it seems simple as hell to me.

Shit, I understood completely all those years when their absence in my life said those same exact words, very loud and very clear. And no matter how much it hurt, I respected the shit out of their request. So why the hell can't they give me that same respect?

But like Grammy always said, guilt is one of the strongest emotions known to mankind and those three are absolutely consumed with that shit at this very moment. So what, I'd almost died from donating an organ to a sister, who in her twenty-eight years on this earth, had never once even bothered to ask me how I was doing. *So, what?*

Like I'd told Kenyan earlier today when the newest arrangement arrived, even in my present state and given everything I went through following the procedure, I would still do it all over again. She's alive and so am I, and that's what my Grammy would have wanted. And maybe my Grammy wasn't perfect, *considering she was slick fucking the deacon and all,* I thought, but what she did do was raise me right, which was a helluva lot more than Janis ever did.

Talking to Kenyan about my personal shit again after all these years wasn't awkward at all. In fact, it almost seems natural when we get into these kinds of conversations. Unlike, Yana, he can relate to not having the unconditional love of one of his parents because his father wasn't shit either. He says his father has gotten somewhat better than he had been when we were teenagers but still definitely not enough for him to earn the title of dad. Actually, his take on the subject is very comedic; yet profound, at the same time.

In the Gospel According to Kenyan, "You are what you answer to. "And when I call my father Mike instead of dad; he answers. Simple as that."

It's funny how men can break complex situations down into such a small nutshell, then literally be done with it. While women, on the other hand, dwell on shit they can't change for forever and day, just to end up with the same results. Looking down at him, now laying in my lap shoving popcorn in his mouth but carefully placing the buttery morsels into mine, I laughed at his candid insight and wished I could be just a little more like him.

Just as he was about to open his mouth and fill my ears with some more of his prophetic wisdom, his cell phone rang in the other room. "Be right back," he said climbing down off the bed from the other side, making sure not to rest his weight on my legs. *Damn, he's fine*, I thought as I watched his chiseled physique stroll out the room." Shit! I exclaimed, "if he's going to stay around here, we have got to establish some house rules or something! His ass is too damn fine and too damn married to be walking around here half naked."

"Did you say something, Hiri?" I heard him yell from the next room."

Oh, Shit! I grimaced. "No, my bad, I was just talking to the tv." I was laughing so damn hard at myself, thanking God he had not heard me...but when I heard him say, *"Heyyy, Baby,"* into the receiver, my laughter immediately ceased. *Fuck.*

She must've said something funny as soon as he got on the line, because he burst out laughing so hard. The kind of laugh I've never heard from him, and I knew right then that she held a special place in his heart, a place no other woman will ever be able to touch...and certainly not me.

Not wanting to invade his privacy, I turned the volume up louder on the television mounted on the wall between our rooms, hopefully it will drown out the unmistakable sound of unconditional love vibrating off the walls of his room. *Someday, someone will love me like that,* I thought as I stared up towards the heavens.

I'm not actually sure when I finally dropped off to sleep, I just remember seeing Kenyan's shadow exiting my room after turning off my television and removing the half-empty bowl of popcorn from my bed. He stood in the doorway looking at my motionless form for a couple of minutes before finally tipping away from the door. Peeking over at the digital clock on my nightstand, 4:15am glared back at me, causing a nauseous surge of jealousy to pierce through my soul.

J'Sat Necolle

Smitten

Sleep never over-took me again. For the rest of the night, all I could think about was all the times he and I had laid in my bed and talked until the sun came. We used to talk about everything...our hopes, our dreams and even our fears. When he was a boy on the cusp of manhood, pointing out the faults he'd observed in his own father and making a vow that he would never hurt his kids that same way, it made the fatherless child in me long to be the one he fathered children with.

But now, all these years later, he and the woman he left me for have that same kind of bond. The kind that makes you talk on the phone until the sun comes up. The kind of bond that makes you keep holding on to the phone; hours after you've grown tired and sleepy, just to keep being within earshot of that other person's voice and when you are both spent...neither one of you wanting to be the first to say goodnight, so you vow to say it at the same time.

By the time daylight forced its way through my bedroom window, my heart was so full. On one side I was mourning a love that I never fully got to exercise and on the other side of my heart, I felt genuine happiness for Kenyan. I suppose what my Grammy always said was right, when you truly do love somebody, you want them to be happy...even if it's not with you.

I never thought I would find myself far enough out of that place of hatred and betrayal to come to this kind of actualization but considering the kind of friend Kenyan's been to me throughout this entire ordeal, it would be selfish to wish him anything other than complete and utter happiness. And even though I still can't stand Christine's ass; shit, if he likes...I love it.

Determined to get to a place of happiness myself, I did something I had not did since the day before my surgery. "Alexa, play *I Wanna Dance With Somebody* by Whitney Houston." The wireless device confirmed my selection from Amazon Music and the next thing you know my bedroom was filled with the sultry voice of the incomparable Whitney Houston and my mood immediately improved.

Within minutes Kenyan was at my door, his face covered in curiosity. He stood and watched as I exercised my left arm with the elastic band my therapist had given me. Then I used my left hand to stabilize my right hand the best I could. While, I was aware of his presence, I didn't let it stop me. I did it the way the therapist had taught me to the best of my limited ability, and I must say I was proud of myself for taking the initiative on my own.

It's time I became more proactive in my own treatment, I thought to myself. *I can't let them want this more for me than I want it for myself,* I thought, as I slowly used my left hand to place the small, blue ball into the palm of my right hand, and squeeze my fingers around the sphere. I slowly pressed the little round ball the best I could. When I got tired, I stopped for a moment, regained my breath, then started again.

As Whitney's voice was fading off, signaling the end of the song, I finally looked up into his awaiting eyes and saw the remnants of glistening tears escaping his eyelids. "Good Morning, You," I said, feeling better than I had since the surgery.

"Good Morning, You!" He said, obviously impressed by my morning work-out routine, because he blessed my eyes with the most amazing smile I've ever seen. His glistening-white teeth looked like they belonged on a Colgate commercial and has always been an aphrodisiac for me, instantly making my heat rise. *His wife probably feels the same way*, I thought to myself.

Removing his relaxed body from the door frame where he'd been perched, he began walking towards the bed smiling from ear to ear. Then I heard his deep, baritone voice slice through the now silent room, "Alexa, play *I Wanna Dance With Somebody*, again." Then he glanced down at a surprised me and said, "because I wanna dance with somebody who loves me, too." A small gasp escaped my throat.

As the funky, up-tempo beat filled the room again, his strong muscled arms reached down and pulled my body off the bed. Carefully placing each one of my feet on top of his size fourteen feet, he pulled my body close to his and swayed to the beat of the music. And just like that, all that bullshit nonsense about wanting him to be happy with someone else went out the window. Oh, I want his ass to be happy alright...I just want it to be with me. Suddenly, that self-revelation literally scared the shit out of me, but for the moment, I allowed myself to just be lost in this moment.

When that song went off, he requested another fast tempo for Alexa to grace us with. Even though I'd seen him Tootsie Roll our first night home from the hospital, I honestly never had any idea he was such a great dancer. Back in the day, guys didn't really dance, they just rocked backed and forth to the beat, all cool and shit. Surprisingly though, Mr. Warner here really had some moves. "Okay then, McSteamy, I see you," I teased as he rocked and swayed us both to the rhythm of the beat. He threw his head back in a fit of laughter.

"So, you like my moves, huh?" He asked, gazing down in my face, awaiting the compliment he just knew was coming.

With a coy smile, I peeked up at him through my long lashes, "They a'ight."

"Oh, snap!" "Okay, then," he laughed, then suddenly stopped moving to the beat and looked down into my eagerly awaiting eyes and said, "Hating is not cute on you." Then started back bouncing again to the rap song escaping the speakers. All I could do was laugh as he bounced over to my sitting room area and sat me down on the chaise lounge I rarely ever got a chance to use anymore.

"Alexa, close the blinds," his voice penetrated the room and in a matter of seconds, the soft amber glow that was sun-kissing my bedroom was no more.

"Alexa, turn the volume all the way up." Grinning from ear to ear, I had no idea what to expect but judging from what I know of him so far, only God knows what he's got up his sleeve now. Just as that thought entered my mind, butterflies started making figure eights in the pit of my stomach. *Oh, shit.*

"Alexa, play… *Dive In*, by Trey Songz." The gleam in his eyes was priceless as he watched me intently as a shock wave washed over my face. As Trey Songz' voice hit the first note, Kenyan licked his lips and looked at me, then grabbed a water bottle off the mantle and started talking in the pretend mic like he was Trey Songz himself… *"I was thinking about taking a couple laps, I just wanna dive in….."* I giggled as he began to roll his body, grinding slowly as the sensual sounds echoed from every wall in my bedroom; trepidation and excitement anchoring my eyes in one place…on him.

As the intro of the song dropped, I almost went crazy in amazement as Kenyan unexpectedly held the Dasani bottle over his head and poured the clear liquid all over his body just as him and Trey sang simultaneously,

"Splash, baby girl that's your waterfall..." and as he continued to sing, the bass in his voice vibrated deep inside my soul as he expertly rolled from the side to side in front of where I sat, making sure not to touch me. As he continued to sing, he slow-rolled his body in every direction, gyrating in ways I never knew was possible.

The entire time his eyes were fixated on me and had me frozen in time. With every thrust of his body, my body became even more heated, but I could not tear my eyes away. He wasn't smiling whatsoever as he intently sang every word of the first verse like he'd written it himself...just for me.

And just when I thought it couldn't get any worse, the chorus dropped and he yanked his shirt off and backed away a little, suddenly his dance moves simulated straight fucking; as he pumped hard and sensually, while grabbing his dick inside his scrub bottoms, he sang dead into my eyes *"Girl, you got me wanting to go... deeper than you'll ever know...wanting to feel the way you flow."* Then in one swift motion, he was in the chair with me, straddling me, and touching me, and grinding on me as he nibbled my ear lobe singing, *"...Ooh you got that look up in your eyes...what we bout to do ain't no surprise..."*

He stayed there, rolling his ass so seditiously slow and seductive, never putting the weight of his full body onto my legs, while he sang the course of *Dive In* right in my ear. The next thing I knew his tongue was in my ear and his finger was in my mouth as he gyrated his groin on me. I hungrily sucked his fingers as I rolled my upper body right along to the slow rhythm, he had set on fire inside of me.

As moans escaped my mouth, he switched to the other ear, his hand encircled my breast, then when his mouth engulfed one of my nipples while his thumb jiggled the other one, I knew I was in trouble. The next thing I knew, he was down on his knees in front of me, looking up into my face, sexily biting his bottom lips with his hands on each of my knees. He gave me the most pleading look and started singing again, *"Watch me stroke left, stroke right, stroke back stroke...Girl, I'm bout to dive in..."*

Then his eyes suddenly swelled with emotion as he felt movement, then immediately looked down, just in time to watch me strain every fiber of muscle strength in my body to slowly open my legs for him.

As the sound of Trey Songz drowned out my cries, I got lost in the magic that is Kenyan, as his ravenous mouth suckled every part of me. Moisture secreted from every pore in my body especially the one that belonged to him and him only, as he flicked his tongue in and out, while blowing sporadically. Once his mouth located my clitoris, his tongue meticulous stroked it back and forth and just as I was about to release, he quickly removed his tongue and inserted his two pointe fingers and slowly glided them in and out

265

of my cavity, leaving an opening just small enough for him to continue to blow air inside of me, followed by an occasional flick of his tongue. I wanted to scream out in joy but the erotic tingling sensation erupting from my body left me speechless.

I had never felt something so amazing. When he suddenly felt my left hand on the side of his face, he stopped feasting on my core and looked up into my longing eyes. And when I licked my lips and slowly motioned with my left hand, he knew just what I wanted. His eyes grew three sizes larger, then that sexy smile enveloped his face, "Are you sure?"

The one nod I gave him was all he needed, as he lifted himself slightly off the floor and pulled both his scrubs and black boxers down in one swift motion. Carefully straddling both my legs over his shoulders, he looked at me, trying to see if I had changed my mind; with eyes begging me not to, then slowly entered me and the heavens and earth began to move.

First, he was masterfully slow, steadily looking at me, making sure he wasn't hurting me, but when I began to roll my hips against his pelvic, he could not stop the full-on penetration and I promise it really did feel like he'd gone deeper than any man before...including him. I rode his wave of ecstasy as he grinded deeper and deeper inside my pool and just when I thought I would die from pleasure, he flipped me

J'Sat Necolle

over on top, while never removing his manhood from inside the walls of my sweet abyss.

Fear pierced my entire body as I looked at him defeatedly, knowing my partial paralysis would not allow me to ride him into a place of pleasure; but then he thoughtfully reached up and lifted my chin, wiped unshed tears from my eyes and said, "Trust me, Ma. I got you."

And with that, he bit his lip as he slowly rolled his hips deeper and deeper inside my honey pot, grinding left, right...deeper and deeper. His strong hands gripped my ass and gyrated it slowly around and around, squeezing it tightly as my walls pulsated around his stiffness. Our intensity had me spiraling out of control, causing a massive vibration from deep inside my woman hood. Reaching out and grabbing his head, I had to feel his mouth on me...his lips captured mine and as his tongue assaulted the folds of my mouth in a tantalizing seduction. Convulsions began to ravage through my body, causing me to cry out his name in pure ecstasy. As I felt the warm secretions erupt from him, he let out a brutal cry from deep in his loins and I relished in the sweet sensation of the only man I've ever loved.

.

Chapter 38

*Y*esterday had unequivocally turned into one of the best days of my life. Kenyan and I had stayed in bed the entire day. We talked, we laughed, we touched...we made love. Then we did it all over again.

Lying here next to him in the wee morning hours almost feels like something out of a fairytale; but as much as I try to put the thought out of my mind, I knew it wasn't real and there would be no happily ever-after for Kenyan and I.

Looking down on him as his chest heaved up and down with each shallow breath, I imagined what our lives could have been like if he had never gotten Christine pregnant all those years ago. Would he still be the man of my dreams, still be the man for me? Would he still be my lover, my babies' father, my lifetime partner...and my friend? *Hell nawl, bitch. He would still be cheating on you, just like he's doing her...* the epiphany hit me like a ton of bricks.

My Grammy told me a long time ago to never confuse good sex with love, which is what she thought I was doing with Vani. Little did she know though, I was not with Vani because his sex game was tight, quite the opposite. I was with him because he treated my pussy like it was a gourmet candy shop. There was no lick too big or too small to keep him from getting to the center of my tootsie roll pop.

Hands down though, The Kenyan Warner was the best sex I ever had...then and now. And what Grammy didn't know is that I fell in love with him right under her roof. *And if I'm completely honest with myself,* I thought, as I looked over at his sleeping form, *he's the only man I've ever truly loved.* And now, the fact that he has stepped his game up since back in the day and is now taking long, earth-shattering trips downtown too...shit, I doubt I will ever love anyone else.

As he rolled over and draped his arm around my waist and pulled me closer to him, snuggling his head up against my back, I felt the tension rise in my chest again as I heard my grandmother's words, louder and clearer than the last time, "Baby, God will send you a lot of things, but he won't send you someone else's husband."

Suddenly my heart began to beat faster and sweat began to ooze from my pores. "Kenyan, Kenyan," I whispered breathlessly. "Can you please run me some water and help me get into the tub?" I asked closely to his ear.

Immediately stirring up from his sleep, he gave me a kiss on both of my eyelids and climbed from the bed and headed to the bathroom. *I wish getting him to give me his heart had been that easy,* I thought, while trying to tear my eyes away from his muscular body, but no matter how hard I tried, a magnetic force kept drawing my eyes back to him. "The man is perfect," I said aloud. *Except for his wife and kids.*

It took everything I had in me to fight off his advances and his pleas to join me in the hot bath, but I held my ground; still hearing my grandmother's voice ringing in my ears, I had to get some distance between us. After he finally retreated from the bathroom in defeat, I commanded Alexa to play 80's and 90's R&B love songs and sank deeper into the tub as the sultry sounds flooded the air. As I sat there being serenaded from one beautiful melody to another, my heart drifted down memory lane and back to our present time, and I didn't feel any better about the situation than I did a few minutes ago when my grandmother scolded me from the grave about loving a married man.

Then, out of nowhere, I believe Alexa's petty ass started reading my mind, and for the next three songs in a row, she gave it to me raw and uncut. First, she hit me with the accusing sounds of *My Little Secret,* then the heifer followed that with the mournful melody of *Have You Ever,* but when that trifling robot played, *My Sidepiece,* I knew then that Amazon was on some *Big Brother* shit, because that song wasn't even in the 90's...Alexa was just all up in my fucking business.

I screamed to the top of my lungs, "Alexa... shut the fuck up!" And for the next thirty

J'Sat Necolle

minutes, I sat there in complete silence with my head resting on the tub contemplating my next move. But just as I was coming to the conclusion that there was nothing I could do about my current situation until I could at least take care of myself, I heard Kenyan on the phone, laughing hysterically. Pangs of jealously shot through my soul as I thought of the kind of bond they obviously shared, being that he could stay gone so long and she still be this understanding. It seemed as though they had something really precious; yet rare. In a time when so many people took their relationships for granted, it seems these two have withstood the test of time. Then a revelation crossed my mind and tore my heart to shreds, *He didn't marry her because she was pregnant, he married her because he loved her...and still does.*

Reluctant to call Kenyan in to help me, I sat in the water until I felt a shiver erode from my soul and my toes began to wrinkle up. "I'm ready!" I yelled, then sat there tentatively waiting for him to come rescue me from the frigid waters. But instead of Kenyan walking in, Yana strolled in like the cat that had swallowed the canary. And while, I definitely wasn't in the mood for her shenanigans today, her face was a welcomed sight at the moment. "Oh, thank God it's you!" I said.

"Well, I'll be. I can't believe you'll rather see me than McSteamy, but shit, I'll take it." We both laughed, me; more so to keep from crying.

Smitten

Quickly wrapping the towel around my upper body as she noticed the chill bumps surfacing all over my body, she said, "Damn Elsa!" "Why the hell you sitting here in Antarctica?" "McSteamy got you that hot and bothered?" Then she went on a rant about how cold the water was, but she was mainly ranting to herself because I really wasn't listening, lost in thoughts of my own. Then as she tried to lift my naked body from the tub, she lost her footing on the damp, marble tile and with one loud screech, she was head first over in the tub with me.

Screaming to the top of her lungs as the cold water assaulted her body, she yelled for help, while I could not stop the laughter from erupting from deep within.
"Kenyan, Help!"

Rushing into the room, Kenyan stopped dead in his tracks, startled by the sight of a disheveled, soaked and wet Yana, straddling my naked body in the large tub. Instead of reaching in to help, his limp body fell back against the wall in fits of laughter, "Now, some men...not me of course...could only fantasize such a sight." And the more Yana cursed, the more both he and I laughed.

Finally grabbing some dry towels, he headed over to us, carefully helping Yana off me and out of the tub. He looked her eye to eye and said, "I told you God don't like ugly," and burst out laughing again, while gently rescuing me from the freezing waters.

J'Sat Necolle

Chapter 39

Yana, Kenyan and I emerged from the bedrooms at the same time, with us still laughing and her still pouting. As Kenyan carried me down the stairs, she said out of nowhere, "I hope he drop your ass."

And what did she say that for, because his knees buckled as fits of laughter overtook us both. Thoughtfully he grabbed the black wrought-iron rails to keep us both from tumbling down the stairs. As he carefully steadied us both, we laughed so hard at her obvious torture. She was really salty, like I meant for her to fall in the water. This was typical Yana though, she could dish the shit but has never been able to take it, but Kenyan didn't make it any better when we finally reached the end of the landing. "I'm sorry, that wasn't funny...Ariel." Then burst out laughing again at his Little Mermaid joke.

"Ha-ha, hell," Yana pouted. "I bet you won't hop your happy ass down to Fox News and call my black ass the little mermaid. Those racist bastards will hang your ass on national television."

Smitten

We all laughed at how idiotic most of white America is sounding right now, all pissed off at Disney about casting a person of color to play The Little Mermaid in their new movie. Did they not realize, Disney don't give two fucks about what their racist ass thinks...they're going to be busy laughing all the way to the bank off our black coins. I let out yet another sarcastic laugh at the irony of it all. *Shit, you'd think these crackers would know by now...Black Girls Rock! Disney damn sure does.*

This laughter was certainly good for my soul, until she hurled a pillow off the couch, aimed straight for his head. Quickly he tossed me onto the sofa and pulled my dress down, instructing me not to be showing his goodies, and handed me a pillow so we could tag-team her ass. The pillow fight was just what the doctor ordered, it helped me to release my frustration with my lack of mobility and my feelings for Kenyan.

Surprisingly, I'd had gained a great deal of strength and control with my left hand because I was tossing pillows for her head like I was an All-Star pitcher for the Atlanta Braves. "Oh, Bitch, so it's like that?" Yana asked putting her hands on her hips. "So, you just gonna turn on me for some..." But before she had finished her sentence, two more pillows were headed straight for her face, ducking behind the recliner, just in time, the pillows hit one of the luxurious potted plants and black potting soil went tumbling out everywhere.

J'Sat Necolle

Smitten

Gasps of 'Oooh's' escaped from Yana's and Kenyan's mouths at the same time, like they were both three years old. Then without hesitation, she fired two rounds at our heads, and yelled, "Fuck, that shit, tell them crackers you ain't dead no way!" We all laughed uncontrollably. Suddenly the sound of the doorbell jarred all of us from our three-way war. Each of us looking around trying to figure out who was expecting a guest.

With a shrug of his shoulder, Kenyan headed towards the door, while Yana and I retreated to our respective fortes and attempted to catch our breaths. Eventhough both Yana and my back were turned away from the door, as soon as the boisterous laughter echoed in the hallways, we both said, "Cleve!" at the same time.

She was just as excited to see him as I was. She'd told me how supportive he'd been during my hospitalization, but I wasn't at all surprised because I knew he was nothing more than a gentle giant.

After working so closely with him on the Hope House Project, and now getting to know Kenyan better over the past few weeks, I can see how their friendship has lasted for so long. According to Cleve, they both met in the Marcy Projects back when they were nine and ten years old and have been down ever since. He said, the hardest two years of his life was when Kenyan got sent away to Georgia. I can remember him telling me one day when we were looking at some flooring samples and talking about the value of friendship, "Yo, my mans always had my back, and after he left, I just felt empty...like a part of me was missing." I wanted to tell him, shit, he left me feeling the same damn way, but I wasn't going to be petty like that. Besides, I really liked Cleve, and mines and Kenyans shit didn't have anything to do with him, so that topic was completely irrelevant in our budding friendship.

"Heyyy, Beautiful," he said coming down into the den where Yana and I was sitting. "Oh, shit, what up with you too, Yana?" He said, surprised to see Yana sitting on the opposite end of the couch.

Before I could return our customary greeting, Yana was already firing in on his ass, "Oh, it's like that?" "So, that bitch gets a 'heyyy Beautiful', but all my ass get is a 'what up'!"

Everybody started laughing except Yana, who kept on with her tirade, her pouty mouth laced in a scowl. "So, why, didn't I get just a 'what up' that night at the hospital when you were trying to get at a sistah?" She glared at him with pure disdain etched across her beautiful face.

Cleve's mouth dropped past his chest, while Kenyan's and my eyes popped out of our sockets in sheer surprise.

Smitten

"You did what?" Kenyan shot in Cleve's direction.

"Yeah, tell ya' boy, Cleve!" Yana exclaimed. "Tell him how I was the most beautiful woman you'd ever seen that night. Remember how you said my intelligence and compassion were both a turn-on for you."

Finally, able to get something to come out his mouth, Cleve shouted, "Man, why you lying?" He started laughing so hard until he started crying. Our gazes shifted from Yana, back to him and then to Yana again, who looked as serious as a heart attack.

"Oh, I'm lying!" "I'm lying!" she shouted. "Negro, please!" "Tell them how you begged me to let you taste it just one time."

By now, both mine and Kenyan's heads were spinning like we'd both got caught up in the ghetto version of the Twilight Zone. Poor Cleve was on his knees in hysterics and I couldn't tell if it was a stalling tactic or if Yana had just busted his ass out so bad in front of us that he just didn't have a comeback, or an explanation for that matter.

My mind immediately started spinning out of control with the idea of someone I'd grown to consider a good friend, hitting on my girl; or any girl for that matter, over my lifeless body. The fact that Cleve would do such a thing was completely atrocious. *Damn, just when you thought you know someone,* I thought to myself, as I watched his large frame crouch even more in uncontainable laughter.

Looking at the repulsive scowl on Kenyan's face, he was just as surprised as I was. Probably even more so, since he'd known him much longer.

We all stood there starring at Cleve, who was now breathlessly trying to pull himself off the floor, saying "Oh, my God!" "Oh, my God!" with tears streaming down his face. Yana, who was now standing with her hands planted firmly on her ample hips, stared down at Cleve, still obviously pissed, did not say another word.

The tension in the room mounting by the minutes as we all watched Cleve as he attempted to regain his composure. By the time he was fully back in an upright position, he turned to face Yana; who suddenly broke out in the biggest smile and said firmly, "See what you get for looking over me!"

Confusion registering immediately over both mine and Kenyan's face, as the two of them laughed even harder as they exchanged hugs.

"ShyYana Tamilia Yearwood!" I shouted, sounding just like Mrs. Yearwood did back in the day when Yana's antics had gone too far. "I know damn well you didn't just lie on this man like that!" I screamed, totally shocked by her little

performance. *This girl really has some fucking
problems,* I thought to myself.

"Man, you need to get yo girl!" Kenyan said,
now also bubbling over in laughter himself,
grabbing Cleve in a warm hug as they both
doubled over in laughter. "She is really sick. Ya'll
really need to get her some damn help...and
fast," he said in between bouts of laughter, tears
rolling down his face.

I'm certainly glad they thought that shit was
funny, because I sure as hell didn't. In a matter of
seconds, that fool had me second guessing
everyone in my life. Shit, if my judgement could
be that off about Cleve, who the hell else wasn't
who I thought they were. Just for that, I aimed
the pillow dead at her head, firing the best shot
of the night. And just like that, pillow war was on
again.

After an hour or so of aiming, ducking,
dodging and fussing, we were all spent.
Exhausted bodies decorated my usually vacant
den. I was stretched out on the large sectional,
while Kenyan's head was touching my feet as his
lean body folded across the chaise. All six-foot,
three inches of Cleve's massive body was
stretched across the plush Burberry carpet in the
middle of the floor; while Yana's tired form laid
back in the adjacent recliner. Heavy breathing
and painful moans filled the room as each of us
realized we were well beyond the age to be
pillow fighting. Finally, Kenyan pushed himself to

his feet and headed towards the kitchen, while the rest of us continued enjoying our rest.

At some point, I assumed I must've drifted off into a good sleep because the next thing I knew, my nose was been accosted by the most amazing aromas. When the aromatic sensations tickled my nose the first time, I assumed I was still dreaming that Kenyan and I were eating Hibachi at Tokyo, my favorite Japanese hole-in-the wall out in Stockbridge. It doesn't have all the glitz and glamour that comes along with the high-end spots in Atlanta, but their Hibachi and fried sushi could make a blind man see. That shit is dope, and as soon as that thought entered my mind, that same wonderful scent accosted my nostrils again, but this time even stronger, causing my eyes to spring open instantly.

As my eyes adjusted to the bright light coming through my floor-to-ceiling glass doors leading out to my upper deck, I could not believe what sat before my eyes. The entire dining room was filled with food. From where I sat in the den, I could not tell exactly what all was in there but whatever it was smelled hella good! Cleve and Yana must've finally woken too, because both of them sprang to life at the same damn time.

"What in the world..." Yana sat up, looking around in a daze, trying to figure out where the intoxicating smells were coming from.

Cleve, on the other hand, sat up and immediately said, "Myyyy Nigga!" Sounding like

Denzel Washington himself. Yana's and my head both jerked in his direction, looking at him like he'd lost his mind. Judging from our reactions, he could tell we were lost, then said, "Fo-sho...my boy gets down with those pots." Just before he yelled out, "Yo K., you need any help in there?" Yana and I was mesmerized.

"Yeah, man, come help me get the plates to the table, and we can eat."

Cleve's ass jumped up from the floor with the expertise of an Olympic skater and headed towards the kitchen door. Then Yana got up and damn near sprinted to the bathroom sitting off the den. *Where the hell is she going?* I wondered.

Before my mind could continue though, she sprinted back in the room like she was Florence Griffith-Joiner, holding baby wipes in her hand. *Whatdawhat,* I thought as I looked at her, but then she came rushing right up on me, then took the damp cloth and started wiping my face. My arms couldn't move fast enough to stop her motions, but I managed to get out irritably, "Girl, what the hell are you doing?"

"I'm looking out for your nasty ass," she said, never relinquishing her circling motions on my face.

"What are you talking about?"

"Girl, you see how good this man can cook and the way he takes care of you, he's a fucking keeper!" Then she started giggling, "I can't let you be sitting up in here with all that dried up salvia around your mouth!" Thankful she caught a glimpse of me before the guys did, I shut my mouth and let her do her thing. But then she said, "And now this big ass booger gots to go, too!" My eyes stretched in horror.

"Oh, my God!" "I got a booger in my nose?"

"Bitch, you 'been' had a booger in your nose!" She said, laughing hysterically.

"Ho, why didn't you say anything?"

"Since you wanted to be all Team McDreamy and shit, I was waiting for him to tell you, with your nasty ass!" "See, what you get for fucking with me!"

She makes me fucking sick, I said to myself as I stared at her with my mouth dropped open, while she laughed herself to death, then continued on, completely unbothered that she had me pissed. "Hell, I knew McDreamy was a good care-taker and all, and he'd fixed your broken pussy and shit, but I had no idea his ass could cook-cook. Bitch, we can't let him get away!" she adamantly whispered in my face.

This fool was as serious as a hard attack, too; and if I wasn't so pissed at her about the damn booger, I would be killing myself laughing, but at the moment, all I could do was roll my eyes. She waved her hand dismissively at my actions and was about to say something else, but, just as soon as he heard the guys headed in from the kitchen, she quickly rushed the wipe up to my nose and whispered, "Blow, bitch. Blow!"

Quickly tucking the wipe in her pocket as she stood, she reached out to help me get up into a seated position. "I'll be right back, Booh," she cooed sweetly, just loud enough for the fellas to hear, like she was auditioning for Bestie of The Year or some shit. *But had just let me sit here with a damn booger in my nose for hours.* She returned almost immediately though with hand sanitizer for me. *Oh, now the bitch wanna be thoughtful.* But I played her game, as she reached down for me to grab her hands as Kenyan had instructed us. I glaringly shot daggers in her direction as she walked me towards the dining room table.

As I got a closer view of the amazing feast Kenyan had prepared for us, hell, I didn't have time to stay pissed at Yana's spiteful ass, shit I was ready to eat!

Seated beside Kenyan, he whispered loudly in my ear. "You have nothing to be embarrassed by here. We all love you. You eat, I'll assist." Those words hit me like a ton of bricks and when I looked up into the awaiting eyes of Yana and Cleve, who had yet to touch their food, I gave a mere nod of my head in acceptance of their gesture. Then everyone dug in, including me.

Smitten

At first, I had to make several attempts to get the food to my mouth with my left hand, without dropping anything, but soon I got the hang of it. When I did lose some of the morsels off my fork, Kenyan just swooped in with the assist and kept talking, we all did.

No one was staring or making me feel self-conscious and before too long, I felt less and less like I was a spectacle and more like myself. We sat around the table for hours, telling stories of our past, sharing thoughts of our futures and reminiscing on our present. *Life is good,* I thought, as I looked around into the faces of my old friend and my new friends. *It could be better...but it's still good.*

J'Sat Necolle

Chapter 40

As the days turned into nights, and the nights turned into the best days of my life, Kenyan and I fell into a routine. Most of our days were spent together, with the exception of the few times he could not pass one of his patients off to his partners' rotations, for whatever reason.

First, we'd start every morning with breakfast out on the veranda, then after that, we'd begin our physical therapy session. What had started as long, gruesome hours in my home gym, had quickly turned into relaxing walks in the park, talking about any and everything. Or some days we'd take long trips to the local farmer's market, casually walking the aisles, touching and smelling the wonderful produce of nature. Then other times, we would indulge in long massages at Spa Sydell...when we were not making love.

I kept asking him how he could miss so many days off work and it not be a problem. He explained to me that he was his own boss and set his own schedule; besides, his partners were definitely not complaining about the extra client billings they were getting in his absence. I wish I could muster up the nerve to ask him how he could spend so much time from home, but I just could not get up the nerve; afraid the answer to my question would hurt more than just ignoring the obvious.

Now, when he got his late-night phone calls, I'd retreat to another part of the house and pretend to be doing something else. I was so thankful when I finally got to the point of being able to walk with the use of my walker though, because prior to that, I would just have to lay there and listen to his chuckles from the other room, as he sat on the phone all night, going from one subject to another.

In fact, the only times he'd used the other room lately is when he was on his phone calls, other than that, he slept in my room. Occasionally, though, some of those phone calls would last to the wee hours of the morning and when they did, he didn't bother waking me up to climb in bed with me. He just stayed where he was.

Those nights seemed to be the longest and the most torturous. For hours prior to falling asleep, I'd try to do everything in my power to drown out the outburst of laughter and endless mumbles of chatter I heard from the other room. And when I could not stand it any longer, I would turn on Pandora on my phone and put my earbuds in my ear to drown out the noise...and the pain.

Last night, though; last night took the cake. Instead of him just going into the next room like he always did, he didn't bother to move at all.

J'Sat Necolle

Smitten

When the call came in around 10pm, which had become the norm for her calls; He and I were just getting out of the shower. When he heard his cell, he raced out the bathroom to get to the phone, which was laying on his side of the bed.

Not waiting for him to come back and help me out of the restroom and continue getting dressed for bed, I grabbed my walker and went about the task alone. When I finally emerged from the bathroom, instead of him being in the room next door like always, his long, languid body was sprawled across my bed, just chilling, enjoying his conversation. In fact, he was so enthralled about whatever they were talking about that he never even bothered to look up and acknowledge my presence in my own room.

Don't sweat it, Hiri, I told myself as I sat on my side of the bed. *He was just waiting within earshot if I needed him while I was still in the bathroom,* I told myself. Eventhough, I was thankful for his thoughtfulness for my safety, I was anxious for him to carry his and his dearly beloved's conversation to the other room, so I hurried as fast as I could moisturizing my feet and climbing into bed. Rolling over, my right hand extended out slowly to turn off the light. *Everyday my body is getting much stronger,* I thought to myself, then I heard him burst into laughter before uttering, "Girl stop!" teasingly into the phone. *And my heart is getting weaker,* my thoughts continued on.

Smitten

Praying silently that once the light was out, he'd excuse himself to his room like he'd done a million times before in the last month and a half, I shut my eyes really tight, hoping to expedite the inevitable. But it never came...

That night, I lay motionless as the man I love laid in bed next to me talking to the woman he loved... his wife.

J'Sat Necolle

Chapter 41

*W*hen the sun finally attacked my eyes the following morning, I could not believe the desperate turn my life had fallen into. Things I swore I would never do, had now became my new normal. So much so, that not only was I becoming complacent with being the other woman, I damn near felt like a sister-wife, after allowing last night's transgression to ever take place. "What's next?" I asked myself under my breath, "Will he be inviting her over for us all to hold hands and sing kumbaya?" *Oh, hell nawl,* I thought to myself, *the dick ain't that damn good.*

Looking over at his sleeping form, still lying peacefully next to me, a series of emotions cursed through my soul. A part of me loathed him for the stunt he'd pulled last night, but the other part of me was beyond indebted to him for being here for me when I need him most. *As much as I hate to admit,* I thought to myself, *I love this man.* If it were not for his wife and their late-night phone calls, my life would be damn near perfect right now.

Kenyan's thoughtfulness was completely amazing. He never left anything to chance, if he even remotely thought I needed something, he made it happen. Unlike most of the men in my past, he did not wait for me to ask him for something, he made sure to always be one step ahead of me in fulfilling my needs. And that was both physically and emotionally; which is something I've never had in a man. They either had little dicks and emotionally over-compensated for their short-comings; or they had big dicks, which gave them the big head; therefore, they never took my needs into consideration. Either way, no man as ever pleased me in my entirety the way Kenyan has.

Just as thoughts of our lovemaking sessions clicked on in my head, his massive body started to stir next to me. Watching him intently as he welcomed the gift of a new day, I wondered if he was even apologetic about last night. With his eyes still closed, he reached out his long muscular arms in a relentless stretch that immediately caused his biceps to flex and his pectorals to harden; instantly causing a tingling sensation down my spine.

I watched intently as he blindly reached his arm to my side of the bed. Amusement striking me immediately as his mouth quickly turned into a grimace when he did not feel my naked body life always. As fright partook his handsome face, his eyes sprang to life desperately, until he looked up into mine from my perched seated position. "Girl, you scared the crap out of me," he grumbled.

Yeah, right! I thought to myself, as he pulled me back down next to him. Everything in me wanted to scream, *"If you cared, you wouldn't have disrespected me like you did last night."* But the words would not escape my lips. I don't know if I was more afraid of him leaving; or more afraid of who I'll become if he stays.

Unsure if he could sense my apprehension or if he just knew he'd fucked up last night, but as soon as my face was near his, he began showering me with kisses. As much as I wanted to push his body away from mine, the magnetic chemistry that fused us together would not let me muster up the strength to turn him away. With fingers as graceful as a pianist, he strummed by body with delicate touches, followed by slow lingering kisses, yet I held solidly onto my anger.

Then he slowly rolled me over and began trailing kisses across my shoulder blade. Massaging my head with his strong hands, he groped me neck tenderly as his tongue made a sensual voyage down my spine, still I was pissed.

However, when his soft tender kisses began to grace my round backside, the surge in my spirit slightly began to shift. "You won't believe how much I'd missed you," he said, in between each loving peck he adorned on my ass. *Don't give in, Hiri.* I scolded amidst more kisses. "I didn't think I'd ever see you again." *I refuse to give in,* I chided, as his lips caressed my ass. "And when I saw you in that exam room that day..." his large hands spread my butt cheeks, "I knew I had to have you..." his warm tongue darted inside, and he began work the same electric magic he'd relinquished on my pussy so many times before. His moans became louder and needier as he feasted on every crevice of my being. My legs curled inside, almost causing my body to coil into a fetal position, part of me trying to get away and the other part of me fighting to stay.

With his mouth never vacating my insides, he abruptly reached his strong arm under my waist and pulled my body back up until I was completely trapped and perched on all fours.

There he devoured me from the front to the back for what felt like hours. His tongue created a magical pathway from my ass to my pussy that he and he only had the map. My knees trembled relentless as he suckled my sweet nectar from both ends and just when I could not stand it any longer, he entered my vaginal walls with the force of an African warrior.

"Oh my God!" "Oh my God!" I screamed over and over again. Causing him to dive deeper and deeper into my abyss. His balls crashed ferociously up against my swollen lips with each stroke, causing another wave of unexpected sensations to curse through my body.

All my anger and resentment dissipated as guttural screams erupted from deep within my soul, as I called out Kenyan's name over and over again.

J'Sat Necolle

Breathless confessions of love filling the air as he emptied his contents into my awaiting reservoir. *Lord don't let me become a sister-wife,* I thought to myself, just as sleep overtook my body. *Actually, the dick is that good...*

Chapter 42

*W*hen Kenyan and I finally emerged from upstairs, which was hours later, our love-making session leaving us both exhausted, we were both surprised to see Yana's ass lying peacefully on the couch, like she was Sleeping Beauty or some shit.

It was good to see her though, given how strained our relationship had been since our big blow-up two weeks ago.

Eventhough, most of Kenyan and my days were spent together, occasionally, he did still call Yana to come over and babysit me when he could not get out of an appointment. Although, he could see how frustrated I'd begun to get with the 24-hour surveillance, he still insisted I wasn't ready to be left at home alone.

But listening to Yana talk non-stop about how she thinks Gavin deserves another chance was just plain sickening. She'd go on and on for hours about how he was now doing this, and now doing that. Hell, I wanted to tell her ass that those are the things husbands should do. I wanted to tell her that if she wanted to be stuck on stupid again, then knock herself out, but that bastard wasn't getting no damn cookie from me for finally doing the shit that he should have been doing from day one.

But she was my girl, and I'd learned a long time ago just to let her do her. So, I didn't say shit, just like I've done most of their marriage. But, the last straw came last Wednesday though, when she was over here "babysitting" me; yet again, and his trifling ass called to get the account number to her separate account.

The account that we; as in, she and I, started together the day before we left for college over thirteen years ago. The same account that we; as in, she and I, had both deposited our hard-earned cash into every fucking month for the past thirteen years. The very account that did not have his damn name anywhere on it; and not one of his fucking pennies in it. It is our account; as in, she and I...so when I heard her giving him our account number, I nearly lost my fucking mind.

Nawl, scratch that. I did lose my fucking mind. And when I say I read that heifer for everything she knows. I mean, I read her ass. I went back so far reading her ass about how she'd let this trifling ass man shit on her from day one, that I almost forgot how much our friendship meant to me. All the shit that I'd held in for years trying to spare her feelings came bubbling out in the urgency of an erupting volcano.

J'Sat Necolle

Smitten

As tears welled up in the corners of her eyes, I could see my words burned like lava, too. And even though I could hear my grandmother's voice scolding me in the back of my head about how sometimes God sends you what you need when you need it, which is what she always used to say about Yana's and my friendship, at that moment, I didn't give two fucks about what Grammy or Yana thought.

All I knew was that, that no-good, trifling, hood-rat ass, missing-in-action negro now had access to my fucking money, and she had given it to him. And I didn't appreciate that shit one damn bit.

I told her that she was stupid as hell for passing up on a second chance to spend her life with a man like Brandon that loves the ground she walks on, and if she stays in this marriage, she's going to lose everything else in her life; including herself.

I knew I was going too far but I just couldn't stop myself when I told her about how she was so judgmental and cold towards her dad after he'd done what he done to her mother; yet she refused to see how Gavin, in no way, shape or form even measure up to half the man her dad was.

"Real talk, yeah your daddy may have been a ho… but what he did do was take care of his family. He put you and your mother on a pedestal and to my knowledge, he never disrespected her by calling her out her name; nor did he treated her like she was a fucking dog, that he could just walk on!"

"In fact," I went on, shooting daggers across the room right into my best friend's tear-stricken face, "In fact, when your mother entered a room, your daddy's eyes lit right up with pure affection. His words to her were always kind and his words to others about her, were even kinder...but you became too hypercritical to even see that!"

"If you ask me," I continued, anger oozing from every pore of my body as I walked slowly towards my best friend in revolt, "compared to the bullshit you call a marriage, your parents' marriage looks fucking perfect!" I yelled right in her face. "That's right, they're damn near, Obama-Like, compared to yours!" I yelled again, this time flailing my arms in the air for added effect.

"Zahiri!" Kenyan yelled with so much force from the entryway, he stopped my tirade mid-sentence. My eyes never left from the piercing eyes of my best friend, who still stood frozen in place, heaving for her next breath. Another guttural sob escaped her parted lips just before she abruptly began to run towards the front door, pulling her limp body out of Kenyan's grasp as he tried to stop her as she fled my home. Running behind her he yelled, "Yana, stop. She didn't mean it. She didn't mean it!"

J'Sat Necolle

Smitten

I watched from the doorway as he banged on the windows of her SUV, pleading with her to let him drive her home. He kept insisting she was in no condition to drive, but frantically she just threw the vehicle in reverse and plowed out the long driveway.

For the remainder of the night and into the next day, Kenyan did not say two words to me. If I asked him a question, he'd just nod his answer, yes or no.

When I attempted to explain to him my side of things, he'd just put his hand up to shush me, which really pissed me the fuck off; but I couldn't even speak on that.

Nevertheless though, I could not wait for the bank to open that following morning, having been checking our account every thirty minutes since she'd ran out the house. I couldn't stand the idea of losing both my best friend and my money. *Gavin's ass might get one, but it'll be over my dead body before he gets both,* I thought, right before I checked the balance every single time, scared as hell that the automative teller would eventually report a zero balance.

When 9am registered on the alarm clock perched on my nightstand, my soul quivered deep inside. And as I pressed the many prompts and waited for a real person to get on the line, I prayed like I've never prayed before. And once I gave my credentials and the representative finally verified that I was an account holder, I prayed even more.

In the moments it took for her to confirm the account transactions and balances, I tried to imagine my life without Yana, and I couldn't. Sadness enveloped me at the mere thought of it, and when the young lady came back on the line and said, "Ms. Jones, there has been no withdrawals on this account...ever. All I see is two monthly deposits every month, for the life of the account.

Thank you, Jesus. Lord, I thank you. I repeated over and over in my head. Whatever the young woman was saying on the other end of the line about setting up a money market account was going in one ear and out the other, but when she finally asked if there was anything else she could help me with, indicating the call was about to ended, I started to ask her if she could help me get my best friend back; which only reminded me why I'd had to call in the first place...

"Yes mam. I need you to please put a freeze on this account immediately."

Chapter 43

*M*uch like Sleeping Beauty, Yana's lifeless body did not stir at all as Kenyan and I entered into the living room. "She must be really tired, we won't wake her," Kenyan said, as he motioned for me to follow him to the kitchen with my walker. Starring at her for a few more seconds, I reluctantly turned away; just thankful that I was able to set eyes on the one constant in my life once again.

I've tried calling and texting her since the day after my explosion, but she hadn't returned any of my calls or texts. To say she was ghosting me was a total understatement. Although she'd been at work every day since then, except the day following the argument, she continuously came up with clever excuses to Julia to explain her not taking my calls. Knowing me well enough to know that I wasn't about to put my office in our personal business, I just left casual messages here and there, in hopes that she'd eventually call. She never did.

It's only been two weeks but has felt like a lifetime. Kenyan's ass didn't make it any better either, because he constantly reminded me how fucked what I'd said to Yana was. In the gospel according to Kenyan, you don't take what others have shared with you in confidence or experience and throw it back in their face, just to hurt them. And no matter how much I tried to explain that what I said was not out of spite, but because she needed to hear it, he stuck to his stance that it was fucked up... "If you wouldn't say the shit from fear of hurting her before...why would you say it when you were angry?" Eventually, I began to see it from his perspective. I just prayed it wasn't too late.

Kenyan and I went about preparing a hearty lunch, anyone that knows Yana knows that food is the way to her soul. That chick could eat. And unlike me, the extra pounds always hit her in just the right places. Me, on the other hand; hell, if I even smelled half the calories she consumes, my ass would be one French fry away from a heart attack.

Laughing at the thought, I handed Kenyan the head of lettuce as I took on my accustomed role as executive sous chef. Before him, I'd never enjoyed cooking. I suppose the feminist in me shied away from most things that are considered to be women's work. With Kenyan though, I really enjoyed cooking, or at least assisting him while he did so. What I loved most about him is that he doesn't show any ounce of male bravado and that shit is sexy as hell to me. He's just as at ease cooking or washing dishes as he is trimming the hedges or mowing the lawn. I love a man who is confident in his own masculinity, and don't feel the need make sure everyone else knows just how much of a 'real man' he is.

Hell, I was beginning to think this kind of brotha had become extinct, so I'm ecstatic to finally get me one. *But now that I've got one, I plan to take full advantage,* I thought, as I used my walker to guide me over to the counter where he was skillfully cutting the vegetables for the salad.

Instead of reaching up for the knife handle that he'd turned in my direction, I turned my walker around and glided my butt down onto the seat instead. Then I slowly slid my hands up his thighs and onto the crouch of his scrub bottoms. Looking up into his handsome face, I seductively licked my lips, a gleam of mischief sparkling in my eyes.

Recognizing my sultry expression, he immediately knew he was in for a treat. "Ah, come on, Babe," he said throwing his head back trying to contain his hearty laughter, while trying to stop me from pulling out my newest BFF. "Yana might hear us," he said amusedly, while still trying to keep my hands off his growing member.

"I thought you said this was my dick earlier." My eyes fixated on his caramel-coated gaze.

"I did." He licked his lips as he looked down at me, with a lump growing in his throat. "But..."

"Ain't no buts...it's either mine or it's not." My gaze never leaving his.

Smitten

With a slight gasp escaping his parted lips, his eyes penetrated through to my soul as he dropped the knife on the counter and reached down and withdrew his shaft in one swift motion. Saliva salivated in my throat as he and I both watched it harden right before our eyes. His breathing became more labored as I gawked at his penis in pure, unadulterated amazement. *Damn, he's got the prettiest dick I've ever seen*, I thought, just before he grabbed my head from behind and slowly ushered my mouth down to take final possession of the magnificent beauty he said only belonged to me.

Upon initial contact, I would not allow him to push my head any further than the head of his massive membrane. The more he urged for me to go further down his shaft, the more I resisted by suckling even harder on his head, knowing the small nerves encircling it were now sending tingles all down his shaft. Once the sensations reached their final destination, his dick stiffened even more in my mouth and his hold on my head loosened as he threw his head back in ecstasy.

As moisture drizzled down his hardness, I encircled his girth with both of my petit hands, slowly stroking up and down and round and around, then up and down. The soft moans escaping his lips were causing a spontaneous combustion in my pussy, and just when I felt he could not stand it any longer, my mouth swallowed his dick in one long gulp. Slowly pulling up the elongated shaft, I tickled his balls with my fingers. Just as I reached the top of

J'Sat Necolle

Mount Rushmore, I quickly descended the giant again, and again, and again. Both his hands now encircling the curly tendrils of hair in my head as he manipulated my head up and down on the dick I've grown to love. Up and down. Up and down. Again, and again.

"Oh, Shit!" he whispered louder and louder as I quickened the pace. "Oh, shit, Hiri!" "I'm about to cum, I'm about to cum," he cried breathlessly, as he quickly pulled his majesty from my mouth just as he erupted all over the dish towel he'd grabbed from the counter top.

As I sat there trying to regain my composer, I could not believe I'd just sucked this nigga's dick in the middle of my gourmet kitchen, when just six weeks ago, I'd never sucked a dick in my entire life. *Damn, what a difference a confident man can make.*

"Umm, um," we suddenly heard throat clearing from the doorway. My eyes stretched frantically, as Kenyan jumped, quickly trying to shove his dick out of site, burying it in the dish towel he'd been using. "Man, ya'll some nasty asses!" Yana exclaimed, then casually strolled away from the doorway where she'd been perched for God knows how long.

Completely mortified, we just stared at one another as he quickly replaced his junk inside his pants. We cringed as she continued to laugh uncontrollably from the next room, "Since, ya'll done made 'me' work up an appetite, ya'll need hurry the hell up; a bitch is hungry!"

Joining in on the laughter, we both set in motion to finish the lunch of grilled Ribeye salad and garlic toast. *Thank God, Yana's back,* I thought, just as we emerged from the kitchen with food fit for a queen.

Yana, true to her nature, dived right into the plate as soon as we sat it before her, then abruptly stopped eating. "Oh, Lord, forgive me," she said seriously; quickly bowing her head she began saying her grace, "Lord, please bless this food that I'm about to receive," she paused and looked up at us momentarily, then continued, "and please tell me you cleansed the hands that prepared it. Let it be prepared for the nourishment of my body, not from seeds sewn of loins from the nourishment of Hiri's pussy. These and many blessings I ask of you, in your name's sake. Amen."

Laughter erupted from both Kenyan and me. This fool hasn't changed one little bit. *I can't believe she just pulled the Lord in on her foolishness.*

"You're going to hell for that," Kenyan chided between bites, still shaking his head at her stupidity.

While, I just smirked at her antics, not the least bit surprised. I'm not sure if her catching us was such a terrible thing because she had one joke after another, which made our reunion a little more pleasant than it would have been otherwise. While, I know we can't pretend like nothing ever happened, it felt good for things to feel normal between us again.

Like old times, she caught us up on what was going on at work; then the office gossip and after that, we just skipped from subject to subject, enjoying each other's company. With our bellies full and the wine flowing, our afternoon was in full swing, the misery of the past two weeks having finally escaped the premises. When the doorbell rang out of nowhere, it startled the shit out of all of us because Kenyan was right in the middle of telling us what it was like the first and last time he'd spent the night in jail, when he was arrested on a possession charge at twenty.

After we gained our composure, Kenyan stood and went to the door, leaving Yana and I alone for the first time.

"Yana, I'm so sorry!" I spoke up first, my voice filled with unshed tears and regret. "I..." My voice trailed off.

Sitting with my back to the door, I had no idea who had just entered my house and was approaching my dining room with Kenyan, but the muffled voices, loud sounds of clacking heels on my polished oak floors; along with, the stark-white expression blanketing Yana's angelic, heart-shaped face was an indication that this was going to be interesting.

305

"What are you doing here?" Kenyan's deep, baritone voice dulled the clacking sound momentarily.

"What am I doing here?" "A better question is what the fuck are you doing here?" I heard a woman's voice hiss vehemently back in Kenyan's direction. And even before I could turn my head, I already knew that shrill of a voice could belong to no one other than, Mrs. Kenyan Warner. Christine was in my fucking house.

I turned just in time to see Kenyan snatch her by the $2000 Michael Kors bag straddling her shoulders, stopping her dead in her tracks. She was dressed impeccably from head-to-toe, with the exception of her disheveled hair, which I assumed got messed up while tousling with Kenyan, who was obviously trying to deny her access to my home, because they both were clearly out of breath. Nevertheless though, her make-up was still flawlessly applied, and the bling popping from her hands and her ear lobes made her look like she was worth a million bucks.

"I knew it was you!" She said as she looked me dead in my eyes, as Yana approached my side quietly from the other side of the room.

"You're damn right, it's me," I spat. "And what the fuck are you doing in my house?"

"That's right, Chris," Kenyan's voice interrupted. "You had no business coming here. Now, come on, let's go!" He tried yanking her towards the door.

"First of all," she said with unyielding emphasis, her eyes still locked in on mine, "I'll go anywhere I damn well please...especially, if my husband's here."

"Oh, hell nawl!" Yana and I both screeched at the same time, right before Yana lunged in her direction. Immediately sensing the oncoming danger, Kenyan quickly shoved Christine out the way of a lunging Yana, whom he then reached out to catch to break her fall.

"Damn, Yana!" "Stop it...you're only making matters worse."

"You want Yana to stop," I hissed at the now crumpled over Kenyan, under the weight of Yana's massive hips. "You should have told your bitch to stop it before she graced my fucking doorstep!"

"You, pathetic bitch!" Christine yelled, as she heaved herself up from the floor in a fury, scrambling to her feet. "After all these years, you're still okay with being his sloppy seconds!"

"Bitch!" "Oh, I got your bitch!" I yelled back, never having felt so helpless in my life as my eyes frantically searched for something to fend off the on-coming threat quickly approaching. I reached over and picked up the largest of the three candle holders on top of the mahogany dining room table where I was sitting, and not even waiting to see if Kenyan or Yana, who were both on her heels, would be able to catch her, I hurled it straight at her head with as much strength as my left hand could muster.

She ducked her head just in time; I missed her by an inch. But, the next one landed dead in the center of her forehead, causing her to stop dead in her tracks. Stumbling backwards, Christine grabbed her head and immediately bent over in pain as blood suddenly gushed from her wound.

I didn't feel one iota of remorse either. *That's what the fuck she gets...strolling all up in my shit like she's paying bills here.*

"Oooh shit!" she moaned, as Kenyan hurried to her side, frantically assessing her injury.

"Oooh shit, my ass!" I yelled. "You better get the fuck out my house before that's not all you get." My knees began shaking so fast, while my heart began breaking into a million pieces as I watched Kenyan lovingly tend to her.

"And take your husband too!" I hissed, in a voice barely above a whisper; yet so forceful it made everyone's head snap up and look into my solemn face.

Smitten

Unable to walk or even move, for that matter, the only thing I could do to wash out the scene happening before me was close my eyes. Leaning my head back against the sectional, I created my own version of Alexa in my head. Mentally shuffling from one love song to another, my humming became louder and louder, until I'd completely drowned out every plea leaving Kenyan's mouth.

It was an hour later when Yana lightly touched my arm and said they were gone, that I was finally able to cry.

Chapter 44

It had been three weeks since Kenyan and his lovely wife scrolled out of my home amidst the humming tunes drowning out my misery. According to Yana, Kenyan was straddling my legs begging me to stay, while Christine was straddling his legs begging him to leave. To let her tell it, the entire ordeal looked like a scene out of *The Twilight Zone,* but for the life of me, I can't remember shit, except for the last song in my head when Yana finally tapped me on my shoulder. And ever since then, I have had Alexa playing *The Wrong Side of A Love Song* on repeat, to remind myself to never open myself up to be played ever again.

My home phone and my cell phone had both been ringing off the hook for the past three weeks. If it was Kenyan's number, I didn't answer. If it was Cleve's number, I didn't answer. And if it was a blocked number, I didn't answer. I didn't want to see his face or hear his voice until the day after the day that I die. Sadly though, it has felt like I've been dying a slow, agonizing death every day, since the day he left. Without fail, every time I closed my eyes, I saw his face, I heard his voice, but not only that, I could have sworn I felt his touch. I miss him so much that at times his presence is so strong and so real that I could swear I smell the scent of his cologne.

J'Sat Necolle

Smitten

One day during one of my strenuous therapy sessions, I almost kissed my trainer, Raphael, because his voice sounded just like Kenyan's in my ear motivating me not to give up and to keep going. I remember it so vividly. I suppose because I was so humiliated by my actions. While, Yana, on the other hand, thought it was funny as hell.

When she got off work and came by my place that night like she has done for the past three weeks, Mrs. Lois, whom I had called back the day after Kenyan left and have grown to love, did a play by play of every humiliating moment. She was laughing so hard, she could hardly complete her little performance for Yana as she reenacted how I had closed my eyes and was counting off the steps I was taking on my walker and how Raphael was urging me on with every single step. Then, after finally climbing my stairway all by myself, I turned and quickly wrapped my arms around my trainer's neck and veered in for a kiss.

She was snickering so hard her entire body was shaking up and down, reminding me of my grandmother. She described the look on Raphael's face as pure horror when he realized what was happening. Slapping Yana on the shoulder playfully, she finished her narration teasingly saying, "Chile, you know that boy is gay as the day is long, he didn't know what in the world to do with all them titties pressed up against his chest." According to Mrs. Lois,

Raphael damn near skipped out the door trying to get the hell away from me.

"Man, I don't know what I was thinking," I explained, laughing at my own foolery. "I was just so proud of myself and with every step, Raphael's voice was being drowned out with my memories of Kenyan coaching me the very same way. I never imagined getting this far without him...and shit..." I continued, with a shrug of my shoulders. "Shit, I forgot he was gone..." My voice trailed off as the humor turned into sorrow, something I've grown accustomed to lately.

Both jumping to their feet simultaneously, both Yana and Mrs. Lois came over and wrapped their arms around me. Mrs. Lois rocked me silently in her arms, while Yana stroked my hair and began telling me how great I am doing.

"Why don't you just answer the phone and talk to him?" Mrs. Lois finally asked.

"I can't."

"You can and eventually you're going to have to..."

"Is he still calling every day?" Yana asked inquisitively.

Still sobbing on Mrs. Lois' shoulder, I merely nodded my head.

J'Sat Necolle

"He's not just calling, he's calling...all day, every day," Mrs. Lois chimed. He showed up last Friday when I went to get the mail. Almost scared me half to death."

"He did?" Both Yana and I asked curiously.

"Yes mam, he did." Not offering any more information than she had to.

"Well, why the hell didn't you say something?" Yana asked aggressively.

"He asked me not to."

Finally raising my head from her shoulders, I looked at her in shock. "Mrs. Lois, so you just weren't going to say anything just because he asked you not to?"

Looking me square in the eyes, she said, "Well, you told me never to let him in, which I didn't. You told me never to answer his call, which I haven't, but you did not tell me to never to talk to him, which I did."

Shaking our heads at her candidness, Yana tried to contain her snort but to no avail. Something she always did when she found something funny but knew she shouldn't laugh. "Well, she 'was' respecting your wishes," she said in response to the harsh eye roll I'd just shot Mrs. Lois.

"So was he," Mrs. Lois chided. "When he saw me going to the mailbox, he called my name and waved for me to come out to the street where he was parked. He apologized for just popping up but confessed that he was just so worried that he did not know what else to do. My heart went out to him, I had to pull him into a warm embrace and reassure him that you were going to be okay and I was going to take good care of you."

"You shouldn't have told him shit, he needs to worry.

Both Mrs. Lois's and Yana's head spun around on their shoulders so fast as they stared at me in awe, like I'd suddenly grown three heads.

"What?" I asked, completely baffled by the unspoken judgement they were hurling in my direction. Ignoring their obvious displeasure, I carried on, "He doesn't deserve to know shit about me. If he cared that damn much he wouldn't have left in the first fucking place."

Quickly raising her hand to speak, like she was in the first fucking grade. "Umm...Bitch, you really didn't leave him much of a choice."

"There's always a choice," I hurled back defensively.

"Are you sure you're talking about now, or fifteen years ago?" Yana asked, rather matter of fact.

J'Sat Necolle

If my heart wasn't aching so badly, the look of shock that had registered on Mrs. Lois's face when Yana brought up mine and Kenyan's past would have been absolutely priceless but given the fact that I presently felt like the valve around the aorta in my heart was slowly closing, I couldn't even appreciate the humor of her surprise.

"There's no way in hell," Yana continued, "did the man have a choice other than leaving. He begged your ass, in front of his wife I might add, to please let him stay. He declared his love for you, confessed he'd never stopped loving you and that he wanted to spend the rest of his life with you. Again...in front of his wife, I might add."

After staring at the floor for what felt like hours, with both women gazing down on me, I finally muttered, "He had a choice, and he chose her."

Frustration pulsating from every pore, Yana sprang up from where she'd been sitting, her voice now echoing off the wall, "Hiri, the only choice you gave that man that day, was to either leave or call the cops to 10:13 your ass! The way you were rocking back and forth, humming one sad song after another, sounding like a wounded animal, he and I both was scared shitless that you'd finally had a nervous breakdown. And given all the shit you've been through over the last few months, the possibility of that happening was not that far-fetched, and we both knew it."

I just stared into space as my best friend continued on with her tirade.

"And when I finally convinced him to just leave, the man had tears streaming down his face," she said, her tone quieting down as she remembered the despair she'd witnessed. Reaching out, Yana grabbed my shoulders with both hands and shook my entire body, forcing me to look up into her solemn face. "Hiri, that man loves you. You hear me? HE-LOVES-YOU!"

When she saw the sour expression still gracing my face and my eyes still rolling scornfully in the back of my head, she released me abruptly, then angrily turned on her heels and headed towards the front door without one glance back in my direction. She hurled over her shoulder, "For someone that thinks she knows everything about my fucking relationship, you're sure doing a piss-poor job with yours!"

Reaching out and turning the door knob, she stopped momentarily and finally turned to look back at me, then yelled, "Hiri, he's not Janis!" "He did not leave, you pushed him way!" "Now, wake the fuck up and realize you are worthy of being loved, before you fuck up the best thing that has ever happened to you!" She slammed the door forcefully behind her, without the slightest gesture goodbye.

J'Sat Necolle

Chapter 45

That night was one of the longest nights of my entire life. After Yana had stormed out the door, the tension that filled the room was utterly deafening. While Mrs. Lois didn't say anything else about Kenyan and I, I could feel her sentiment exuding from her body just as intensely as the tension in the air.

Finally feeling my emotions drain the last bit of strength I had left in me, I reached for my walker and scrounged up all my strength to help pull myself to my feet. Before Mrs. Lois could chastise me as she scurried to get to her feet from the rocking chair she'd claimed as her own, I waved to her that I got it. Cutting off her words mid-sentence, she did not return to her seat as I had motioned, but she also did not move any further to aide me in my quest.

Every step I took was strategically calculated and completely draining, but each step made me feel more liberated than the last. And for those ten minutes it took me to conquer the stairway on my own, there was no tension in the air. Neither was there a disloyal lover, judgmental friend, or even the slightest bit of a broken heart. All I felt was triumph. Pure, unadulterated triumph. Something I needed even more than my next breath.

Smitten

My bedtime regimen that usually took Mrs. Lois and I about twenty minutes to complete in its entirety, had taken me a good forty-five minutes to an hour, but I didn't care the least, little bit. All that mattered is that I had done it by my damn self, and right now, that meant more to me than anything. *Or almost anything.*

J'Sat Necolle

Chapter 46

ℱor the rest of the week, I was completely
miserable. No Kenyan, and no Yana, had me so
deep in my feelings, I felt like I was drowning in
quick sand. This morning though, was the worst
day yet. I didn't even have the strength to get out
of bed. Despite Mrs. Lois' repeated commands
that I need to eat something, I chose to stay in
bed and sulk in my misery.

"Lord, why do you hate me so much?" I
groaned towards the ceiling, knowing what I had
to do, but dreaded even the thought of it. I wish I
could talk to Yana, but this was the first time in
all the years I've known her that I could not
depend on her. She's been my confidant and my
rock for as long as I could remember. Shit, as
dysfunctional as she was, I feel completely lost
without having her to lean on. It's amazing how
we tend to take people for granted, but the
moment you have to do without them, you
realize just how important they are to your own
happiness.

"Hiri," Mrs. Lois called out from the bottom of
the stairway, snapping me out of my wayward
thoughts. "Hiri, you have a visitor." *Damn.* I
thought.

"Now, she knows damn well I'm not in the
mood to be bothered with anyone today," I
mumbled aloud, not even attempting to get up

from the fetal position that I was still curled up in. Calling back down stairs, I yelled to Mrs. Lois and whoever the hell it was she had let into my home, "I'm sorry, I'm not feeling well. Can you come back tomorrow?"

I was greeted by silence. Mrs. Lois did not say another word and for a quick moment, I thought my exploits had worked...right up until I heard footsteps coming towards my bedroom, the plush carpeting nearly muffling the sound of clacking heels.

It's probably Julia stopping by for her weekly check on me, I thought, glancing over at the clock on my bedside table, noting that it was only three-thirty, a little early for Julia to have made it all the way up to Alpharetta from my office down in Buckhead...*unless something was wrong.*

Fright immediately taking over my mind, *Lord, let everything be okay,* my mind instantly started raking over everything that could possibly be wrong. *Lord, I've worked too hard to build my brand to just lie here and watch it all go down the drain. I'm going to work next week, come hell or high water. My legs are broke, not my fucking brain, and I be damn if I'm about to lose everything I've worked for.*

My mind was racing faster than my common sense could keep up. Despite all the good reports I've gotten from Yana, a surprise visit from Julia in the middle of the day was saying otherwise.

J'Sat Necolle

Smitten

"Hurry up, come on in Julia, I yelled out into the hallway, hoping she'd put a little pep in her step, so she could hurry and tell me what the hell was going on. The longer it took her to make it down the long hallway, the more I regretted not following my contractor's suggestion and shortening the foyer. A thought that had crossed my mind more and more since the stroke and now...Just when my imagination was about to get the best of me, the door to my bedroom finally pushed open.

Whatdafuck! Whatdafuck! Whatdafuck! I yelled over and over in my head; but for the life of me, I could not make a sound escape my parted lips. *What the hell are you doing here,* I yelled, but nothing came out. "*Who in the hell let you in my house?*" I yelled, still nothing came out. "*What the fuck do you want?*" Rang out in my head, yet again, no sound graced my lips. For what felt like hours, we both stared at each other, each frozen in time.

The hurt, the pain, the humiliation, the rejection came hurling through my soul all at once. As my body shuddered over, the bile began to rise from the depths of my intestinal walls, I attempted to reach out to grab the small garbage bin I had been using all day, but this time with no success. The thick, amber liquid erupted from my mouth in a rage. The waves of nausea crashing against my stomach with a mounting fury, still though, I tried to wade off the oncoming help. "*Don't fucking touch me,*" I yelled., but my words remained trapped inside my head.

Smitten

Suddenly, electricity shocked my skin as I felt the gentle touch pull me near; soothingly holding me tight, while rocking away my pain. Tears frantically rushing down both of our faces when the one word I could not remember ever uttering before, finally graced my lips... "Mama."

"I'm so sorry, baby. I'm so sorry," Janis cried over and over again, as she rocked my body and held me tighter than I'd ever been held before.

I held onto her as if my life depended on it as I sobbed, "Mama, Mama," from the pits of my soul.

I could not explain my actions or my emotions, but at this moment, Janis was not the mother that gave me away, the one that never wanted me, the one for whom I wasn't good enough. At this moment, she was just Mama...*and I've never needed my mama more than I do right now.*

J'Sat Necolle

Chapter 47

"Zahiri," Janis yelled from downstairs the following morning. "Do you prefer your eggs scrambled or fried?" *If you had raised me, you would know how I like my fucking eggs,* the thought immediately flooded my brain. Despite our long talk yesterday, and the way she'd taken care of me through the night, I guess my mind just isn't ready to forgive and forget; and this entire scene felt like something from the *Twilight Zone.*

"I prefer fried. Two please, the yolk slightly running and a piece of cheese in the middle." I yelled back, with as much strength as I could muster. Never in a million years would I have imagined when I woke up yesterday morning suffering with a relentless broken heart, fueled by a horrific bout of morning sickness, that it would be my very own mother to swoop in and save the day.

Once we'd both cried our eyes out yesterday morning, she set about get me cleaned up. I must admit, it was funny as hell watching her trance around my bedroom in her red bottoms, and her cashmere sweater; cleaning up vomit like she was a housekeeper or something. It was also quite surprising to find out that she was actually pretty funny, too. Like Yana, she had a very smart mouth, and her come back game was quick as hell. Nothing at all like I'd imagined.

Smitten

I'd listened while she was on the phone talking to her husband, and boy, did she give him have the business when I assume, he'd suggested that she come on home, instead of staying overnight to take care of me like she'd offered. Oh, she let his ass have it. In fact, my heart almost burst into a million piece when I heard her yell into the receiver from the other room, "Listening to your stupid ass where 'my' child is concerned is what got me where I am in the first fucking place. So, please, just do me a favor, and keep my baby's name out of your fucking mouth from now on!"

I tried to act normal after that, but I could feel my anger begin to dissolve. Reluctantly, it dissolved even more as I listened to her tell me about how she had fallen head over heels in love with my father, her high school sweetheart, but also about how he'd cheated on her during her pregnancy with me. She said she'd never been so hurt and humiliated in her life...yet, she still loved him.

According to her though, the ultimate betrayal came when she found out when I was about eight months old that not only had he fucked just about every other girl in the school while she was pregnant, but he was also fucking her best friend.

"I'm not trying to make any excuses for leaving you, because there's not one big enough; but I was in a place where I wasn't fit to be love or to love anyone else; hell, I couldn't even love

J'Sat Necolle

myself." Tears moistened her eyes as she continued on. "I thought leaving town was going to help me get over him and the hurt, but even when I took you and went up north, I still couldn't make the pain go away."

"I literally cried myself to sleep for years. And to make matters worse, every time I looked at you, he was all I could see." Her voice became sadder and quieter, as she looked up into my face with tears dredging down her cheeks, "After a while, I couldn't stand to look at you."

Hearing my mother admit after all these years that she could no longer stand to look at my face was the reason she'd brought me back and left me with my Grammy wasn't as hurtful as I'd imagined it would be. In fact, it was actually rather therapeutic. All this time, I'd just assumed she'd never loved me and never wanted me, but that wasn't the truth. My father had broken her and looking at me growing up in the spiting image of him had eventually become too much for her.

"Bringing you and leaving you with Mama was the toughest thing I've ever had to do," she'd said. "At first, it was just supposed to be for a week, just so I could get a break. But then the week turned into two, then the two turned into a month; and before I knew it, I was moving on past the hurt he'd caused me and was out in the world finally living...just, without you."

Smitten

The pit of my stomach felt like a torch was festering there as I listened to my own story of abandonment from her perspective. To let her tell it, the longer she'd stayed gone, the easier it got to just stay away. She said she'd tell herself I was better off without her; and eventually she'd stopped calling her own mother, just to not be reminded of the horrible thing she'd done to me.

She said she used to tell herself some times that my father was actually better than she was because he'd wanted to be in my life; but my Grammy had told him and all his people that if they ever said one word to her daughter or her granddaughter that she would kill them, and everyone knew my Grammy meant what she said. According to Janis, my father and his entire family lived two blocks away from me my entire childhood but were too afraid to even say 'hi'.

Now, that revelation did something to my soul. All this time, I'd just assumed that neither of my parents wanted me, him nor her. "Why would my Grammy do such a thing?" I asked, unable to fathom the fact that she thought I was better off without having the love of at least one of my parents.

"She was just trying to protect you, Sweetheart," she said, while rocking me in her arms and rubbing my back. "That night when I came home with my heart completely broken, after finding him in bed with my best friend, Mama became so angry no one could calm her down. She held you in one of her arms and

J'Sat Necolle

rocked me in the other, as I cried and cried. She'd called her friend, Sister Gracie, from the church to come over and sit with us, saying she had to go see a man about a dog.

The next thing I knew, Deacon Knight was dragging her back into the apartment about an hour later, drenching in sweat. The side of her face was bleeding slightly, and her gun was clutched tightly in her right hand.

She did not say one word, she just came over to where you and I was lying on the sofa, me still crying my heart out, and regained her position of rocking us both. The following morning, my Uncle Bill was at our front door, waiting to take me and you back to Detroit with him, per the request of my mama."

"Word?" was all I could muster, looking up at her puzzledly.

"Word." She said, her dainty voice barely above a whisper, sounded funny using urban slang. "I finally heard years later that she'd gone over to Marcus' mom's house and pistol whipped him, his mama. They say by the time Deacon Knight had made it around there, she was walking up on your father's teenaged sisters telling them she'd been wanting to whip their high yella' asses anyway, so she wished they would jump.

To let the streets tell it, the McCray's were talking mad shit when the deacon was pulling mama out their yard, but when she almost got away from him, then threatened to blow all their fucking brains out if either of them ever came near me or my baby again...they said everybody, including the dog...shut the hell up and hauled ass back in their house."

She and I both laughing. "Damnnn, I knew Grammy was gangster, but I didn't know she was gangster-gangster!"

Our laughter filled the room, both of us with our own sordid memories of Grammy invading our thoughts.

Then, out of nowhere, I said, "Sooo, Marcus McCray...off Elms and 5th... is my daddy?"

Nodding her head up and down, Janis confirmed my lineage, as my newest revelation hit me in the chest like a ton of bricks.

Whatdafuck... Christine is my sister...

Chapter 48

I woke up with the mother of mother of all headaches. Still praying I was stuck in a bad nightmare, I glanced over to see the bedside toilet that I used to use perched right up next to my side of the bed. *No, that's the same toilet my mom put next to my bed last night, just in case my stomach decided to start tripping again.*

Just then, the word "mom" ran back through my brain, and I prayed that all this could still be an object of my imagination, but the movement of the mattress next to me was an indication that God had ghosted my prayers...again.

Turning over slightly, careful not to upset my stomach, I turned to look into the sleeping face of my very own mother. As I lay there starring at her, I became more aware of just how much her features matched my own. We had the same round face, the same pouty lips, and the same narrow nose...how could she look at me and see him.

Will I look in my own child's eyes and see Kenyan? The question penetrated my mind so quickly, I did not have a chance to halt its intrusion. "You cannot have this baby, Hiri," I chastised myself quietly, trying not to wake Janis, but trying to speak loud enough that the message resonates in my brain...and my heart.

Smitten

Her motherly intuition obviously kicking in, Janis suddenly stirred from her sleep…just in time to keep me from going into a full panic attack. When she looked over at me, sweat had begun cascading down my forehead and my heart was beating loud enough to hear it through my chest, "Calm down, baby. Calm down." She pulled me close and began lightly stoking my hairs. "It's going to be okay. Everything is going to be okay."

Feeling the warmth and sincerity of my mother's love, something I never thought I would have, the pains in my chest began to subside, but in the back of my head I could still hear my Grammy's voice, "Child, God might send you a lot of things, but he ain't gonna send you someone else's husband…and he damn shole' ain't gonna send you your sister's husband."

Tears sprang to life in my eyes as I lay in my mother's arms wondering why the universe seemed to hate me so much. My mother's revelation of who my father was only reiterated what I already knew I had to do.

Aborting my baby was going to be the single, most difficult thing I've ever had to do, besides burying my grandmother; but from the time I figured out I was pregnant a week after Kenyan left, I knew I had no other choice.

For weeks now I've been contemplating on how I was going to go about such a feat being that I had limited use of my limbs and could not

J'Sat Necolle

go alone. Nor could I call Kenyan, he was with his wife. Nor, could I call Yana, she was with her husband...and she'd lost three babies in the last five years.

No matter how strained our friendship was right now, I know if I asked her, she would do it...but it would be the most hurtful thing in the world for her, and there was no way in the world I would succumb her to that kind of pain.

In fact, given the amount of morning sickness I've been having, Yana getting mad at me was the best thing that could have happened because I wasn't sure how much longer I could hide it from her.

Especially given the fact that Mrs. Lois's noisy ass had figured the shit out long before I did. She was tactful and never said anything directly, but indirectly, she let me know in no uncertain terms that she knew I was with child. In fact, that day, right before Yana blew up at me, I liked to shitted bricks when Mrs. Lois made the remark in front of Yana that I was gonna 'have' to talk to Kenyan sooner rather than later.

As soon as the words left her lips, she knew she had messed up because my eyes got bigger than the diamond on Oprah's hand. I thought for sure Yana was going to catch it, but she was so irritated with me that she completely missed that slip of the tongue. And boy, was I happy because I'd felt a full-blown heart attack coming on.

That following day was so miserable for me because I knew I could not hide my indiscretion for much longer; and with the new Georgia abortion law on the horizon, I had to make it happen sooner rather than later. I lay in that bed all day with a list of possible culprits to help me pull off my plan, but one by one, I marked their names off the list for one reason or another.

My last hope was Cleve. I knew he would not like the idea, but I knew he would respect my decision as a woman to do whatever I saw fit to do with my own body. The issue was going to be; however, his loyalty to Kenyan. That was his boy. Hell, they'd been friends longer than Yana and I, so I knew I was going to be taking a big risk asking him to help me...but for the life of me, I could not think of anyone else. That is...until Janis walked in.

At first my little reunion with mommy dearest was stifling to say the least. Part of me wanted to pull her hair out for having the audacity to scroll up in my shit, like she was mother of the year. Yeah, that fraudulent shit worked downstairs with Mrs. Lois because she didn't know any better, but when I saw her light-bright ass grace the door of my bedroom instead of Julia, I'd immediately wished like hell that I wasn't so fucking secretive.

If I'd only mentioned it in casual conversation with Mrs. Lois that my birth mama wasn't shit and had bowed out both mine and my Grammy's life, then she wouldn't have fell for her mommy of the year bullshit when she'd darkened my front door. I will admit though, Grammy's philosophy that my business ain't everybody's business bullshit really saved the day this time.

Mrs. Lois was just as protective as a pit bull, and if she'd known that my mother had abandoned me, she would have never let her in my house. But Grammy said, God will always send you what you need, when you need it...even when you don't even know you need it.

Of course, it hadn't taken her long to realize I was pregnant, but she never said a word until I finally felt comfortable enough to discuss it with her. In fact, most of our day was compiled of her wiping up vomit, washing soiled bed linen and preparing food.

At first, I felt bad that she was having to do all that for me, but then I thought, hell; better late than never. If she had raised me, all this shit comes with motherhood 101. It was her fault she'd failed and now was getting a crash course in credit recovery. Besides, it was her bright idea to give Mrs. Lois the rest of the day off without my permission. The joke was on her.

It took a great deal of convincing, but she finally agreed to be my accomplice. Once I told her about Kenyan being happily married and all, she understood more of why I felt like I had no choice. And when she asked why Yana hadn't taken me, I had to tell her about my best friend's difficulty of carrying full-term; and what helping me could do to her.

She was lying across my bed listening intently as I spilled my heart out to her, my emotions were all over the place. She said she could not imagine being in my situation.

According to her both her pregnancies had been planned. She went on to tell me about my conception..." Your dad and I were so in love, or at least I thought we were. But, when I told him I was late, both of us was scared to death. Every day he would call before football practice to ask me, 'has it came yet' and when I'd say 'no', he'd just let out a sigh and say 'okay.'"

"One Wednesday afternoon though," she continued, "I called him before he could call me and as soon as he answered the phone, the words, 'it came' hurriedly escaped my lips. He'd said 'okay', just as he'd done all those days before, but that night he didn't come see me at all.

The following day, when he should have been at football practice, he was at my front door. Knowing my mother's schedule, he came inside and sat down on the couch without uttering a word. We sat side by side for a while before he finally pulled me into a warm embrace, then looked down on me with tears in his eyes and said, "I know we're too young and everything, but I really hate your cycle came on."

J'Sat Necolle

And with that confession, tears immediately sprang to my eyes, because I too, had secretly felt the same way. We kissed and confessed our undying love to each other, but when he stopped kissing me and held my face close to his, looked me dead in the eyes and whispered, '*I want you to have my baby, that way, no matter what...I'll always have a piece of you,*' I fell in love all over again!"

"Four months later," she whispered, "I got pregnant with you."

"Damnnn." I whispered, completely enthralled by my parents' love affair. "Ya'll really had some Harlequin Romance shit going on, huh," I said, looking over at her lost in a trance, remembering it like it was yesterday, tears threatening the corners of her eyes. I watched her face intently as she lay beside me silently remembering her past. I could feel her emotions intensify with each flutter of her eyelids.

Subconsciously, she reached over and began rubbing my belly without ever placing her gaze on me. As she rubbed, she hummed, her eye lids still flooding in memories. Then suddenly she looked over and locked her gaze on mine, "Yes, sweetheart, it was good...until it wasn't." Then she propped her elbow up and sat up slightly, placing her head in her hand. "The moral of our story is though...sometimes what you think will have a happy ending...doesn't."

Smitten

Then she rubbed my stomach once more before removing her hand slowly and said, "And sometimes what we think is not meant to be...is."

Her words were so simple, yet so profound; their magnitude if their weight falling upon me like a ton of cement.

As she slid down off the bed, with tears now clearly glistening in the corners of her eyes, she looked at me warmly and said, "I'll do whatever it is you need me to do...I owe you that. But only after you've prayed long and hard because this my dear, will be the toughest decision of your life. And take it from me, if you make the wrong decision, you don't get a do-over."

With an undeniable sadness in her eyes, she walked over to the bathroom and then spoke softly over her shoulders before closing the door, "Alexa, play Babyface... *Never Keeping Secrets.*"

J'Sat Necolle

Chapter 49

*B*eing pampered by a mother that abandoned you for most of your life is quite awkward, yet rather refreshing at the same time. I've wished so many times over the past few days that I could call Yana and share this experience with her. I must admit, though, that I am really surprised that she hasn't tried to call or text me since our little disagreement, but maybe that's for the best. *As soon as this is over, I'll reach out to her*, I thought, as I continued getting dress, determined not to let anything distract me from what I had to do.

For the past few days, I'd prayed and prayed for God to send me a sign, but my final resolve was that he'd sent my sign when he'd sent Janis to my door...armed with the knowledge that my child's father is married to my sister.

And even though being of blood relation has not made me change my stance on Christine, having Kenyan's baby was just not an option for me. Under normal circumstances, I'll admit, nothing in the world would have made me happier...*but ain't nothing normal about this Jerry Springer, trailer park trash shit*, I thought to myself.

Being her usual nosey self, Mrs. Lois had a million questions when she saw Janis and I emerge from my bedroom, where we had been fully isolated for days. "You girls finally got tired of being closed up in that dere room?" She'd asked as soon as she saw Janis helping me down the stairway.

Trying to throw her off our scent, I kept my response nonchalant, "Yeah...we decided to get out and get some fresh air."

"So, you're feeling better?" She asked, peering at Janis more than at me.

Knowing her well enough to know she was fishing for something, I said, "Not really, so Mom made me a doctor's appointment to make sure everything's okay."

Looking at me, she started beaming from ear to ear, "Halleluiah!" she threw her hands in the air, giving God praise. Then quickly pulled first me, then Janis into a warm embrace. Going along with the frolic, Janis peered at me from behind Mrs. Lois's back, not knowing what to expect next.

"Let me fix you both a plate before you leave. I've got grits, eggs, sausage..."

"Please stop, Ms. Lois," placing my palm in the air for her to stop talking. "Just the mere mention of food is making me sick to my stomach," I said, grabbing the center of my stomach to sell my performance a little better.

Smitten

Eventhough I was hungry as hell, I knew we only had about half a minute at a breakfast table with Mrs. Lois before she'd get the God-awful truth out of both of us about what we were about to do. It was amazing how in just the few minutes she'd been in her presence the day she'd gotten here, even Janis had seen just how much Mrs. Lois and Grammy had in common. About two days into her stay, we got a belly full of laughs at how much the two of them were alike.

"Now, I knew that woman always had to be in control, but damn, I never thought she'd be sending someone from her grave to watch over you."

"Damn, you see it too. Yana said that was the craziest shit she'd ever seen, I had to agree."

Picking up on my clue, Janis brushed past Mrs. Lois, rushing to my side. "Come on, dear, let's get you to the doctor. They'll be able to give you something to help you with the nausea." Grabbing my backside, she spotted me perfectly as I glided the walker towards the front door.

We'd almost made a clear escape, when I heard Mrs. Lois yell behind me, "Zahiri." I turned to see her still standing frozen in the same place, sadness emanating from her eyes. "Baby, God don't make no mistakes."

"Yes mam." I lowered my head, then closed the front door. The magnitude of my decision cursing through the depths of my soul. And

Smitten

suddenly the nausea I'd just faked, was now reigning true. Holding tightly to the ivory stucco ornamenting my front porch, I leaned over and puked behind the bushes until I felt like my insides would come spilling out.

"It's going to be okay, honey. You don't have to do this."

I stood there glaring into eyes that were so much like mine for what felt like an eternity. Weighing my odds for the umpteenth time, I finally said, "Yes, I do."

As my mother and I rode in silence, I could not help but to think about the first time I'd gone to an abortion clinic. Is this how Dominique felt? Was she in love with Mr. Yearwood? Did she want more than anything for him to be in love with her and not with his wife? I gazed out the window absently as thoughts of my own fate filled my mind. The ride to the south side seemed quicker than usual, and before I knew it, we were pulling up in front of a run-down brick building that almost looked abandoned.

As we entered the structure, I noticed the theme of abandonment was carried on throughout the interior space as well. From the receptionist desk, that had seen better days, to the worn, blue patient chairs filing the waiting area, right down to the lifeless faces of the women and teen-aged girls staring blankly at the clipboards they held in front of them, sealing their fates.

J'Sat Necolle

Smitten

As I directed my walker towards two empty seats in the back of the room, I thought about Kenyan. As I answered the questions for Janis to fill in on the consent forms and medical history, I thought about Kenyan; and even when the nurse took me into triage and asked me all those personal questions, I still only thought of Kenyan. Finally, I was seated back in the waiting room, glancing around at all the other abandoned women...I then thought about me.

Lost so far in my thoughts, I completely forgot Janis was sitting next to me, until she grabbed my hand and began to stroke it as she touched my legs with her other one, stopping me from shaking them. Looking around the room, I realized that I was only one of three women, that had someone by their side supporting them through this ordeal. The other twenty-two or so patients, just sat there with no one to comfort them. *How sad.*

Just when my mood was reaching another all-time low, my cell phone vibrated in my purse, indicating that I had a text message. Reaching down and grabbing my purse, Janis looked inside and gathered my phone and handed it to me. Stuck on an emotional rollercoaster, I couldn't muster the strength to even take the phone from her hand. Sensing my distress, she turned the phone over to look at the screen, "It's from Ms. Lois."

Smitten

Absently, I waved for her to ignore the text, figuring it was probably a bible verse or some shit. *Hell, I'm already sitting here trying not to have another stroke, I ain't got time for Grammy's ass trying to boss me from the grave.* "Turn it off."

Looking at me for more confirmation, I nodded my head solemnly, right before laying it on her shoulders. With a squeeze of her hand, she let me know that she had me. My mother finally had me.

Quickly she responded to Mrs. Lois text for me, then silenced the phone and began stroking my hair lightly, while humming beautifully in my ear.

After what felt like hours, the receptionist finally called my name to come to back. In any other circumstance, I would have been raising hell about how long it took to see a doctor, but given the magnitude of this procedure, I suppose they really are giving women a final chance to change their minds if they want to.

As we sat there waiting, it gave me time to think about everything. I began to wonder if it was a boy or a girl; and what he or she would look like. Will she have Kenyan's chestnut skin or my wavy hair. Will his personality be sweet and loyal like me; or would he a charismatic cheater, like his father.

Just when I felt my stomach begin to turn flips again with nervous anxiety, I had to

J'Sat Necolle

reassure myself I could go through with it. What choice did I have? I couldn't bring a child into this world, knowing he or she would have to endure the same kind of pain and rejection I had to endure as a child. *"But you'll be a wonderful mother,"* A tiny voice echoed in my head. "Yeah, but he won't have a father. I can't teach my son how to be a man."

"What was that my dear?" I heard Janis say from behind my back, as I slowly entered the hallway on my walker.

"Oh, my bad. I was just talking to myself."

A few more steps, Hiri. You can do this. I began using the self-motivation techniques we'd learned during our last team-building session. Lord knows, when I chose that employee training exercise, I never in a million years thought I'd be using it myself, especially not to help me kill my unborn child. *Who are you fooling? You can't do this,* the tiny voice once again echoed in my head.

"Yes, I can." I said aloud, before I even realized.

"What was that?" Janis and the nurse both asked simultaneously.

"I'm sorry, I was just going over my to-do list in my head," I said absently, as the tiny voice said, *"Since when is killing babies on your to-do list?"*

343

Smitten

Tears instantly sprang to my eyes, trying to conceal it from the nurse, I quickly turned my face towards my mother. Quickly noting my distress, Janis chimed right in, providing me with the distraction I so desperately needed. "Excuse me sweetheart," she turned in the nurse's direction, "Is there any way you can get her a drink of water while I help her get out of her cloths?" "We're still getting used to her new...condition, so it takes us a little longer dressing and undressing," she chimed sweetly.

Clearly sympathetic to my handicap, the petit nurse nodded her understanding and immediately left the room, closing the door behind her. Not saying a word, Janis pulled me into a tight embrace and stroked my hair softly as the sobs that I'd been holding in came cascading out.

"How did I get myself in this situation," I cried. "I've always been so careful." My body shook at the mammoth weight bearing on me. Janis still not saying a word, just rocked and stroked. "This is going to drive me crazy," I cried. "But I can't let my baby feel like I felt..." I tried to catch my words, but it was too late. Janis froze momentarily, then commenced with her rocking and stroking regimen.

I cried even harder, not meaning to hurt her. I didn't want to hurt anyone...especially my baby. The thought of that brought on yet another bout of tears and hysteria. *Either way it's going to get*

J'Sat Necolle

hurt." The voice crept back inside my head. "You're right!" I said, my voice steadying, as I regained my composure. "I'll rather hurt it now and take it out of its misery, than subject it to a lifetime of pain."

Reaching over on the bed, I picked up the exam gown the nurse had laid out. I turned my face to Janis and said, "I'm better now." She gave me a slight nod and began helping me take off my cloths.

When the nurse finally came back into the room, I was in complete control. I was attentive, listening to every word that came from the young woman's mouth. I then answered the final questions she had to ask before the doctor came in. I'd finally came to the resolve that if I can't give my son or daughter a better life than what I had, I rather not give it life at all.

Chapter 50

*A*s Janis and I slowly walked towards the blinking exit sign, I asked the Lord to please forgive me for my sins and I made him a promise that I will never again find myself in a place like this as long as I live. I must admit though, I don't feel any better going out as I did when I came in. The magnitude of the entire ordeal had taken its toll on me and I'm not sure if my life will ever be the same again.

Janis's motherly intuition automatically kicking in, she reached out to push the tinted glass door open with one hand, while pulling me in close with the other hand and placing my head on her shoulder. "Everything's going to be okay, honey. You had to make the best decision for..."

"For who?" "For you?" Janis's and my head both snapped up instantaneously, our eyes immediately being met by the angry glare of non-other than my best friend, standing in the doorway of the clinic.

"I should have fucking known your trifling ass would be down for this bullshit," Yana yelled at Janis, abruptly drawing her fist back in one swift motion.

"Nooo, Yana. No." I yelled while trying to move the walker out the doorway and ease my body in between Yana and my mother.

"Fuck that!" Yana yelled, tears streaming down her face.

"You don't understand." I cried.

"Oh, I understand perfectly well." She hissed, finally looking at me, disgust written all over her face.

"Well, I don't!" A deep, rich voice suddenly chimed in, causing Janis's and my head to immediately snap in the other direction. There, still holding the door handle was...The Kenyan Warner.

My heart immediately sank into the pit of my stomach as he glared at me with daggers in his eyes. Cleve standing on his heels, just dropped his head.

The way Kenyan looked at me made my emotions swell up yet again. Tears instantly formed pools in the corner of my eyes, as a lump the size of Texas crept of my throat. "Ke-Kenyan..." I stammered. "I can..."

"You can what?" He cut me off angrily, his eyes boring a hole in my soul. "You can explain!" "How the 'fuck' do you explain how you killed my child?" "Oh, nawl... ain't no way in the hell you can explain that!" He shouted, releasing the door abruptly, causing Janis, Yana and myself to have to scramble to get out the way of the tinted glass.

"Man, I can't believe this shit!" He moaned, as he grabbed his head and bent over in agony, now stumbling back into the crowded parking lot. Cleve, shaking his head in disbelief, rubbed his friend's back, quietly urging him to come on before they called the cops.

"I can't believe you let this bitch talk you into this stupid shit!" Yana hissed directly in my face.

"Yana!" "Don't call my mama no bitch!" I said, bravery inching up through every core of my body as I watched how Janis's confident demeanor diminished under Yana's scornful words. She may not have been there for me my whole life, but she was there when I needed her most.

Letting out a sarcastic laugh, Yana chided, "Ohhh, I see. I see. So, she's your mama now."

"Come on, Yana. Cleve yelled, now pulling Kenyan towards his truck.

"Kenyan, wait!" My tear-stricken voice finally managed. "Wait, Kenyan."

But my pleas fell on deaf ears. He never turned around. "What the fuck did you expect?" Yana hissed through clenched teeth, as she brushed past Janis and me.

J'Sat Necolle

Smitten

I watched as my best friend in the world angrily walked towards the SUV, where the love of my life and baby's father was about to leave forever. In a matter of seconds, memories of being a motherless and fatherless child filled my head. Every birthday. Every Christmas. Every day...

"I didn't do it!" I yelled as loud as I could as soon as Yana opened the truck door.

All three heads snapped up at once, each confusingly looking in my direction, as Janis rubbed my back, encouraging me to continue. With tears now flowing full speed, I yelled again, "I couldn't do it!" My knees beginning to buckle.

My confession slowly registered in their minds, as smiles began to appear on each of their faces. Instantaneously, they all jumped out the vehicle, running full-speed in my direction. Janis intuitively reaching her arm out in a shield of protection for her unborn grandchild. The gesture resonating with each of them, as they each calmed their excitement, careful not to injure the mother-to-be. Both Yana and Cleve, moving to the side and allowing Kenyan first access.

Watching the joyous emotion take ahold of his face was the most beautiful sight I'd ever seen. Slowly he reached up and cupped both sides of my face with his large hands. Pulling me close, he placed a gentle kiss on first one, then

Smitten

my other eyelid as I finally uttered the words,
"Kenyan, we're having a baby."

J'Sat Necolle

Epilogue

*A*s Kenyan and I lounged in the cabana he and Cleve had barely completed in time for the twin's first birthday party, I could not believe how much my life had changed in such a short time. Reading my thoughts, he gingerly strummed his finger across my bare shoulder and said, "Can you believe in less than a month, you will finally become Mrs. Kenyan Warner."

"Hmm... Mrs. Kenyan Warner. That does have a nice ring to it, but I think I like Zahiri Jones-Warner much better." For almost twenty years, I'd imagined being nothing other than Mrs. Kenyan Warner, but now the title seems a little less desirable; especially since that fool Christine insists on still calling herself that.

To let Cleve tell it, and it's funny as hell when he does; her silly ass was still using that for her signature four years after their divorce. He said he'd tried to tell Kenyan that she had lost it, but when she showed up to a charity event at his practice, introducing herself to his guest and employees as Mrs. Kenyan Warner, she'd raised awareness for more than just kidney disease.

According to Cleve, Kenyan had no idea she was doing it, that is until one of the kids came over and told Kenyan what they'd overheard her saying numerous times throughout the evening.

351

Smitten

Kenyan, true to his nature, not wanting to hurt her feelings or cause a scene, waited until most of the guest had left before confronting her. Cleve said she went all the way ballistic on his ass, informing him that she'll always be Mrs. Kenyan Warner, and she didn't give a fuck how he felt about it.

He finally realized then and there that she was certifiable. So, he went down to Fulton County Courthouse the very next morning and filed a petition with the clerk to amend their divorce decree. He wanted his name back. Cleve loves to mess with him, telling him he'd marched up in that courthouse like he was Tina Turner and Christine was Ike. I swear, every time Cleve told the story, he added more drama than all the times before and it gets funnier and funnier every time. So much so, that even Kenyan can't help but to laugh.

Hell, I wouldn't be surprised if all Cleve's little added on renditions of what actually happened at the charity event or the courthouse aren't true, and Kenyan is just too noble to tell it, not wanting to cause his ex any more embarrassment. Especially, given the way her koo-koo for coco puffs ass had scrolled up in my shit, repossessing a husband that hadn't been hers in over six years, it really ain't no telling what she'd did up in that courthouse. *And to think, you'd almost aborted your babies fucking with that ho.* The thought immediately caused anger to curse through every pore of my body. *The audacity of that bitch.* I thought, as I snuggled

J'Sat Necolle

even closer to Kenyan, just happy that things worked out for the best.

Glancing over at Raquel and Dale, who seemed to be enjoying their roles in concessions, serving the kids popcorn and snow cones, I said, "Babe, I'm so glad the kids could make it home for the party."

"Yeah, me too." He confessed. "The twins absolutely adore them. I just wish they were going to school in-state, so we could see them more often. But maybe now that you're fully recovered, and the twins are walking, we can go visit them more."

"Oh, that would be great!" "Hope couldn't have found a better person to leave her kids to."

"I don't know about that," he said, shaking off the compliment. "I just wish their mom could see how great they turned out. When her cancer came back with a vengeance the second time, she knew she wasn't going to make it. Even before any of us was willing to admit it; even me.

She'd gracefully adopted the resolve of, "Why not me." And for the next six months, the strength and resolve she showed was astounding." His voice cracked. "She loved those kids with every ounce of her being and to watch her trying to etch every memory of them in her brain forever was heartbreaking."

Trying to lighten his mood, he suddenly chuckled and said, "And I can't believe you thought my late-night conversations with the kids, was me romancing a wife I hadn't had in years."

Slapping him lightly in the chest, I chirped, "I bet you wouldn't be laughing so hard if you knew how many of those nights I thought about stabbing you in your sleep...especially the night you didn't go in the next room, and I thought you were laying in my bed next to me, and chatting it up with the love of your life, like I wasn't shit."

He threw his head back in a fit of laughter, "Girl, you must think I'm crazy. Only white women let you get away that kind of shit!"

Laughing a little, I playfully pinched his thigh. "It's your fault though, 'cause you never explained to me that you were divorced."

"No hell it ain't my fault!" "Shoot, every time I tried to bring up the past, you just shushed me like you was mama or something, so I just figured you knew everything."

"And, just how would I have known about your life, Kenyan Warner?" I asked curiously. "Especially with her ass all up on your job sites, mean-mugging me and shit...why would I think ya'll were no longer an item?"

Chuckling, he said, "Shit, I thought everybody knew. And I told you, the day you saw her at The

J'Sat Necolle

Hope House was the anniversary of our baby's death. We were on our way to visit his grave together, something we do every year."

"Yeah, I know that now. But it damn sure didn't look that way then. When she opened that door and saw me standing there, she looked at me like she wanted to whip me ass"

"Man, I told you that girl is crazy," he said, lightly kissing me on top of my head. Then his words suddenly getting somber, he continued on, "Real talk, Hiri...those kids over there mean the world to me. I love them like my own."

"I know you do."

"In fact, they're the reason I finally filed for a divorce in the first place."

"Really, why?"

"Well, when I first brought Hope and the kids to live with us, Chris was royally pissed. At first, I understood because I knew it was an unexpected surprise. So, I did everything to make sure she did not have to help with anything. I hired a full-time nurse for Hope and a nanny for the kids. But even that didn't satisfy her.

Eventually though, I finally figured out the problem was that she was just one fucked up individual. I'd taken it as long as I could, but after a while, her bigotry got to be too much to ignore. She'd make all kinds of snide remarks to the kids and to Hope, too. And it all boiled down to the fact that, that heifer really thought she was better than them. She acted like her ass didn't grow up in the hood like the rest of us."

"Are you serious?" I asked, completely flabbergasted. "Eventhough I can't say I'm surprised. Shit, she didn't just get that way, that bitch has been like that her whole life. Hell, I never understood what you saw in her in the first place."

"Well, she did have a fat ah-."

"I wish you would," I hissed up at him, between clenched teeth.

"I'm just tripping, babe, he said, laughingly planting a kiss on my forehead. "For real though, that really is all I saw in her. You gotta understand baby, I was just a horny teenager, and she was giving it up."

"So, that's all it was?"

"Honestly Hiri, that is all it was, that is...until she got pregnant. I was so messed up back then. I didn't want to hurt you, but I couldn't fathom the idea of leaving my kid like my dad left me." Tears seeped into his voice again, "That night when we made love, I swear that was not my intention. I came over to come clean and tell you about the baby, but when I saw the look in your eyes when you pulled the cover back, it tore a hole in my soul and I just had to have you. I know that sounds selfish, and it was, but I just couldn't help myself. The next morning though, I felt like a complete ass, and I didn't have the balls to face you. So, I did the only thing I knew how to do...I left."

"I told you, Love, we don't have to talk about this."

"No, I want to talk about it once and for all." Pulling my face closer to his, "I want you to know that leaving you was the hardest thing I ever had to do. And when the baby passed away, my whole world turned up-side down. I'd lost the only girl I'd loved, and I'd lost the baby I'd left her for. If it had not been for Cleve, I probably would have lost it. I spent more nights at his house than I did at home with Chris...crying over you... and my child. I eventually dropped out of school and was just spending my days hustling on the block, smoking weed and chasing women, until that night in jail gave me a reality check"

"So, how did Christine feel about that?"

"About what," he asked confusingly.

"About you chasing other women?"

"Shit, she was doing her thing too. Just imagine her country ass in New York City for the first time, and she'd never been any further than Conyers." Chuckling lightly, "Yeah, baby girl was busting it open," he continued, "besides, she didn't give a fuck who I was with, as long as it wasn't you!"

Well, I'll be damn. "That bitch has known the whole time."

"Known what?"

Reluctantly, I laid back on his chest and relayed the sordid details of what my mother had told me the night she came to my home about who my father was."

"Well, I'll be damn."

"My sentiments exactly. Shit, you, talking about a sister rivalry. Hell; Venus and Serena ain't got shit on us!" "While, they're tossing around tennis balls, me and my sister are tossing around good dick."

"Oh, so I got some good dick?" He questioned humoredly.

"Man, shut the hell up...good dick was the only take away you got from all that!" I said, playfully slapping him in the face, then running my finger threw his new beard, that I was finally getting accustomed to.

Looking over fondly at my mother as she played gleefully in the ball pit with the twins and their other little friends. Looking up at Kenyan, I whispered, "Babe, I am so thankful for my mother."

J'Sat Necolle

Following my watchful eye over to where Janis was playing with the kids, he said, "I know what you mean, Sweetheart. If it weren't for her, none of this would be happening. I don't know what I would have did if she had not sent Mrs. Lois the address to that clinic that day."

"And to think, she never said a word. For a woman that needed all the extra points she could get with the child she left behind, you would've thought she would hurry to take the praise for our reunion, but she never said a word. If I hadn't been looking for Mrs. Lois' cheesecake recipe, like I really needed it, I would never have gone through my old text messages and ran across the single text that literally saved my life."

"Yeah, that says a lot. I think she really does regret leaving you all those years ago."

"Yeah, I do too." I said somberly, somewhat feeling sorry for Janis. "Now, that I've gotten to know her, she's actually pretty cool. She was just a young girl that could not get over her first love...and it cost her dearly." My thoughts lingered on Janis's account of how I was conceived and by whom... *I can't believe that bitch intentionally went after my man all those years ago, about a daddy I didn't even know I had. Ain't that some shit!*

Just as I was about to get sucked in an emotional roller coaster, Yana and Cleve announced that it was time to cut the cake.

Invading my mind's thoughts again, Kenyan said, "Who would have guessed when we asked those two to be God Parents to Kayla and Kyla, that they would have taken their roles so literally; and now are expecting a child of their own."

Teasingly I slapped him on his thigh, "Damn nigga, get out my head!" "I was just thinking the exact same thing." We both laughed.

"Cleve is my dog and all, but I gotta admit, I didn't see that shit coming. Real talk, I do feel sorry for B though. I was hoping they were gonna work out this time around."

"Yeah, me too. I think it was just too much for him though. When she went back to Gavin after my stroke, I think that was the final straw for Brandon. He told me that he still loves her, but he'll do it from a distance from here on. And even when her and Gavin did finally call it quits, Brandon still wouldn't bulge, claiming only a fool gets hurt three times."

"I can feel him on that."

"Yeah, me too." Giggles escaping my parched lips, I excitedly declared, "I'm just happy as hell that she finally saw Gavin for who he really was and kicked his trifling ass to the curb, once and for all!" "Won't He do it!"

"Oh, don't act like that. You know you enjoyed being Gavin's responsibility."

J'Sat Necolle

Smitten

Slapping him lightly up side his head for reminding me of that bullshit. The surgery, the stroke...it all seemed so long ago. *Lord, I thank you for bringing me through.* My Grammy always said, slow and steady always wins the race.

Smitten

To My Home Team...

You guys are the real MVP's! I want to sincerely thank each of you for running out and purchasing my first novel, without a second thought. You all had no idea if I could string two sentences together, let alone write an entire novel; but you supported my project nonetheless. That was such a humbling experience and I sincerely appreciate each and every one of you!

You all have kept me encouraged since that debut novel; making me believe writing is a path I should continue to pursue. You all have been pushing me for the next novel for years; and I'm sorry it's taken me much too long. Honestly, that grandbaby of mine was the first big distraction but then my writer's block took precedence over everything. Believe it or not, you all weren't the only ones who fell in love with Jermaine. Shit, so did I; which made it darn near impossible to come up with another catchy story line... without our Sexy Chocolate!

When you all fell head over heels in love with Jermaine... to the point that some of you read the book in a day or two, some of you chose to read while you were at work. Others of you would not share your copy with your family and friends, instead insisted they purchase their own copy, just to make sure I got all the support I could. Then there were even those of you who were about to mess up your happy homes by comparing Jermaine to your man... (Not a good look, ladies).

And to those of you who used my novel as an example for your children to encourage them to follow their dreams too...

And to my customers, who became friends, that couldn't pick up your dessert orders without asking about Jermaine and my next book...

J'Sat Necolle

Smitten

And to my church folk who told me that just because they were saved, did not mean they weren't still a woman...and my cursing didn't offend them at all...

And to the fellas who purchased the novel, some of you did so just because I'd written it, but fell in love with the characters and plot just as much as the ladies did...

And to my family members that had to close their eyes and skip over the nasty stuff...

And to my ex, who rushed to Amazon the day it was released, wondering if I talked about you... not so much in the first one, BUT honeyyyy...this one's for you! KSW

I said all that to say this...you all know who you are, and I want each of you to know that this entire experience has been a dream come true, and I have you all to thank for that! And even if I never write another successful novel, I'm perfectly okay with that, because you all made my first experience, the best experience ever!

J'Sat Necolle

Smitten

Coming Soon
(I promise 😊)

A Change Gonna Come

Join the discussions, visit...

J'Sat Necolle @ Facebook.com
J'Sat Necolle/twitter

J'Sat Necolle

When I take my last breath, I want to be remembered as a loving mother, grandmother, daughter, sister, aunt, friend and above all else; a child of God!

Accolades, fame and success are all nice, but these are the things that matters most to me!

Made in the USA
Columbia, SC
04 September 2019